FAIR WARNING

Sheriff Keal looked up and met Frank's eyes. "Morgan, I've known some bad ol' boys in my time. I've marshaled in some tough towns. But if just half the things I've heard about you are true . . . you've got to be one randy gunslinger."

Frank chuckled. "Believe about one tenth of what you hear about me, Sheriff."

"You pretty well destroyed the Dooley gang here in California."

"But I didn't get Val."

"He's operating in Texas, and New Mexico. Down along the Mex border."

"So I heard."

"And from here, you're heading where, Morgan?"

Frank smiled at that. "New Mexico. But I'm looking for land, not Val Dooley."

"But if you run into him?"

"I'll finish what I started."

"Good luck." The sheriff pushed back his chair and stood up. "He's up to his old tricks, Frank: kidnapping women and selling them into prostitution. Young boys too. Val Dooley is one sorry son of a bitch."

"I know that only too well, Sheriff."

"When you find him, put one bullet into him for me."

"I'll try, Sheriff."

"Good hunting, Frank Morgan." Sheriff Keal turned and walked away.

Frank rolled a cigarette and refilled his coffee cup. "This time, I'll get you, Dooley," he muttered. "If you get in my way, I'll kill you."

BOOK YOUR PLACE ON OUR WEBSITE AND MAKE THE READING CONNECTION!

We've created a customized website just for our very special readers, where you can get the inside scoop on everything that's going on with Zebra, Pinnacle and Kensington books.

When you come online, you'll have the exciting opportunity to:

- View covers of upcoming books
- Read sample chapters
- Learn about our future publishing schedule (listed by publication month *and author*)
- Find out when your favorite authors will be visiting a city near you
- Search for and order backlist books from our online catalog
- Check out author bios and background information
- Send e-mail to your favorite authors
- Meet the Kensington staff online
- Join us in weekly chats with authors, readers and other guests
- Get writing guidelines
- AND MUCH MORE!

**Visit our website at
http://www.kensingtonbooks.com**

THE LAST GUNFIGHTER: RESCUE

William W. Johnstone

PINNACLE BOOKS

Kensington Publishing Corp.

http://www.kensingtonbooks.com

Six feet of land was all that he needed.

—Leo Tolstoy

One

Frank rode into Los Angeles and stabled his horses at the best livery in town, telling the stable man to rub them down, wash them, and feed them hay and oats. Dog, the big cur, would stay in the stall with the Appaloosa, Stormy.

Frank walked to a nearby café and got a sack of scraps for Dog. That done, he got a room, a nice hotel, then dropped off his suit and some shirts at Wo Fong's Laundry, then headed for the nearest barbershop for a long, hot soapy bath and a haircut and shave.

A couple of hours later, feeling and smelling a damn sight better, Frank, dressed in a black suit, white shirt, and red kerchief, and with his boots polished, stepped out onto the boardwalk and looked around him at the rapidly growing town.

Frank had been told by a proud desk clerk that the population of the town was about fifteen thousand, and when the railroad arrived in a few years, that would more than double, maybe even triple.

Frank whistled and shook his head. "That's too many folks for this cowboy," he told the clerk.

Frank was a cowboy, and a damn good one. He'd started off as a cowhand in Texas. Then he'd been forced into a fight when just a boy and killed a man. The dead man's brothers came after him. Frank killed all four of them. His reputation as a fast gun grew and spread rapidly. He was still in his teens when the Civil War split the country. Four years later, at war's end, Frank was a captain of Confederate cavalry. Rather than turn in his weapons, Frank headed west to become a part of the untamed frontier. In Colorado, he married a beautiful young lady, but the girl's father broke it up. It was years later that Frank learned he had a son. But the boy didn't much care for his father, so Frank left it at that and drifted. That's how he got his nickname: the Drifter.

He became a legend: Frank Morgan, the fastest and deadliest gunfighter west of the Mississippi River.

Frank asked directions to the nearest bank, and after talking with a teller there for a moment, was shown into a private office for a meeting with the bank's president.

"Are you really Frank Morgan?" the bank executive asked.

Frank smiled and laid an oilskin pouch on the desk. "It's all in there."

The executive opened the pouch and studied the contents carefully for a few moments. He smiled and nodded his head. "A pleasure to meet you, Mr. Morgan. I guess the stories are true about your being a wealthy man."

"My ex-wife left me some stock in various companies. The stock has increased in value somewhat."

"Somewhat?" the bank man said, arching an eyebrow and smiling. "That is an understatement, Mr. Morgan."

"I guess it is."

"Do you know how much you are worth?"

"I have a general idea. I have people who take care of that for me."

"Yes," the banker said dryly. "The most prestigious law firms in San Francisco and Denver." He sighed. "What can I do for you, sir?"

Frank pushed a piece of paper across the desk. "I want a couple of bank drafts in those amounts and a thousand dollars in cash."

The banker glanced at the amounts written on the paper. "That will be no problem at all."

"I'll pick them up sometime tomorrow."

"At your convenience, sir. Mr. Morgan?"

Frank looked at him.

"May I say something of a personal nature?"

"Go ahead."

"Your son, Conrad Browning, is becoming quite the entrepreneur. He's branching out in all directions. Were you aware of that?"

"No," Frank said. "My son does not much care for me. We are not close and never correspond."

"I see. I heard as much. I'm sorry."

"No need to be. He has his life, I have mine."

"Mr. Morgan, forgive me for becoming personal, but I have to ask: What kind of life do you have?"

"What do you mean?"

"You drift, sir. You don't have a home . . . that I am aware of. You just, well, wander."

Frank smiled. "I enjoy wandering, seeing the country. I've done it for years." Frank pushed back his chair and stood up. "I'll pick up the bank drafts tomorrow. Thank you, sir." He walked out of the office.

"Excuse me, Mr. Spencer," a man said from the open doorway, seconds after Frank had exited.

"Yes, Blanchard?"

"Was that Frank Morgan the gunfighter?"

"Yes, it was."

"What did he want, a loan?"

Spencer laughed and shook his head. "Not hardly, Blanchard. He was arranging for some bank drafts."

"And you honored the request?"

Spencer waved the man to a chair. "Blanchard, you're fresh from the East, new to the West, so learn this now: Don't judge a man by the clothes he wears or the rumors you might have heard about him. Frank Morgan is a very wealthy man. He owns stock in factories, gold mines, railroads, and numerous other businesses."

"I didn't know, sir."

"Now you do. Close the door on your way out."

Frank walked down the street until he came to a saloon. But the place was filled with fancy men in suits and high collars and polished shoes. Not a pair of boots in the place. Frank walked on until he found a cantina on a side street. He stepped inside and stood for a moment, letting his eyes adjust to the sudden dimness. When he started his walk to a table in the rear of the cantina, the patrons fell silent. Frank didn't fool himself; everyone in the place knew who he was. Every eye was on him. Only when he was seated did the buzz of conversation resume.

A man came to his table and said, "Señor?"

"Beer," Frank said. "And something to eat."

"Beans and tortillas?"

"That'll be fine."

Frank sat sipping his cool beer, waiting for his food to arrive. He was conscious of the furtive glances he received from many of the men in the saloon. It didn't bother him. He was used to it. He was also sure that sooner or later, someone in the place would approach him. Hopefully, for conversation and not gunplay.

Frank had eaten only a few bites of food when he heard a chair being pushed back not far from where he was seated. Boots clumped across the floor and the man stopped in front of Frank's table.

"You're Frank Morgan, ain't you?" The question was tossed at him.

"That's right."

"You got a lot of nerve, showin' your face around here."

"Why is that?"

"You kilt my brother, that's why!"

Frank sighed and laid down his spoon. "What was your brother's name?"

"Jim Elgart."

"I never heard of him. Now go away."

"You kilt him, damn you!"

Just one time, Frank thought. *If I could spend a few days in some town without being confronted by someone ...* "Where am I supposed to have done this?" Frank asked.

"Texas. Early last year. Down along the border."

"Sorry, friend," Frank told him. "But it wasn't me."

"The hell you say! I was told it was you. I been lookin' for you ever since. Now stand up and settle this."

"It wasn't me," Frank insisted.

"You done turned yeller, Morgan. Git up, damn you!"

Frank shoved the table hard, the corner of it catching the man in the belly. The irate stranger grunted and doubled over, all the air driven out of him. Frank shoved the table again, and the man sat down hard on the floor. Frank rose quickly, jerked the man's pistol from his belt, and tossed it on the table, then sat back down.

"Hell," a man said. "I was wantin' to see Morgan in some gun action."

Frank ignored him. The man Frank had put on the barroom floor was helped to his feet and led off, cussing Frank as he went.

"Thought I might finally get to see the famous Frank Morgan in action," a man said from the open doorway of the cantina.

Frank looked up as a deputy stepped inside and walked to the bar.

"Beer," the deputy told the bartender. He turned around to look at Frank. "I was sorta lookin' forward to arrestin' you, Morgan."

"On what charge?"

The deputy smiled. "Oh, I 'spect I could think of somethin'."

Frank returned to his beans and tortillas without replying.

The deputy walked over and sat down at the table.

"Please have a seat," Frank said very sarcastically.

The sarcasm was lost on the deputy. "Thanks, Morgan."

"What do you want, Deputy?"

"You out of town."

"I'll be leaving about midday tomorrow."

"You'll leave when I tell you to leave, and I'm tellin' you to leave right now."

Frank knew a roust when he heard one, and he didn't like to be rousted. "Deputy, you go right straight to hell," Frank said softly, so only the deputy could hear.

The deputy flushed. "No one talks to me like that."

"I just did. Now why don't you drag your butt out of that chair and leave, so I can finish my meal in peace?"

"When I get you in jail, I'm going to teach you a lesson. You're under arrest, Morgan!" the deputy hissed at him.

"Try to take me in," Frank tossed back at him.

For a moment, Frank thought the bigmouthed deputy was going to try him. But the wind suddenly left the man and he slumped in his chair. "You bastard!" he said to Frank in a very low voice. "I'll see you again. Bet on that. No man talks to Vince Barlow like that."

"Hang up that badge, Vince. If you don't, it's going to get you killed. You've got the wrong attitude to wear it."

"I don't need any advice from you, Morgan." Vince pushed back his chair and stomped out of the cantina.

Frank finished his beans and tortillas, then signaled for a refill. While he waited for his second helping, he sipped his beer. He was just finishing his second plate of beans and sopping up the juice with a tortilla when a big man with a star on his vest strolled in. He asked the bartender something. The barkeep pointed at Frank, and the lawman nodded and headed toward Frank's table.

Frank sighed and waited.

"Frank Morgan?" the man asked.

"That's me."

"I'm Sheriff Keal. Mind if I sit down?"

"Not at all, Sheriff. I was about to order a pot of coffee. Want some?"

"Sounds good." Keal motioned for the barkeep to bring them both coffee.

The bartender nodded and in a couple of minutes, set cups and a fresh pot of coffee on the table. Keal sugared his coffee, tasted it, and smiled. "I do like a good cup of coffee. Morgan, I spoke with Spencer over at the bank. He told me you were in town. I always wanted to meet you."

"Well, thank you, Sheriff. I was thinking you were here because of your deputy."

"Which one? No, let me guess. Barlow? Has he been in here?"

Frank told him what had transpired between the two.

"That dumb, hammerheaded peckerwood!" Sheriff Keal said. "He had no call to speak to you that way. I'll talk to him. Or fire him. I think I'll fire him. He's not working out."

"Wait until I leave town, please. I don't want to have to face the man in a shoot-out."

Sheriff Keal smiled. "No. I don't want to have to bury the fool."

"I would appreciate that."

"You in town long?"

"Leaving tomorrow. Early afternoon probably."

"I'll wait until you're gone before I fire him."

"Thanks."

Sheriff Keal fiddled with his nearly empty cup for a few seconds. He looked up and met Frank's eyes. "Morgan, I've known some bad ol' boys in my time. I've marshaled in some tough towns. But if just half the things I've heard about you are true ... you've got to be one randy gunslinger."

Frank chuckled. "Believe about one tenth of what you hear about me, Sheriff."

"You pretty well destroyed the Dooley gang here in California."

"But I didn't get Val."

"He's operating in Texas and New Mexico. Down along the Mex border."

"So I heard."

"And from here, you're heading where, Morgan?"

Frank smiled at that. "New Mexico. But I'm looking for land, not Val Dooley."

"But if you run into him?"

"I'll finish what I started."

"Good luck." The sheriff pushed back his chair and stood up. "He's up to his old tricks, Frank: kidnapping women and selling them into prostitution. Young boys too. Val Dooley is one sorry son of a bitch."

"I know that only too well, Sheriff."

"When you find him, put one bullet into him from me."

"I'll try, Sheriff."

"Good hunting, Frank Morgan." Sheriff Keal turned and walked away.

Frank rolled a cigarette and refilled his coffee cup. "This time, I'll get you, Dooley," he muttered. "If you get in my way, I'll kill you."

Two

From long habit, Frank checked his back trail often. It didn't take him long to pick up on the man who was following him. He didn't know if it was the cowboy who claimed Frank had killed his brother, or Deputy Barlow, or who. But he got tired of it very quickly.

Frank reined up, got his field glasses from the saddlebags, and began studying the still-distant figure. After a few moments, the image became clearer and Frank could make out some of the man's features. He didn't know who it was; had never seen the man before. But the man was definitely following him. Frank decided to wait for him. He got his rifle from the saddle boot and waited.

When the man got within a dozen yards from him, Frank stood up and the man reined up.

"I don't mean you no harm, Morgan," the man said. "I just want to talk."

"You must have seen me back in town. Why didn't you talk then?"

"Couldn't. Too risky."

"You want to explain that?"

"I was once a friend of Val Dooley. That tell you anything?"

"Maybe. Go on."

"Can I dismount?"

"Go ahead."

The man swung down from the saddle and looked around. "They's a spot of shade over yonder. Want to talk there?"

"Lead the way."

The men squatted down in the shade and the stranger looked at Dog, sitting close by. "That dog's got a mean look in his eye. Do he bite?"

"He's been known to. What's on your mind?"

"You lookin' for Val?"

"Not really. But his name keeps getting tossed at me."

"I grew up with Val. We was neighbors back when we was boys. Then we become men and both of us hit the hoot-owl trail. But Val was too randy for me and I broke away from him. I'd run into him ever now and then and we'd talk. Val always seemed to have lots of money and he'd give me some; kept wantin' me to rejoin up with his gang. I never did. Then he told me 'bout six months ago he was gettin' tarred of California and was thinkin' 'bout headin' down to New Mexico-Arizona way. Had him a plan to kidnap women and sell them into whorin'. Then you showed up and Val had to hit the trail a bit sooner than he wanted to. You really busted up his gang, Morgan."

Frank nodded his head and waited for the man to continue.

"And you can bet he knows you was in Los Angeles and knows you done left. He knew it hours ago."

"How?"

"Telegraph wires, Morgan. You know they's strung all over the West now."

"He hasn't had time to set all that up. I just ran him out about a month ago," Frank said dubiously.

"It was already in place. Outlaw by the name of Mason come up with the idea and set it up some months ago."

"What happened to him?"

"Val had him kilt and took over his gang. Val's a mean one, Morgan. And he's a planner and a schemer too. He plans to become king of the outlaws someday. And the way he's a-goin', looks like he might make it."

"And you're going to join him?"

The stranger shook his head. "Hell, no, Morgan. Not me. I'm headin' for San Diego. Get me an honest job and try to find me a good woman to marry up with. I just wanted to warn you 'bout Val."

"And I thank you for that."

"Don't think nothin' 'bout it. Val's crazy, Morgan. And he's killin'-mean. He's done brought grief to a lot of people. He's got to be stopped. I figure you're the man to stop him. That is, if he don't kill you."

"A lot of people have tried that, stranger. What is your name?"

"I ain't a-tellin' you. Val might capture you and torture it out of you. Then he'd come after me. And he likes to torture people. I'm tellin' you, the man is crazy."

"I've had a number of people tell me that."

"Well, you can add me to the list. And I know firsthand. I've seen some of the things he done. Made me puke. I hope you kill the son of a bitch. If any man on this earth needs killin', it's Val Dooley." The stranger stood up. "You be careful, Morgan. I'm tellin' you, Val knows you're on the way.'' Without another word, the man turned and walked to his horse. He mounted up and rode off toward the south.

Frank didn't know whether to believe the man or not, but he wasn't going to take any chances. He mounted up and headed out, this time more to the east than to the south. Val Dooley could be somebody else's worry for now. Right now, Frank wanted to get into Northern New Mexico and check out some land. He would follow the stage road east into Arizona and then cut some north to Wickenburg. Frank loved the northern parts of Arizona and New Mexico, and had always thought that someday he'd like to settle there. Maybe this trip would be the one that would hold him in one place. He hoped so.

But for now, he had days of long, hot riding ahead of him.

Weeks later, a very tired and hot and dirty Frank Morgan rode into Wickenburg. His horses were tired and Dog was just about pooped out. All Frank wanted was a long, hot soapy bath, a change into clean fresh clothing, and something to eat. Then to sleep in a bed, on a nice feather-tick, for about ten hours.

What he got, almost right out of the saddle, was trouble.

Frank had just left the livery, after arranging for the care of his animals, and was carrying his saddlebags, stuffed with dirty clothes, heading for the laundry and then a bathhouse. A shout stopped him in the street.

''Turn around and face me, Morgan. I been waitin' a long time for this.''

Frank immediately dropped his saddlebags and slowly turned around, his pale eyes narrowing at the sight before him. He knew the man as Ray Hayden. He was a gunfighter, so called. But mostly he was a paid assassin.

"Ray," Frank called as people scurried to clear the street. "When did you crawl out of your hole?"

"I'm gonna kill you, Morgan. I ain't forgot the last time we met."

"Oh, yeah, Ray. I remember now. That's when I took your guns away from you and used them to pistol-whip you."

Ray Hayden cussed him loud and long.

Frank laughed at him. "Is that the best you can do, Ray? Or are you just trying to work up enough nerve to pull on me?"

"I said I aim to kill you, Morgan!" the man shouted.

There were no locals left visible in the line of fire in front of Frank. He had no way of knowing about any behind him.

"Do you want me to turn my back to you, Ray?" Frank said with a smile. "Would that make it easier for you?"

"Damn your eyes, Morgan!" Hayden shouted.

The day was very hot in the high Sonoran Desert, and Frank could see that Ray Hayden's shirt was soaked with sweat. It was hot, but not intensely so. *The man's scared,* Frank thought. Then he mentally added: *But that might only serve to make him even more dangerous.* And Frank knew that while Hayden normally was a back-shooter, he was a fast gun when pushed.

"The marshal and his deputies are out of town, Morgan," Hayden called, stepping a few feet closer. "Some trouble out in the country."

"Here, now!" a citizen called from a store entrance. "You men stop this right now!"

"Shut up!" Hayden shouted. "I aim to kill Frank Morgan."

"Frank Morgan!" another citizen shouted. "Here in Wickenburg?"

"He's gonna be buried here too," Hayden said. "So you best advise the undertaker to get ready."

Frank waited for Hayden to make his move, something the man did not seem in any hurry to do.

"Hayden," Frank said, "I'm hot and tired and hungry. And I'm tired of your big mouth. Now either make your play or give this up."

"Draw, Morgan!" Hayden shouted.

"This was your idea, Hayden. It's up to you."

"I'll buy the winner a drink," a woman called from a saloon.

"Then you better uncork the bottle," Hayden called. "I'm a-gettin' thirsty." Ray Hayden's hand closed around the butt of his pistol and he pulled.

Frank shot him.

The bullet hit Ray in the belly and knocked him down to the boardwalk. He tried to get up, and managed to roll off the boardwalk into the street. He clawed for his gun and closed his hand around the butt.

"Don't do it, Ray," Frank called.

"Hell with you!" Hayden said. He tried to lift and cock his pistol just as the shock wore off and the pain hit him. He yelled in agony and pulled the trigger. The .44 boomed and the bullet tore into the dirt, sending a huge cloud of dust into the air. Ray began coughing and gagging. "I can't see nothin'!" he finally said. "Somebody point out Morgan. I want to kill him."

"Get a doctor," a local said.

"Get the undertaker," another said. "He's done for, I 'spect."

"I ain't neither!" Ray yelled as a large crowd began gathering around him. "Git out of my way. I ain't done yet." He tried to lift his pistol, and a man reached down and jerked it from his hand.

"Give it up, mister," the local said. "Here comes the doctor."

"Hell with the doctor," Ray mumbled.

"The preacher's comin' too," another citizen said.

"Hell with him too," Ray muttered, the side of his face pressing against the dirt, his breath kicking up dust.

"That ain't a nice thing for a man about to meet his Maker to be sayin'."

"Hell with you too," Ray replied.

The citizen shook his head and stepped back onto the boardwalk. He looked at Frank. "Are you really Frank Morgan?"

"Yes."

"I thought you'd be older."

"It's my clean living," Frank told him. "Keeps me young."

The citizen shook his head. "Town's gettin' plumb filled up with smart alecks."

The preacher knelt down beside Ray Hayden. "Would you like for me to pray for your soul?"

"I'd druther you get me a drink of whiskey," Ray told him. "After that you can get me a whore to pull her dress up."

"For shame, for shame," the preacher admonished him.

The doctor elbowed his way through the gathering crowd and knelt down beside Ray, pulling the man's hands away from his bloody stomach. He quickly checked him. "Bullet went right through the liver. Make your peace with God, mister."

"Gimme my pistol. I wanna kill that damn Frank Morgan."

The doctor stood up. "Some of you men carry him over to my office. He can die in peace there."

Ray groaned in pain and then said, "You ain't much of a doctor, you quack! Why can't you fix me up?"

The doctor looked at Frank. "You should have shot him in the head, Morgan. It wouldn't have hurt him. There apparently is nothing up there to hurt."

Three

Frank lounged around the town for a couple of days. He provisioned up and bought another packhorse and packsaddle. He bought another water bag for the trek across the dry country. At first the new packhorse, called Buster, didn't seem to want to get along with Stormy. All that was settled after Stormy kicked him once and bit him twice. Buster got the message.

Frank bought a dozen boxes of .45s, half a dozen boxes of .44-40s, and another bandolier. Then he sat around the town's many saloons and listened to the talk.

"That damn Val Dooley is on the rampage again," he heard one man say. "He's all over New Mexico."

"He knows better than to mess around in Texas," his drinking buddy replied. "The Rangers have make it public that they'll shoot him on sight."

"Somebody damn sure needs to."

In another saloon, Frank heard a man say, "I heard the Dooley gang was operating wide open up in Northern New Mexico Territory."

"I heard the same thing," another man said. "Stealin' little girls and sometimes little boys and sellin' them into slavery."

Both men looked at Frank. "You goin' after Val Dooley, Mr. Morgan?" one asked.

"Not directly," Frank replied.

"What do that mean?" the other asked.

"It means if he gets in my way, there'll be trouble."

"Way I heared it," the first local said, "Val Dooley don't like you. Seems he's been makin' big brags 'bout how he's gonna kill you."

"Then I reckon he's got it to do." Frank drained his beer and walked out.

Outside on the boardwalk, a young man ran up to Frank. "The sheriff wants to see you, Mr. Morgan. He give me a nickel to find you and tell you."

Frank smiled and gave the boy a silver dollar. The boy's eyes widened. "You found me, son. Thanks."

"Have you really killed a thousand men?" the boy asked.

Frank laughed and put a big hand on the boy's shoulder. "No, son. Those are just stories people have made up about me."

"Five hundred?" the boy asked hopefully.

Again, Frank laughed and patted the boy's shoulder. "No, boy. Not five hundred either. You run along now. Thanks for telling me about the sheriff."

At the sheriff's office, the sheriff was quite blunt and came right to the point. "I want you out of this town, Morgan."

"Why?"

"Because I just got word that some of Ray Hayden's friends are making plans to kill you. I don't want a bloodbath on my streets."

"Hayden died?"

"Just after dawn this morning."

"You worried about whose blood getting spilled, Sheriff: mine or theirs?"

The lawman smiled. "I seen you back in '67 or '68, Morgan. At that old tradin' post in Colorado. When them five gun-handlers from West Texas braced you. When the smoke cleared, they was all dead or dyin' and you had a little nick on the left leg and a cut on your cheek from flyin' glass. I'm not a damn bit worried about your blood, Morgan. But when the lead starts flyin', innocent people tend to get hurt."

Frank nodded his head in agreement. "I agree, Sheriff. All right. I'll pull out later on this afternoon. Soon as I can pack up."

"Thanks, Morgan. That's mighty white of you. You really goin' to New Mexico to try to buy some land and settle down?"

"News gets around," Frank said with a grin. "Yes, I am."

"Good luck to you."

"Thanks."

Frank was packed up and riding out of Wickenburg two hours later.

Frank fixed an early supper the first night out, and then rode on for a few more miles, using up another couple of hours of daylight, all the while checking his back trail. He made a cold camp just before dark, and slept the night through without being disturbed. Dog sounded no alarms during the night. Indeed, the big cur was still asleep when Frank awakened.

Frank fried some bacon and ate that, then sopped up the grease with a hunk of store-bought bread, then had a pot of coffee and a couple of cigarettes. There was not a single cloud in the sky when Frank saddled up and pointed Stormy's nose north, toward Prescott. Frank didn't anticipate any trouble in Prescott, for that was Arizona's territorial capital and was well policed. Prescott was the territorial capital first in the early 1860s; then the capital moved to Tucson for a time, then back to Prescott in 1877.

At noon of the second day out, after checking his back trail every ten minutes or so, Frank knew he was being followed, and grew tired of it very quickly. "Probably Ray Hayden's pals," Frank muttered, and began looking for a good place to set up an ambush. It didn't take him long to find the ideal spot.

If those behind him were merely travelers on the road to Prescott, and they might well be, they could ride on and never know they were in his gun sights. If they were trouble-hunters, they would know instantly where Frank had left the trail and would know just as quickly they were in big trouble.

Frank left his horses in the shade of some pines just off the trail, and taking his rifle, took up a position on the crest of a rocky upthrust. He waited motionless and watched as four men came riding slowly into view. When they drew closer, Frank could recognize one of the riders: Till Brackman. Frank grunted softly. Till was a bad one, for a fact, quick and deadly. He didn't know the other three. And Till was a longtime friend of Ray Hayden . . . or had been, that is, now that Ray was busy rolling dice with the devil.

The four men reined up abruptly almost directly below Frank's position in the rocks.

"He's left the road," one of the men said, his words carrying clearly to Frank.

"No shit?" Till said sarcastically. "Well, I'll tell you boys what you'd better do. You'd better keep your hands away from your guns, 'cause you can believe Morgan's got us in gun sights right now."

Frank had edged closer to the rim and was looking down on the riders. "Believe him, boys," he said. "Sit your saddles easy now."

Four sets of eyes looked up into the cold gray eyes of Frank Morgan, looking down at them over the barrel of a .44-40.

"Can't a man even ride a road in peace, Morgan?" Till asked.

"Not if you're following me," Frank told him.

"Who says we are?" one of the riders with Till asked.

"I do," Frank replied. "You have a name?"

"Mack."

"Mack . . . what?"

"Mack Smith, Jones, Johnson. Whatever suits me at the time."

"These other two are the Crow brothers," Till said. "Todd and Boyd."

"Heard of them," Frank said. "Montana gunhands. Like to shoot farmers in the back, so I'm told."

"You ain't never heared of me?" Mack asked.

"Can't say as I have. You famous, Mack?"

"I got a rep," Mack said sullenly.

"Where would I find it, carved on the walls of whorehouses and outhouses?"

"I'll get you for that, Morgan," Mack flared right back.

"Feel like doing it now?"

"Naw, I'll wait."

"Until my back is turned?"

"Goddamn you, Morgan. I ain't no coward."

Frank cut his eyes to Till. "You boys looking to avenge the death of Hayden?"

"He was a pal."

"He was a loudmouth trouble-hunter, Till. And you know it."

"He was still a pal."

"Ride on, Till. All of you. Leave me be. I'm not looking for trouble."

"I'm gonna ride on, Morgan," Mack said. "After I kill you."

"Shut up, Mack," Todd Crow told him.

"You shut up, Crow. I aim to kill Morgan."

"You're a fool," Till told him.

"Oh, yeah?" Mack yelled. "Well, watch this!" He grabbed for his pistol.

Frank shot him. At this range, the .44-40 slug blew a hole in Mack's chest about the size of a silver dollar and knocked him backward out of the saddle. Mack was dead before he hit the ground.

Till looked at his dead former riding pard. "He's got kin, Morgan. The Bookbinder brothers was Mack's cousins."

"And you think they'll come looking for me?"

"I *know* they will. All three of 'em. Jules, Kenny, and Al."

"You boys bury your pal and then turn around and head the other way. Don't follow me. If I find you on my back trail, and I'll be checking often, I'll lay up and wait for you and I'll kill you. All of you."

"Oh, we got time, Morgan," Boyd said. "Nothin' but time. We'll be a-seein' you. Bet on that."

"Dismount and take off your gun belts, hook them on the saddle horns, and then start digging," Frank told them.

"I'll just be on my way. Don't dog my trail, boys. I mean it."

When they'd dismounted and had their gun belts hanging on the saddle horns, Till Brackman looked up at Frank. "You don't have to worry about me back-shootin' you, Morgan. When I kill you, it'll be face-to-face."

Frank climbed down from the rocks and walked over to his horses. He rode back to the stage road and looked at Till and Boyd as they dragged Mack's body off the road. Todd had gotten a shovel from their packhorse and was digging a hole a few yards off the road.

"You boys bury him deep now," Frank called. "You wouldn't want the critters to dig him up and eat him now, would you?"

"Go to hell, Morgan," Todd called back.

Frank put his back to the three gun slicks and turned Stormy's nose toward Prescott.

Frank's ride to Prescott was uneventful after the confrontation on the stage road. He stabled his horses, got Dog a sack full of scraps from a café, and then got a room in a hotel. After a bath and a change into clean clothes, Frank stepped out onto the boardwalk.

Two men stepped up to stand beside him, one on either side. "There's another man right behind you, Morgan," one said. "Just stand easy."

"All right," Frank replied. "What's on your mind and who are you?"

"We're deputies, Morgan. And preventing trouble is on our mind."

"I'm not here to cause any trouble."

"We only have your word for that."

"My word's been good enough for many years, boys. If

there is any trouble, I won't be the one who starts it. You mind if I roll me a smoke?''

"Go ahead."

Cigarette lit, Frank asked, "Why the concern about trouble?"

"You got people looking for you, Morgan. We heard about the trouble on the stage road."

"Stagecoach driver spread the word?"

"That's right. Till Brackman and the Crow Brothers was nightin' at a way station."

"What'd they say about it?"

"Just that you killed a pard of theirs."

"That pard was a man named Mack. He pulled on me after I took exception to the four of them doggin' my trail."

"The sheriff figured it might have been something like that. But he couldn't figure why the other three didn't buy into it and drag iron."

"Maybe they figured it wasn't a good day to die."

The deputy chuckled and relaxed. "That would sure be a good reason, I reckon."

"I killed Ray Hayden after he braced me in Wickenburg. Till and the others were friends of his."

"I don't know much about the Crow Brothers," the deputy said. "But Till Brackman is a sure-'nuff bad one."

"He's quick and he's mean, for a fact. But I don't think he'll show up here in Prescott while I'm here."

"If he does?"

"Then I reckon there'll be trouble."

"I'll keep an eye out."

"Thanks."

The three lawmen walked away.

"Starting out to be a very interesting trip," Frank muttered.

Four

"I'm headin' north in a few days," the man said to Frank over a beer. "But I'm told some renegade Indians are raiding north of here. Looking for some men to ride along with."

"I'm heading north in a day or two," Frank told him. "Little settlement called Flagstaff. 'Bout ninety miles from here, so I'm told."

"Any particular reason for headin' that way?"

"I was going due east, over the Muggyown Rim. But that can get kind of rough. I changed my mind."

"Want to ride along with us?"

"Sounds good to me."

The man smiled and stuck out his hand. "I'm Jack Barnes. Got my wife and kids with me. My woman's a good cook. You won't go hungry."

"Now I know you got a deal."

"We plan to pull out day after tomorrow, at dawn. All right with you?"

"That's fine. How many others do you have lined up?"

"Two other families. We're all in wagons. You sure we won't slow you down, put you off schedule?"

Frank smiled at that. "I'm sure. I'm on no schedule. But are you sure you want *me* to ride along with you?"

Jack grinned. "Why not? Are you a wanted man?"

"I'm Frank Morgan."

The smile on Jack's face slowly vanished. He blinked a couple of times. "*The* Frank Morgan? The gunfighter?"

"I reckon so."

Slowly, the smile returned to the man's face. "My girls will be thrilled, Mr. Morgan. And so will my wife."

"Drop the mister, Jack. It's Frank."

"All right . . . Frank. Done. We're camped just outside of town. On the north side. We'd be proud to have you for supper. Can you make it?"

"I'll be there, Jack. Thanks."

"I'll see you about five then. Golly, I can't wait to tell the others. See you later, Mr. . . . ah, Frank."

"See you then, Jack."

As he watched the man walk out of the saloon, Frank thought: *People are moving all over the country, looking for . . . what?* Jack Barnes's clothing was not worn or patched or dirty, and he did not speak as an uneducated man. So what was he looking for in life, for himself and his family? *For that matter,* Frank thought with a silent sour note, *what the hell am I looking for?*

Julie Barnes was a very attractive woman, in her mid-thirties, Frank guessed. Their two daughters were Rebecca and Susan. Rebecca (Becky as she preferred to be called) was sixteen, Susan had just turned fourteen.

Frank couldn't keep up with all the other kids' names, but the adults were Roland and Joan Sutton and Dick and Ruby Carter. Between them, they had six kids, two boys, four girls. Frank figured that eventually he'd get all the kids' names straightened out. Maybe by the time they reached Flagstaff.

Supper was a feast for Frank. Julie had fixed some really good homemade stew and lots of it, with fresh-baked apple pie for dessert. Lots of fresh-baked bread and plenty of good coffee. Joan Sutton fried some chicken and boiled some potatoes and fixed up some lip-smackin'-good gravy. Ruby cooked up a mess of vegetables and fixed some rice puddin'. The kids all made a big fuss over Dog, and hand-fed him until he was so full he could hardly walk.

"Pig," Frank whispered to him.

Dog showed him his teeth.

The boys all wanted to see Frank's Peacemaker, but Frank could tell that Joan Sutton didn't much cotton to that idea, and he told the boys maybe later on up the trail.

"My wife is a very devout Christian woman, Mr. Morgan," Roland told him. "She doesn't like guns."

"Do you have any weapons?"

"Oh, yes. I told Joan before we got married that God, guts, and guns were the backbone of this nation and it was our right and duty to have guns. She didn't like it, but she said no more about it."

"This is mean country to be unarmed."

"Don't I know it."

Dick Carter played the guitar and Ruby had a pleasant voice, and they entertained the gathering for a time after supper.

Frank learned that all three families had originally settled

close to each other down near the border, but both Mexican
and Anglo bandits and rampaging Indians had finally convinced them to pull up stakes and head north.

"We're all of us plannin' on doin' some ranchin' and
farmin' over near Santa Fe," Dick told Frank. "We got us
some capital and maybe we can make a go of it. How 'bout
you, Frank?"

"I'm looking to buy some land over in that direction
myself. Might turn out that we'll be neighbors."

"Hey, now," Jack said. "That would be great."

Yes, it would, Frank thought. *A home of my own, with
good neighbors living close by.*

That's a nice thing to dream about, for a fact.

"You never can tell," Frank said. "Well, thanks for the
fine meal and the good company. I'll see you folks day after
tomorrow and we'll hit the trail."

"Good night, Mr. Morgan," the kids chimed.

Frank smiled at them.

The outlaws hit them just north of the Big Chino Wash,
about halfway between Prescott and the main stage road
that ran east and west. The small wagon train rounded a
curve in the road, and the morning's quiet was shattered by
gunfire from a half-dozen locations among the rocks along
both sides of the road. Frank saw Roland Sutton take a round
in the center of his forehead that blew out the back of his
head. The man toppled backward into the covered bed of
the wagon. His wife began screaming in shock and panic.

Dick Carter managed to get his pistol from leather before
a bullet cut him down. The kids were screaming and yelling,
and that was the last thing Frank remembered before a white-
hot pain touched the side of his head and dropped him into
darkness.

Frank awoke to a terrible pain in his head; a deep throbbing that surged through him with every beat of his heart. He tasted dirt in his mouth and opened his eyes. He was lying facedown by the side of the road. He slowly and very carefully turned his head. He looked square into the eyes of Dog, sitting a few feet away, looking at him.

"Hello, boy," Frank managed to whisper. "What the hell happened here?"

Dog came to him and licked his face.

Then Frank remembered the attack.

He lay very still for a few more moments, and then, with what seemed to be a tremendous effort on his part, managed to crawl to his knees. He groaned as his world swayed and shifted all around him. He closed his eyes and waited for a few moments before opening them again. The landscape had settled down.

Frank was thirsty to the bone, his mouth cotton-dry. He tried to spit, and could not muster up enough saliva to even do that. He slowly rose to his feet and stood there for a moment, swaying like a drunk man as his world moved all around him. When everything stopped shifting, Frank took a closer look around him. About a hundred yards away he spotted one lone team and wagon sitting in the road. He heard a snicker, and looked around as Stormy and the pack-horse came out of the rocks and walked up to him. He dropped his hand to his gun butt. It was still in his holster. He searched but he couldn't find his hat.

"Damn," Frank said. "That was a new hat too." Then Frank remembered the women and the kids. "Oh, God!" he muttered.

He picked up the lead rope to the packhorse and managed to get into the saddle. He rode up to the wagon and looked inside. It was empty of everything except the body of Roland Sutton. The outlaws must have taken the contents and distributed the goods among the other two wagons. But where were the others? He didn't like to think about what might have happened to the women and the girls. He felt pretty sure he knew. Staying in the saddle, he circled the wagon and located his hat, off the road a few yards. He dismounted and got his hat and tried to put it on. It wouldn't fit over the lump and the cut on his head. Frank got his canteen and had a long drink, then got back into the saddle and hung his hat on the saddle horn.

He began searching for any survivors of the attack, working in a circle all around the road. It didn't take him long to find the body of Jack Barnes. The man had been shot several times, but had managed to crawl off the road and into the rocks; there he had died. Frank could find no sign of Julie or the girls.

Another five minutes of searching on the other side of the road and he found Dick Carter, shot to bloody rags. A few yards away he found the naked body of Ruby Carter. She had been raped and then killed. No sign of the Carter children.

The remaining two women, the six girls and the two boys, had been taken alive and carried off. Frank pulled the wagon off the road and unhitched the team. He then began burying the bodies. It was slow work, for his head was hurting really badly. He stopped often to rest, but eventually got the job done. Then Frank built a fire and made himself a pot of coffee. He sat down on the ground to think things out as best he could.

While the coffee was making, Frank rolled a cigarette and carefully bathed the side of his head with a wet cloth. He felt some better after doing that. Then two cups of hot strong coffee and another cigarette made him feel even better and he could think straighter.

There wasn't a doubt in his mind but that the women had

been taken by some members of one of the Val Dooley gangs. He'd heard back in Prescott that the gangs were working all over two states. And he'd also heard that the combined gangs numbered close to two hundred and included Mexicans, Anglos, renegade Indians from half a dozen different tribes, and also Comancheros.

"Hell of a volatile mixture," Frank muttered, sitting by the fire and pouring himself another cup of coffee. He looked up as he felt the pounding of many hooves slightly tremble on the ground beneath him.

A dozen or more riders reined up. As they spotted him, Frank lifted both hands to show them he meant no harm.

"That's Frank Morgan!" he heard one man yell.

"Morgan," a man with a star on his chest said as he rode over and dismounted, "I'm the sheriff of this county. You seen any large numbers of men ride through here?" Before Frank could reply, the sheriff squinted his eyes and exclaimed, "What the hell happened to your head?"

Briefly, Frank explained, ending by pointing and saying, "The men and the woman are buried over yonder. I reckon the outlaws took the other women and the kids."

"You think it's some of Dooley's bunch?"

"I do."

The sheriff yelled for his men to check out the graves and carefully mark their locations on a county map, then turned back to Frank. "You need a doctor, Frank?"

"No. Thank God, I've got a hard head. I reckon they saw all the blood and figured I was dead."

"Feel up to giving me a description of the women and the kids? I'll get it out over the wires immediately."

"Sure. While I write them out, why not pull up a piece of ground and have a cup of coffee?"

"Sounds good to me. I'm butt-sore from hours in the saddle. And I'm gettin' too damn old for all this."

"It's only going to get worse until Dooley is dead."

The sheriff paused in his pouring of coffee and eyed Frank. "You have that job in mind, Morgan?"

Frank's smile was thin. "You bet I do, Sheriff. I damn sure do."

Five

The sheriff and his posse rode on, and Frank put out the fire and stowed his coffeepot. He mounted up and began riding in a slow circle all around the ambush site, trying to make some sense out of all the hundreds of hoofprints. The gang that had hit the small wagon train must have numbered about thirty, Frank concluded after sorting out many of the tracks. And they had split up into three groups. One group of eight or ten had headed south. Another group of about the same size had headed west. The final group, which included the stolen wagons and the hostages, had left the road a few miles from the ambush site and headed northeast, straight for some rough country. Frank followed the third group, knowing they would have to abandon the wagons before long. The country would be too rough to get a wagon through, unless someone had cut a road that Frank knew nothing about . . . which was entirely possible, for he had not been in this area in quite a while.

An hour later Frank came upon an abandoned wagon and team. The gang had left the horses still hitched up. "Bastards," Frank muttered, dismounting and setting the team free to search for food and water. He knew that somebody would come along and claim the animals for themselves, for they were good stock.

"So they had hidden horses here," Frank said to the blue and cloudless sky. "Now I wonder if they knew how many women were going to be in the wagons."

Probably, he silently concluded. That meant they had to have spies reporting to them, and if they had eyes and ears in one town, they probably had them in others.

"Hell of an operation," Frank said. "I guess the rumors were true."

He looked up into the sky; still a few more hours of daylight left. But he didn't want to ride into an ambush. He would follow the trail for another hour and try to pick up any shoe marks or stride that would help identify the horse later on. Then he would make camp for the night.

He still didn't know, and probably never would know, why his horses and gear had not been taken by the outlaws. He could only guess that when he was hit and knocked out of the saddle, his horses bolted for the rocks. Dog would have taken off with them, and Dog had probably kept them in the rocks until the outlaws were gone. Dog was more than a pet and a watchdog. He was a survivor, first, last, and always.

Back in the saddle, Frank pressed on, riding slowly, checking the many hoofprints of the outlaws. He found several very distinctive prints from three different animals. "I got you now, you bastards,'' Frank muttered. ''No matter where you go, if you're on these horses, I'll find you and send you to hell.''

Frank rode on.

He made camp about an hour before dark. Over a hat-sized fire, he fixed bacon, biscuits, and coffee. Then he went to sleep and slept soundly until four o'clock. After eating what was left of the biscuits he'd fixed for his supper and drinking a pot of coffee, Frank enjoyed a smoke, and then saddled up and was on the trail just as dawn was streaking the eastern sky. He dogged the trail of the outlaws relentlessly until two o'clock that afternoon; that's when he discovered the body of fourteen-year-old Roy Sutton lying just off the trail. The boy had been shot in the back twice.

Frank spent an hour studying the tracks and broken low limbs and smashed vegetation before he put it all together. The boy had escaped, somehow, and it looked as though he was making a pretty good run for it when the outlaws caught up with him and shot him. Frank doubted the boy suffered. He was probably dead before he hit the ground.

''If you'd only taken to the timber, boy,'' Frank muttered as he was digging a hole to bury Roy in, ''you might have made it.'' *Too late to dwell on that now,* Frank thought, glancing over at the body of Roy Sutton.

He buried the boy and covered the mound with rocks, then spoke a few words over the grave and was back in the saddle again. He was getting closer to the outlaws. Horse droppings were very fresh.

''Now if I only had a plan to get the hostages free,'' he muttered. *A hell of a lot of ifs associated with this,* he thought.

But he knew the plan would come when he caught up with the gang. It all depended on the size of the gang and the terrain.

An hour after burying the boy, Frank reined up when he caught the faint scent of smoke. He sat in his saddle for a moment, sniffing the air, trying to determine where the smoke was coming from. He swung down from the saddle, removed his spurs and stashed them in the saddlebags, then pulled his rifle from the boot.

"You stay," he told Dog. "Stay."

The big cur sat down and looked at him.

Frank slipped through the rocks and timber, the smell of smoke getting stronger. Then he caught the odor of coffee and bacon. A few yards farther and he could hear the faint murmur of conversation. He carefully made his way closer until he could clearly see the camp area. Four men and a woman. Julie Barnes.

"I don't see why we can't have us a taste of this woman," one man said. "Hell, Val's gonna sell her to some greaser anyway."

"Orders, Brit," another man said. "Val don't want 'em all beat up. And you know she's gonna fight you if you try to lift them skirts."

"Well," the man called Brit countered, "why don't you and Tom hold her down and I'll mount her thataway?"

"Leave me out of this," Tom said. "I ain't goin' agin Val's orders. 'Sides, we got whores a-waitin' for us at the main camp."

"That's a hundred miles south of here!" Brit said. "I got me an itch that's got to be scratched right now."

"Hal's right," another man said. "There ain't no woman worth gettin' kilt over. Right, Jeff?"

"I don't know," the fourth man said, looking over at Julie. "That there is shore-nuff one fine-lookin' piece of candy."

Frank was mentally figuring the odds of his being able

to take out all four outlaws without Julie getting hurt. The odds were not good.

Brit suddenly stood up. "Hell with Val," he said. "Hike up them skirts, lady."

"You go to hell!" Julie told him.

The other three men laughed, Hal saying, "She's a regular wildcat, Brit. You bes' leave her be."

Jeff set his coffee cup on the ground and stood up. "I'll hep you with her, Brit. Then I get my turn."

"Damn you!" Julie shouted.

Brit was fumbling with the buttons on his jeans when Frank shot him. The .44-40 slug struck the outlaw on the left side and blew out the right. Brit was dead and cooling before he tumbled to the ground.

Jeff cussed and clawed for his pistol. Frank gut-shot him, doubling the man over just as Hal jerked up a rifle. Frank put a round in him. Hal was knocked backward but not down. He lifted his rifle, and Frank put a second round in him. Hal dropped his rifle and sat down hard on the ground, slowly toppling over, his head coming to rest in the fire. The smell of burning hair filled the air.

Tom raised his hands. "I'm done! I'm out of this."

Frank stepped out of the rocks. "Pull your partner's head out of the fire and then untie the woman. Do it!"

"Oh, I'm hard hit!" Jeff hollered. "Hep me!"

"In a minute, Jeff," Tom said. "Just hang on." He pulled Hal's head out of the fire and then hurriedly untied Julie.

Julie stepped away from the outlaw, rubbing her wrists, and walked toward Frank, being careful not to get between Frank and Tom.

Smart woman, Frank thought. *She knows something about guns.*

"Can I see to Jeff now?" Tom asked.

"Go ahead. But first kick his pistol out of reach."

"Yes, sir, Mr. Whoever-You-Is."

"Frank Morgan."

Tom kicked the six-gun out of reach, and then slowly turned to look at Frank, his eyes wide. *"Frank Morgan!"*

"Yes."

"Frank Morgan shot me?" Jeff asked, both his hands covering the hole in his belly. "You wasn't supposed to be with them movers."

"Well, I was. And one of you bastards shot me."

"It wasn't me, Mr. Morgan," Tom said quickly. "I didn't shoot nobody and I didn't rape that woman back yonder."

"Ruby Carter."

"Whatever her name was. That was some others. They went on ahead with the other women and the boy."

"Who shot the boy I found back yonder on the trail?"

"Ormond," Tom said. "He's a bad one too."

"He certainly smells that way," Julie said. She looked at Frank. "Did you bury my husband, Frank?"

"Yes. I buried all that were killed back on the road."

"I want my girls back."

"I intend to get as many of the hostages back as possible, Julie."

"You'll play hell doin' that, Morgan," Jeff said as Tom helped him stretch out on the ground. "They's too many in the gang."

"Tell me about the gang," Frank said.

Jeff cussed him.

"What are you goin' to do with us, Morgan?" Tom asked.

"I haven't made up my mind about that."

"I know what to do with them," Julie said. "Fix a rope and hang them."

"Now wait a minute!" Tom protested. "I didn't take no part in talkin' 'bout rapin' you, lady. I talked agin it."

"You can't hang me," Jeff said. "I'm a wounded man. I need a doctor."

"There isn't a doctor within fifty miles of here," Frank told him. "You think you can sit a saddle for fifty miles?"

"You just gonna leave me to die?"

"Seems like a good idea to me," Frank told him. "Now shut up." He looked at Tom. "Tell me about the gang, Tom."

"They's five gangs, Morgan. They operate in Arizona and New Mexico. Rangers run 'em out of Texas. Val Dooley's smart enough to stay clear of Texas now."

"How many men per gang?"

" 'Bout thirty-five or forty. Men come and go all the time."

"Why don't you shut your cowardly mouth, Tom?" Jeff groaned.

Tom ignored him. "And it ain't just men south of the border who buy slaves neither. They's men right here in the States buyin' women and girls for ... well ... you know, personal use. And sometimes it's little boys too. And the older boys are used as laborers in mines. They work 'em till they die. Which in many cases don't take long."

"The women are sold here in the West?"

"Oh, no. Not just here. They're shipped like cattle all over the United States. Val worked it all out. They're drugged up real good and kept that way till they get to where they're goin'. Passed off as sick folks. It's worked so far. Val's becomin' a really rich man. He's gonna retire in Mexico someday and live like a king."

"You're a dead man, Tom," Jeff whispered. "Val'll find out who talked and have you kilt."

"But you won't be the one who tells him, Jeff," Tom replied. " 'Cause you'll be long dead."

"Hell with you, you yeller dog."

Dog looked up from where he was lying and growled at Jeff.

"You keep that big ugly hound away from me, Morgan!" Jeff said.

Dog growled again and showed his teeth.

"I don't think my dog likes you very much, Jeff," Frank said.

"Hell with you too, Morgan! Val's gonna kill you too. He's fast, Drifter. Fast as a lightnin' strike. He'll take you."

Frank shrugged that off and turned to Julie. "Rummage around in the men's clothing and see if you can find some britches that'll fit you. We're going to be doing some hard riding and you'll be more comfortable in the saddle wearing jeans."

"All right. Frank?" Julie said.

Frank waited.

"I'm going with you after my girls."

"Julie . . ."

"No arguing, Frank. I can ride with the best of men and I grew up on the frontier, fighting Indians and outlaws. I can handle rifle, pistol, or shotgun. As a matter of fact, one of the dead men has a double-barrel Greener that I've had my eyes on. And he's got a bandolier filled with shells too."

Frank smiled at her. "All right, Julie. But it's going to be rough."

"Don't worry about me, Frank. I can take it."

"Good enough. Now go find something to wear." He looked at Tom. "I'm going to get pencil and paper, Tom. And then you're going to write down the location of every hideout Val's gang uses. Every trail, water hole, creek, and river. Large and small. Don't leave anything out, Tom. Your life depends on it."

"Don't you do it, Tom!" Jeff called, his voice weak.

Frank got a writing tablet and a couple of pencils from his gear and handed them to Tom.

"Get with it, Tom. And make it correct. 'Cause if it's all wrong, I'll come looking for you. And when I find you, I'll kill you."

Six

Jeff breathed his last breath on earth while Tom was busy writing instructions and drawing maps on the tablet pages. Neither Frank nor Tom had noticed. Julie came out of the brush after changing clothes and pointed out Jeff's passing.

"You don't appear to be upset about it," Frank remarked.

"I hope he burns in hell forever," Julie replied.

That got Tom's attention. He looked up from the writing tablet and said, "He didn't have many good qualities, for a fact."

"You known him long?" Frank asked.

"Awhile. I was with the gang when Mason was head of it. Jeff was already in tight when I come along."

"Val killed this Mason fellow?"

"Sure did. Walked right up to him all smilin' and shot him twice in the belly. Left him to die along the trail. Val laughed about it. Val ain't, well, he ain't quite right in the head, I don't think.''

''So I've heard,'' Frank said very dryly.

''Val is a big, handsome feller, so the ladies say. You and him resemble a lot. You could pass for brothers. But Val is mad-dog mean. Likes to hurt people.'' Tom shook his head. ''I never liked to be around him. He scares me.''

''And I hear tell he's fast with a gun too.''

''He is, Morgan. He's as fast as rumors claim you to be. You and him would be one matchup I'd pay hard money to see.''

''We'll see,'' Frank said. ''Finish up with your work.''

''I'm 'bout done. 'Nother ten minutes or so.''

Frank rummaged around the supplies of the outlaws and found a shovel, laying it aside. Tom could use it to dig the graves for the dead. Julie was also rummaging around the gear.

''This Dutch oven belonged to the Suttons,'' she said. ''I've seen Joan use it many times.''

''Set it aside,'' Frank told her. ''We'll take one of the outlaws' pack animals and carry enough supplies to last us for a time.''

''Frank?'' Julie whispered. ''What are you going to do with Tom?''

''Turn him loose.''

''Unarmed?''

''No. Not in this country. Not with the Apaches running wild.''

''He might turn on us,'' she replied, a dubious note in her voice.

''I don't think so. Besides,'' Frank added with a smile, ''I'm not going to give him a chance to do that.''

Tom finished and laid the tablet aside just as Frank and

Julie were done packing the additional supplies. "You gonna bury the dead, Morgan?" he asked.

"No, you are."

"I'll do it. Then what?"

"While you're digging the holes, Julie and I will head out. I've left you with supplies aplenty, and I'll leave you a pistol and rifle."

"That's big of you, Morgan. Mighty big."

"I hope I never see you again, Tom."

"You won't. I'm headin' out, back home to farm. If the tax people ain't seized my pa's land, that is."

"How long have you been gone?" Julie asked.

"Years, ma'am. I heard my ma died some five years ago, but Pa was still in good health and workin' the land. I aim to join him."

"Stay clean with the law, Tom," Frank said, swinging into the saddle.

"I plan on doin' just that, Morgan." He looked at Julie. "I'm some sorry for what's happened to your family. I mean that. And I hope you find your girls and bring them back to home safe and sound."

Julie looked as though she'd like to spit in Tom's face. But instead she nodded her head in acknowledgment.

"It ain't proper for you to be dressed in men's britches, ma'am," Tom said.

"Oh, for heaven's sake!" Julie said.

"Let's ride," Frank said with a smile, and lifted the reins.

"The nerve of that man," Julie said. "A kidnapper, rapist, and thief, lecturing me about the way I dress."

They had ridden about ten miles before making camp for the evening. Frank was frying bacon and boiling water for coffee, and Julie was still seething about Tom's comments.

"Finish peeling the potatoes, please, Julie," Frank urged. "And stop worrying about what Tom said. We'll never see him again."

"I know it," she admitted. "But it takes my mind off what might be happening to my girls."

"I understand. Julie, you know there is a good chance we won't find them."

"I know," she said, slashing at a potato with a knife. "But there is also a chance that we will."

"A chance, yes. But we don't know what camp they were taken to. And we've got to hit them all."

"And the first camp is . . . where?" She stopped her mutilation of the potato, which was now about the size of a small egg, and looked at him.

"About a day and a half's ride from here. It's over by a little creek. Sycamore Creek, I think it's called." He smiled at her. "Careful, Julie. You're about to lose a finger hacking at what's left of that tater."

She looked down at what remained of the potato and flushed in embarrassment. "I guess I got carried away, Frank. I'm sorry."

"No need to be," he reassured her. "I think you're holding up really well, considering all that you've been through."

She got another potato from the bag and began carefully peeling it. "Thank you. Frank, you don't speak or behave like a paid gunfighter. You've had some formal education."

"I'm not a paid gunfighter, Julie. I've never taken money to fight a man. Besides, how many gunfighters have you known?"

"Well . . . actually, none."

"That's what I thought. As to formal education, no, I have none. I left school at a very early age."

"But your manner of speaking . . ."

"Whatever education I have is self-taught. I enjoy reading; usually have one or two books with me."

"I always wanted to be a schoolteacher," Julie said. "My girls knew how to read before they ever went off to the first grade. They both love to read."

A branch popped in the brush and Dog growled low in his throat. Julie stared in amazement as Frank's Peacemaker seemed to leap into his hand.

"Hello, the camp!" a man called faintly from the timber. "I need help real bad. Please help me."

"Get your shotgun and get into those rocks over there," Frank told Julie, pointing. "Take Dog with you."

Frank circled wide in order to come up behind the voice. But there was no need for that. The man had been shot and was stretched out on his back, nearly unconscious, when Frank came up on him.

Frank knelt down. "Take it easy, partner. Let me open your shirt and see how bad hit you are."

The man's eyelids fluttered. "Hard hit. Belly shot. Outlaws took my horse and gear yesterday. But I slipped into the rocks and hid from them."

"Did they have any women with them?"

"Women? No. No women that I seen. Look, mister. They didn't get my money belt. It's around my waist. Bullet hit me right above it. I got near'bouts a thousand dollars in there. I been gold-huntin' and found me a small vein. I cleaned it out and the money's what I got for it. I ain't got no family to leave it to. You bury me deep so's the varmits won't dig me up. Keep the money for your troubles. Will you do that?"

"Of course I will," Frank said. "I don't want your money."

"It'll rot if you plant it with me. What good would that do?"

"All right. Let me get you into camp."

"No! It hurts too bad. I'm done, mister. Smelled your food a-cookin'. Nice talkin' with you." The man smiled, closed his eyes, and never opened them again on this side of the veil.

Frank left him and went back to get his shovel. He told Julie what had happened, and she said, "I'll get a blanket to wrap him in. It's only proper."

Frank pulled the skillet with the bacon off the fire and set it aside. He looked at Dog and pointed. "You leave that alone," he said.

If a dog could smile, Dog did.

"On second thought," Frank said, and set the skillet high up on a large rock, then went and got his shovel. Julie joined him by the body. Frank told her about the money belt. "I want you to have it, Julie. If the man had lived he would have said the same thing."

"All right, Frank," she said softly.

Frank dug the hole and slipped the man in it, then shoveled the dirt over him. When that was done, he spent some time gathering rocks to generously cover the mound. "I didn't think to ask his name. I don't reckon it makes much difference. Dead is dead. In a year or so there won't be any sign of the grave."

"But we'll know where it is," Julie said. "As long as somebody is alive who remembers, he won't be forgotten."

"I reckon that's so, Julie."

When they got back to camp, Dog was sitting staring up at the skillet on the large rock. "Oh, all right," Frank told him. "You can have a biscuit and some bacon."

"The biscuits!" Julie said, looking at the camp oven.

Dog had not bothered the biscuits.

"Good boy," Frank told him. "For that you can have two biscuits."

"What else do you feed him on the trail?" Julie asked.

"Bully beef, rabbit or squirrel if I can manage to shoot one. I have killed a small deer and jerked the meat for him."

"That is a spoiled dog."

Frank smiled. "Yes, he is. He's also very good company on the trail and he's a fine watchdog."

"I've noticed that. How do you keep him smelling so good?"

"Strong soap and bay rum," Frank said with a laugh.

"You're joshing about the bay rum, aren't you?"

"No. I keep a jug of it with me. Dog likes it too."

Julie shook her head at the thought of a dog wearing men's lotion. "I thought I recognized the scent. Bay rum on a dog," she muttered.

Frank got the skillet down from the rock, and once more set it on the rack over the fire. "These biscuits are ready. How about the potatoes?"

"One more to go," Julie said, grabbing up a potato and a paring knife. "Frank?"

He looked at her.

"What if my girls are not at the camp?"

"I'll try to free any who are there."

She shook her head. "That's not what I meant. We go on looking, don't we?"

"Of course. There are five camps. The last one is down along Tonto Creek. According to Tom, it's not far from an old trading post that I'm familiar with. I know the fella who runs it. He was one of the last of the mountain men. Name is Dewey. He ought to be about a hundred years old now."

Julie looked at him dubiously.

"Well . . . in his early eighties, at least," Frank admitted.

"That's better." She placed the peeled and sliced potatoes in with the bacon.

"I have some onions, if you like them in with the fried potatoes."

"I do. You're a good cook, Frank."

"Learned to be. Either that or starve to death. Soon as the bacon is good and done, I'll add the onions."

Julie stood up and stretched. To Frank's eye, the movement did marvels for the men's jeans the woman was wearing.

She turned to look at him, and Frank quicky averted his eyes . . . but not before she noticed him looking at her.

"I'll get that jar of jam out of the supplies," she said softly.

"It'll taste good for dessert."

"Yes. Then I guess we'd best get ready for bed."

"I reckon." Frank watched her walk away. Very handsome woman. Shapely. It was going to an interesting trip for sure.

Seven

Frank spotted the buzzards circling long before they reached the camp of the outlaws. Or rather, what was left of the camp ... and the outlaws.

"I know what it means," Julie said. "I've seen buzzards circling before."

"But have you seen what they can do to a body?"

"Several times, Frank. I told you, I was raised on the frontier."

"Sure you don't want to hang back and keep an eye on Dog?"

"I will if you absolutely insist."

Frank shook his head. "No. I won't do that. We'll ride on in. The buzzards tell me the Indians have left."

"How do you know it was Indians?"

Frank pointed to the ground. "Unshod pony tracks. I've been seeing them off and on for the last few miles."

"If there were hostages with the outlaws?" she questioned.

"They would have been better off being sold into prostitution." He shook his head. "Of course, that all depends on what tribe of Apaches this was. And how old the women are. If they're middle-aged, they'd be raped and then probably killed. Young girls would be taken. Julie, when we get closer, I want you to stay back with Dog for a time until I check the camp out. I'll call you in if it's clear."

"All right."

They rode a few hundred more yards before the smell hit them hard. Dog growled, and Julie frowned and wrinkled her nose.

"The Apaches had some fun torturing the prisoners. They burned some of them alive. One favorite trick of the Apaches is to cut out a man's tongue, then cut the tendons so he can't walk and let him just flop around on the ground. That's funny to them."

"Do you hate the Apaches, Frank?"

"Hate? No, I don't hate them. I don't have much use for them, I'll certainly admit that. The Apaches have just about been brought to their knees. It won't be many more years before they're a conquered people. But even when corralled and put on reservations, they'll always be a burden to the white man. Not just the Apaches, but most tribes."

"Why?"

"Because they resist change. A hundred years from now they'll still be resisting change; insisting on holding on to the old ways."

"And that's bad?"

"In a world of constant change, yes, it is. I doubt the Indian has changed much in a thousand years. Not of his own choosing, that is. That's why the whites are winning, and will continue to win."

Julie waited several hundred yards from the outlaw camp while Frank went in alone, on foot. He waded in among several belligerent and stubborn buzzards, feasting on the bloating corpses, and knocked them out of the way with his rifle. The buzzards were too full of human flesh and innards to fly; they could only waddle away and stare angrily at Frank.

Frank didn't expect to find anyone alive, and he didn't. The Apaches had had themselves a fine time with the outlaws. They had outdone themselves when it came to torture. Frank had never seen any worse than what he saw that day.

He called Julie in with the horses and Dog.

Dog had himself a high old time chasing the buzzards away, and while Dog was doing that, Julie went off behind a wagon to puke. Waiting for her to finish, Frank prowled around the carnage a bit more. He found a few things the Apaches had missed: several boxes of ammunition, a cache of money hidden in a false compartment in a wagon, a bottle of whiskey, and some women's underthings. He pointed out the undergarments to Julie.

"So they had some of the hostages with them," she said.

"Maybe, maybe not. These things just might have been left in the wagon." He showed her the money. "I'll keep this for you, Julie."

"I'm not familiar with that wagon, Frank. It wasn't one of them that rolled with us."

"I know. No telling where it came from. It doesn't matter. The money's still yours."

"Throw those underthings away. I don't want them. I'm not wearing some other woman's drawers."

Frank nodded and tossed the garments on the ground.

"Are you going to bury these men?" she asked.

"I hadn't planned on it."

"Just leave them?"

"No. I'll drag them over to that ravine yonder and dump them in, then try to collapse some earth and rocks over them."

"They're outlaws, Frank. I recognize some of them from the attack and just afterward, before the gang split up."

Again, Frank nodded. "Pick some of that brittlebrush there," he pointed, "and bunches of that owl clover yonder. I'll fix a small fire and you can toss it in the flames. That will help kill some of this dead stink."

"Gladly," Julie said, and hurriedly went to work while Frank set about building a small fire in the center of the death camp.

During a rest break in dragging the bodies to the ravine, Julie called, "I found some brand-new men's jeans and shirts, Frank. They've never been worn. I've got enough clothes to last me for a while now."

"Prowl around some more," Frank called. "No telling what you might discover that we can find a use for."

Frank really wanted to keep her away from the dead men, for some of them, during the dragging, had busted open and the smell was really bad. And the blowflies and maggots were busy working. All in all, it was not a pleasant sight . . . or smell.

Frank finally got all the men over the side of the ravine, and managed to collapse some dirt and rocks on top of them. "Hell with it," Frank panted. "That's going to have to do." He wiped the sweat from his face, for the day was warm and hauling off the bodies had been a job.

The buzzards had either flown off or waddled out of sight, much to the displeasure of Dog, for he had been having a good time chasing them. "You better be glad you didn't catch one," Frank told him, heading for his canteen and a long drink of water. "Those critters have the equipment to be mean."

"Are we ready to go?" Julie asked.

"Any time you are. Did you find anything else you could use?"

"Nothing at all. But I'll be very happy when we find a creek and I can take a bath—get this death smell off me."

"I could sure use a bath myself. And so could Dog. I've got some strong soap."

"And some bay rum," Julie said with a smile.

"Two jugs of that," Frank said, returning the smile. "One for me and one for Dog. Let's ride."

It was sixty miles over some rough and rugged country to the next outlaw camp. It took Frank and Julie just over four days to reach it. Frank saw plenty of signs of Indians, but no Indians. And for that, he was very grateful.

They found the camp of the outlaws, but no outlaws. It had been abandoned.

"Three or four days ago, I'd guess," Frank said after checking the droppings in the makeshift corral.

"Where is the next camp?"

"About thirty-five miles south of here, on the Mogollon Mesa. And it looks as though that's where this bunch took off to."

"I wonder why."

"I don't know. There's no sign of any battle having been fought here."

Julie was prowling around the deserted camp. Frank heard her gasp and whirled around, Peacemaker in hand. Julie was holding a bandanna.

"My Susan was wearing this when we were attacked. It belonged to her father. She was here, Frank. She was *here!*"

Frank walked to her. Julie was holding the bandanna tightly. "We've got to go, Frank. We've got to leave right now. Come on!"

Frank gripped her arm. "It'll be dark soon, Julie. And this is a good place to make camp. That's a little creek over yonder, and we're both tired and could use a good wash. Just settle down and think about it."

Julie struggled with Frank for a moment, then abruptly started weeping and fell against him. Frank put his arms around her and held her.

"They're alive, Frank," she sobbed. "They're alive!"

"I know, Julie. I know."

"We've got to find them."

"We will. I promise you, we won't stop looking."

"Promise?"

"I promise, Julie. We'll search every camp for your girls." He patted her shoulder. "Right now, I want you to settle down and rest for a few moments. I'll make some coffee for us. Would you like some?"

She nodded her head against his chest.

"All right. That's better. Now come on and sit down over here. You rest while I—"

"No!" she blurted out, pushing back away from him. "I'll see to a fire and the making of coffee." She wiped her eyes and took a deep breath. "You've got to take care of the horses and unloading of supplies. Go on, Frank. I'll be all right. Just give me a few minutes; let me collect myself."

"Sure?"

"I'm sure. Go on with you." She managed a smile.

Frank led the horses down to the creek and let them drink, then took them out to a small clearing and let them roll. Then he hobbled them and left them to graze. He walked the short distance back to the camp area, and busied himself rigging a rope for a picket line. He wasn't about to leave the horses away from the camp with Apaches on the prowl.

He heard Julie scream and whirled around, his hand dropping to the butt of his .45. Julie was standing at the edge of the clearing, pointing. Frank ran to her side. His eyes followed her shaking finger.

He could see nothing. He stared at Julie for a moment. "What is it, Julie? What did you see?"

"A girl," she replied in a quivering voice. "Right down there. I swear I did, Frank. I saw a young girl in a very soiled dress."

"Stay here. I'll take a look."

Frank slid his Peacemaker from leather and stepped down into the brush. He looked carefully around him after taking each step. Then his eyes began to adjust to the gloom, and he began to see signs of where someone had moved around . . . crawled around would be more like it. He stepped deeper into the brush and saw a piece of fabric that had been ripped off by a thorny bush. He pulled the fabric from the long thorn. The fabric was soiled, Julie had been right about that. But not by dirt. By blood.

"Do you see anything, Frank?" Julie called.

"Stay where you are, Julie."

"You did find something!"

"Stay put!" Frank yelled.

"Mama!" a girl called from Frank's left.

Julie screamed, and came running as fast as she could through the brush.

"Mama!"

Frank tried to head Julie off. She shoved him out of the way and raced past him, yelling her child's name.

Frank holstered his .45 and ran after Julie, catching up with her just as she stopped and screamed. He ran into her, almost knocking her down.

Susan Barnes lay on the ground in front of them. Her face was bruised and her dress bloody and torn. But she was alive.

Julie fainted.

Eight

Frank caught Julie and lowered her to the ground. He turned toward Susan and took a step. The girl moaned and huddled herself into a ball, crying out, "No! Don't touch me. Don't touch me. Leave me alone."

"Easy now, girl," Frank said. "I'm not going to hurt you. I'm with your mother, Susan. You're going to be all right now. I promise."

Susan opened her eyes and looked at Frank. "Mr. Morgan?"

"Yes, honey. It's me. Let me help you up."

Susan held out a hand and Frank took it, carefully helping the young girl to her feet. She was a mess. Her dress was no more than rags, hanging on her. Her face was bruised. It looked as though someone had used her for a punching bag.

Julie moaned and sat up.

"Mama," Susan said. She knelt down beside her mother and put her arms around her.

Mother and daughter embraced for a long moment before Julie pushed her away and looked at her. Then they embraced again for a few seconds. Susan stood up and helped her mother to her feet.

"How did you get free of those terrible people?" Julie asked.

"I told them I had to go to the privy, and as soon as I was in the brush I started running. I ran until I couldn't run anymore. I guess they got tired of looking for me and left."

"How long ago was that, Susan?" Frank asked.

"Several days ago."

"You must be starved, honey," Julie said.

"I am. I'm so hungry."

"Come on. We'll fix you something to eat and you can tell us everything that happened."

"I'd . . . well, I'd rather not talk about *everything* that happened, Mother. It's absolutely disgusting."

"We understand, Susan," Frank said. "Come on. I'll get you a bar of soap and you can take a bath in the creek and get clean. That should make you feel better."

"Oh, that would be wonderful. But I don't have any clothes."

"I'll find something you can wear," Julie said. "While you're bathing, I'll fix us something to eat."

After rummaging around, Frank found a bar of soap and gave it to Julie, then put on water to boil for coffee. He got out a pot and filled it with water for the beans, then sliced up some bacon. Julie, with her twelve-gauge Greener, was keeping watch down by the creek, as she guarded her daughter with an eagle eye. She had found some men's britches and a shirt for Susan to wear. Frank was glad now that he had taken a spare horse after freeing Julie from the outlaws. He had taken it just in case. It had been a good move.

Susan and her mother soon joined Frank in the clearing. With a pair of too-big men's jeans and a baggy shirt, Susan looked like a lost waif. But she was alive and apparently not too badly hurt . . . at least not physically.

Gnawing on a cold biscuit and drinking a cup of coffee, Susan told her story . . . that is, as much of it as she preferred to tell in mixed company.

"We were all kept together for the first day," the girl said. "Then it was just me and Becky when the others were taken. The outlaws"—she sighed and took a sip of coffee—"had their way with Becky and me until they got tired of us. Then I tried to run away, and they caught me and beat me. The next day I tried to run away again, and they caught me and beat me unconscious. Then they did some things to me and made me do some things to them I'd rather not talk about. Anyway, that went on until I got a chance to escape. When I saw my chance, I took it. That's all I want to say about that right now."

"How is, was your sister the last time you saw her?" Julie asked.

"She was alive, Mama. But they used her bad too."

"Do you know where they took her, Susan?" Frank asked.

The girl shook her head. "No, sir. I don't."

"We'll pull out in the morning," Frank said. "Head for the next outlaw camp."

"How far is that?" Julie asked.

"Couple of days' ride, if we're lucky. It's rough country." He looked over at Susan. "You feel like riding, honey?"

"I feel like killing those men who raped me, Mr. Morgan. And I will if you give me just half a chance."

"I don't blame you for feeling that way, Susan," Frank

replied. "But killing a man is a hard thing. It stays with you for a long time."

"You remember every man you ever killed?" Julie asked.

"I damn sure remember the first ones, Julie. And I will until the day I die."

"Well, let's put it this way, Frank," Julie said. "I'll help her kill those rapists. And I'll do it with a great deal of pleasure."

"We'll pull out at dawn tomorrow."

"That's Buck Mountain," Frank said, pointing to a peak to the west and just north of where they were camped. "Muggyown Mesa is a few miles ahead of us. Enjoy this hot meal and the coffee. It's the last we'll have until we clear the outlaw camp tomorrow."

"I want my gun now, Mama," Susan said.

"What's this?" Frank looked up. "Gun?"

"I can shoot, Mr. Morgan," the fourteen-year-old said. "Papa made sure of that. I was helping fight Apaches when I was ten . . . several times."

"You can shoot a pistol?"

"Pistol and rifle, Mr. Morgan. And I'm a very good shot with a rifle."

Frank slowly nodded his head. "All right. But when I put you in position—both of you—you don't move until I holler and tell you, understood?"

They both did.

Frank got one of the rifles taken from the outlaw camp, and a cartridge belt with every loop filled with .44-caliber rounds. He got a pistol and a belt from the same pack, and looked at it, and then at the petite young lady, then at her mother. "Are you sure about this, Julie?" he asked very dubiously.

"She can handle weapons, Frank. I know that for a truth. And she certainly has a right to be armed when confronting the men who kidnapped and assaulted her."

Frank handed the weapons to Susan, then watched as the girl carefully checked both rifle and pistol. Frank smiled and nodded his head in approval.

"See what I mean, Frank?" Julie asked.

"I'm convinced."

Frank rolled a cigarette, and then refilled his coffee cup and sat down. "About noon tomorrow we should be within a mile or so of the camp. I'll leave you two and scout on ahead, locate the camp. Then I'll be back and get you."

"We'll ride in?" Julie asked.

"We'll walk in. Too much danger of the horses smelling each other and starting a ruckus. Both of you sit down and rest, have some coffee. It's going to be a busy day tomorrow."

"I heard one of the outlaws say the Carter sisters would bring a pretty penny," Susan said. "Said he knew a man in Tucson who would jump at the change to buy them. He's bought girls before from some man called Mason."

"He must be a sorry son of a bitch," Frank said without thinking. He quickly looked up and said, "Excuse my language, ladies."

"That's all right, Frank," Julie said. "No need to apologize. I wholeheartedly agree with you."

"The outlaws said none of the hostages they now held would be sold out of the country," Susan said.

Frank shook his head in disgust. "We've got telegraph wires and something called a telephone now. I'm told that over in Europe they've got machines that chug around powered by something called an internal combustion engine— whatever that is. But around here we've got people buying young girls for disgusting uses. Worse yet, we've got men who will kidnap the girls for profit.''

"Maybe we can put an end to it," Julie said.

"I damn sure intend to try."

"The outlaws said this Dooley person likes to do, well, really bad things to the prisoners," Susan said.

"That's the head of the snake," Frank said. "I've got to kill him and I've got to make sure he's dead."

"A bullet to the heart would certainly do that," Julie replied. "And I would be more than happy to fire the weapon that puts it there."

"Me too," Susan said.

Frank touched the handle of the big bowie knife he carried on his gun belt. "Cutting his heart out was more what I had in mind."

"I'll help you do that too," Julie said.

Frank cut his eyes to her. The woman was grim-faced. She meant it. He looked at Susan. The young girl's eyes had followed his hand to the knife.

"I'll help you, Mother," Susan said.

"I didn't really mean that, ladies," Frank said.

"We did," mother and daughter said simultaneously.

Frank believed them. No doubt in his mind but that they would do it.

Frank guessed the number of outlaws in the camp at about twenty-five. He could not spot any hostages, nor could he see any sign they might be there.

He made his way back to Julie and Susan and told them what he'd observed.

"Are you suggesting we bypass this camp?" Julie asked.

"I'm saying it might be wise if we did just that."

"But you don't know for sure there are no hostages there, do you?"

"No, I don't."

Julie and Susan sat and stared at him. Dog came over and sat down beside Susan and stared at Frank.

"The two of you even managed to turn my dog against me," Frank said with a smile. "All right, all right. We'll all take a look at the outlaw camp. Then we'll make up our minds what to do. Does that suit you?"

It did.

"Get your gear together and let's go." He looked at Dog. "You stay with Stormy. Understood?"

Dog showed him his teeth.

"Does that mean he understands?" Susan asked.

"I reckon so. At least he understands the word stay."

While the women gathered up their gear, Frank unsaddled the horses and rigged up a flimsy corral of sorts. If no one came back from the outlaw camp, the horses could easily break out of the makeshift corral when they got thirsty.

"Let's go," Frank told Susan and her mother. *And pray,* he silently added, *that we aren't making one hell of a mistake.*

Nine

Frank got the women into position, then made his way closer to the camp for a long second look. He visually checked every part of the camp he could see. He could spot no hostages, nor could he see any sign that any of the kidnapped women had ever been there.

He was just about to slip back to Julie and tell her to get her daughter so the three of them could haul their asses out of there when someone in the outlaw camp yelled.

"Hey! They's someone in them rocks over yonder."

"Where?" another man hollered.

"Right over yonder," the man shouted, pointing in the direction of Susan. "It looked like a young boy. Come on. Let's check it out."

"I'd rather it was a young girl," another man said, standing up and picking up his rifle. "I could use me a taste of a young girl."

"It is a young girl," another man hollered. "I seen her just then. Ain't no boy got a butt like that."

The tents that were scattered around the camp area began emptying of outlaws, all of them armed.

One man started running toward the jumble of rocks where Frank had left Susan. "I get furst dibs if'n I lay hands on her furst!" he hollered.

"The hell you say," the man who'd first spotted Susan yelled. "I seen her 'fore anybody else. She's mine, goddamnit."

It was the last thing either of them would ever say, until they met up with Old Nick. Susan's rifle cracked and Julie's shotgun boomed. A blossom of crimson appeared on the chest of the man who received the load of buckshot from Julie. He was stopped in his tracks for half a second, then shoved backward as if hit by a giant fist.

The man who got himself lined up in Susan's gun sights hit the ground minus part of his head. Susan's .44 round had struck him in the center of his face and angled off to the right as it exited, taking with it a glob of gray matter, blood, and bone.

"Good God!" another outlaw yelled, pausing in his running to stare at the man who was missing part of his head. Those were the last words he would speak as Frank's .44-40 sang his death knell. The outlaw crumpled to his knees and died in that position, his arms by his side, hands clinched into fists against the ground.

Outlaws began jumping for cover as Frank, Julie, and Susan opened up, firing as rapidly as they could.

When the last surviving outlaw finally reached cover, there were eight men sprawled on the ground, dead or dying. And Frank knew that several more had been wounded, but were still able to walk or run for cover.

"Wonderful," Frank muttered. "Only about twenty or so to go."

Frank was on the south side of the encampment, Susan on the north side, Julie in the rocks to the west of the camp. To Susan's left there was a clearing. The outlaws would not try to cross that in any attempt to circle around behind them, for it was too wide-open. To Frank's right, there was a creek, then a small clearing before the camp area. Any assault from the outlaws would have to be made head-on, and that was about the only good thing to be said about the position of the three of them.

"Are you boys from what's left of Mason's gang?" someone tossed out. "If you is, we can maybe talk a deal."

"No deals," Frank called.

"Who are you?" another voice called.

"Frank Morgan."

"Frank Morgan!" several men shouted in unison.

After a few seconds of stunned silence, another man called, "What's your trouble with us, Morgan? How come you want to buy into this hand?"

"I was with the small wagon train you bastards ambushed."

"Damn!" another outlaw said.

"But we didn't kill you, Morgan. Hell, that ought to count for somethin', shouldn't it? You ain't got no other stake in this."

"You shot me," Frank said. "And you kidnapped some young girls. I want those girls back."

"We ain't got no girls here, Morgan. They're gone."

"Gone where?"

There was just enough hesitation on the outlaw's part to let Frank know he was about to hear a lie.

"Ah . . . we don't know, Morgan."

"You're a damn liar!" Frank called.

There was no reply to that. Frank didn't think there would be.

"Morgan?" The shout came from another part of the outlaw camp.

"Right here," Frank called.

"We tell you where the girls was tooken, you cut us some slack?"

"Maybe."

"You shet your damn mouth, Barlow!" a man yelled. "Val Dooley will cut off your balls and feed 'em to the hogs."

"Hell with Val Dooley," Barlow called. "Dooley ain't here like we is. Lookin' down the barrel of Frank Morgan's rifle."

"Let's rush him!" another hollered.

No one immediately replied or jumped up.

After a few seconds, a man yelled, "You want to rush him, Jenks, you lead the charge. How about that?"

"It was just an idea," Jenks replied without exposing himself from behind cover.

"Lousy idea," another said.

"Them girls was tooken south, Morgan," Barlow called. "Either right there where the Vedre splits or southwest of the Sierra Anchas, 'tween there and the Tonto. I don't know exact."

"All right, Barlow," Frank called. That jibed with the map Frank had. "Go get your horse and clear out. Ride like the devil is bitin' you on the butt. You understand?"

"I shore do. I'm gone, Morgan. You'll not see nor hear from me never again."

"I'll kill you personal, Barlow!" a man called. "You yeller dog!"

"Hell with you, Sims," Barlow yelled. "I'm gone and by God I'm done with you."

"Hold up, Barlow," another man yelled. "Me and Hank and Reb want to go with you. That all right with you, Morgan?"

"Suits me. Ride out fast and don't come back."

"You don't have to worry 'bout that. We're gone."

"Goddamn you all!" Sims yelled. "You're all dead men. I'll make shore Val Dooley knows what you done. Count on that."

"By God, I ain't runnin'!" a man yelled, and jumped up, both hands full of Colts spitting fire and lead.

Frank shot him, drilled him in the chest with a single rifle shot. The man fell back and kicked a couple of times, then was still . . . and very dead.

The sounds of several horses galloping away quickly faded into silence as those outlaws who chose life over death rode away.

"Now what, Morgan?" Sims called. "Come the night, we're sure to get you all. You gots to know that."

"Come the night, Sims," Frank replied, "you'll all be dead. I do know that."

"Big talk, Morgan! Big talk. That's all it is."

"It's enough for me," a man called.

"Me too," another said. "Them people got the highest ground and they're hid out in the rocks and brush. Me and Irish is gone."

"Cowards!" Sims yelled. "Craven cowards, that's all you is."

A few minutes later, the sounds of horses galloping away reached the trio in the rocks and the outlaws in the camp.

Frank spied what he was sure was a boot sticking out from behind a tree on the far side of the camp. He took careful aim and squeezed off a round.

"Owwww, damn!" a man bellered. "I'm shot, boys. He done shot off part of my foot. Oh, Lordy, it hurts so bad."

"Somebody go help Nick," Sims ordered. "Noah, you be the closest to him. Lend him a hand."

Noah tried. But Susan was right on him with her rifle, plugging him in the belly.

"That's it for me," a man yelled. "I'm out of here. Let me leave, Morgan? I promise you I won't be back."

"Ride out," Frank told him.

"You won't shoot me, Morgan?"

"I didn't shoot any of the others."

"I'll shoot you, you yeller bastard!" Sims hollered. "If I ever see you again, I'll gonna kill you."

"You ain't never gonna see me again. I'm gone. Hell with you, Sims."

Sims was still cussing as the man rode out.

"Seems like your gang is deserting you, Sims!" Frank called. But his eyes had picked up movement near the creek bank. He talked, but kept his eyes on the spot where he had detected movement. "Pretty soon it's just going to be you and me."

"I'll gut-shoot you, Morgan!" Sims yelled. "And stand over you and laugh while you die. What do you think about that?"

"I think it's a lousy idea." Frank lifted his rifle as he again saw movement by the creek. "And it isn't going to happen."

"I think it will," Sims yelled.

Frank sighted in on what appeared to be a shadow in the branches of the trees along the bank and squeezed off a round. He heard a scream and then a lot of thrashing around and cussing by the creek.

"I'm hard hit!" the man called. "Oh, I'm bleedin' bad. Blood's a-pourin' outta me like I was a stuck hog. Help me, please."

"I ain't movin'," a man called from the other side of the

camp. "Them damn people over yonder is too good a shots for me to risk my butt for the likes of Charlie."

"I heard that, you sorry son!" Charlie hollered. "Sims . . . you send somebody over here to help me."

"I didn't tell you to git yourself shot, Charlie," Sims replied. "You're on your own over yonder."

"Damn you to hell!" Charlie bellered. "I'm a-bleedin' to death over here."

"Well, do it quietly," another voice added.

"Hell with you too, Noble!" Charlie said. "You just as turd-sorry as Sims and all the others. You're all a bunch of yeller skunks. Ooohhh!" he yelled. "The pain is awful, I tell you. Somebody come over here and help me."

No one from the outlaw side offered to help.

"So much for honor among thieves," Frank yelled.

"My foot is hurtin' somethin' awful!" Nick yelled. "And I'm a-bleedin', too. My foot is broke."

"Too bad he didn't shoot you in the mouth!" a man hollered.

"You're a low-down skunk, Harwood!" Nick called. "I hope Morgan shoots you in the privates."

Susan's rifle cracked and a man grunted. He stood up in the rocks, his belly bloody, and looked down. "I been shot!" he yelled. "Oh, Lordy!"

Julie's Greener boomed, and another outlaw who had made the mistake of shoving a leg out of cover screamed in agony. "Oh, my God!" he screamed. "My leg is blowed off. My leg is blowed off."

A man jumped up to run to the outlaw's aid, and Susan's rifle cracked. The outlaw went down in a seemingly boneless heap.

"I'm gone!" another outlaw yelled. "They got the high ground and the best cover. We're all just easy targets here. I'm out of this, Morgan. You hear me? I'm done."

"I hear you," Frank called. "Ride out."

A few moments later, after the sounds of a horse's hooves had faded, Sims called, "All right, Morgan. All right. How about the rest of us?"

"What about you, Sims?"

"Can we give it up and ride out?"

"Without your guns, yes."

"This is 'Pache country, Morgan! You can't take our guns away from us. That'd be like handin' us a death sentence."

"Take it or leave it, Sims."

"I'll take it," one of Sim's men called. "That damn shore beats a-layin' here waitin' for a bullet."

"How about you, Sims?" Frank called.

"All right, Morgan," Sims said. "You win. We're comin' out."

"Do it slow and easy, boys," Frank cautioned.

Outlaws began rising up from out of their scant cover on the other side of the camp, hands in the air.

"Don't shoot them, ladies," Frank called. "Let's keep our word."

"Ladies?" Sims yelled. "You mean them others with you is wimmen?"

"That's right, Sims. Pretty good shots, aren't they?"

Sims started cussing.

Julie and Susan began laughing.

Frank stood up.

Sims looked at him for a moment and grabbed for his six-gun.

Ten

Frank shot him from the hip with his .44-40. Sims turned around once as if spun by a mighty hand, then crumpled to his knees, dropping his pistol. He cussed Frank for a few seconds, then toppled over face-first in the rocks, hard hit but still alive.

The other outlaws made no attempt to grab for their weapons. They stood silently, hands in the air.

"That one tried to be nice to me," Susan said, pointing at a young man.

"Which one?" Frank asked.

"The one wearing the black-and-white-checkered shirt. His name is Danny."

"Get over here, Danny," Frank said. "The rest of you get facedown on the ground." Danny walked slowly toward Frank. "On the ground, I said."

The outlaws hit the ground.

"How did this one help you, Susan?" Julie asked when Danny drew closer.

"He didn't rape me. When he wouldn't, the others laughed at him and called him names."

"Is that right, Danny?" Julie asked.

"He's a yeller-bellied, wet-behind-the-ears kid," Sims said with a groan.

"I was in jail when Harwood and Nick broke out," the young man explained. "They made me go with them. Said they'd kill me if I refused."

"What were you in jail for?" Frank said.

"I broke into a general store and stole some clothes back in the spring. I was cold and didn't have no money and couldn't find a job. Judge give me a year in jail. I didn't mind that. Least I was warm and had something to eat ever day."

"Stinkin' coward," one of the bellied-down outlaws said.

"Shut up," Frank told him. He cut his eyes toward Danny. "Get over here and sit down and be quiet."

"Yes, sir!" Danny said quickly.

"If just one of them on the ground starts moving, ladies," Frank said, "start shooting."

"We ain't gonna move!" one yelled.

Frank quickly collected all the guns and dragged the wounded outlaws into the clearing.

"I hurt somethin' awful," the outlaw with the shot-off leg complained. "You ain't a decent man, Morgan, draggin' me like I was a dead hog."

"When we leave," Frank told him, "you can get someone to heat a runnin' iron and cauterize that stump."

"Oh, Lord!" the man hollered.

"How 'bout me?" Sims groaned.

"You're done for," Frank told him.

"I ain't neither!" Sims said. "I'm gonna live to kill you, Morgan."

"Get the horses," Frank told Julie and Susan. He looked at Danny. "You go get you a horse and saddle up. Get ready to ride."

"Yes, sir!"

Frank did not like the idea of turning men loose in Apache country without means to defend themselves . . . even these men. But he couldn't take them with him, and he wasn't going to cold-bloodedly line them up and kill them. So what else could he do? The nearest sheriff's office was several days' ride away.

When the women had returned with the horses, Frank asked Susan, "Did any of these men rape you?"

"Yes. But they're paying for it. Sims did, and so did the man called Charlie. Noah raped me several times, and so did the man Mama shot in the leg. There were others, but they aren't here with this bunch."

"All right. Mount up." He looked at Danny. "Do you know where the next camp is located, boy?"

"No, sir. I ain't been with this bunch very long. Harwood and Nick was regular members. Way I heard it told, they was with this feller named Mason when Val Dooley come along. They plotted with Dooley to have Mason killed."

"Take the lead, Danny. Head south."

"Yes, sir. Does that dog of yours bite?"

"Only if you mess with him."

"I can promise you, I ain't gonna do that."

"Good. Move out." Frank swung into the saddle.

"Mean-lookin' dog," Danny muttered.

"I play with him all the time." Susan grinned at Danny.

"You're welcome to do it," Danny said.

As Danny was leading the women and the packhorses out, Frank turned to the men on the ground. "You all know what's going to happen if I ever seen any of you again, don't you?''

"Yeah," several of the outlaws said. "We're dead men."

"You got that right. See to it that you don't ever meet me again after today."

"I'm gonna meet you," Sims groaned. "I'm gonna kill you when I do."

Frank lifted the reins and rode out without looking back.

Late that afternoon, after the horses had been allowed to roll and graze, Frank rigged up a picket line close to camp. Susan was helping her mother fix supper, and Danny was sitting off to himself, his back to a tree.

Frank got a cup of coffee and sat down. "We were real lucky today, ladies. So don't get cocky and think all the outlaw camps will be as easy as this one was."

"We won't," Susan said. "Me and Mama been talking about just that very thing."

Frank looked over at Danny. "Get yourself some coffee, boy. Join us."

"Thank you kindly, sir," he said, getting up and walking over, pouring a cup of coffee. "Coffee would taste good."

"Where are you from, Danny?" Frank asked.

"Up in Iowa."

"You're a long way from home."

"Pa was mean as a snake, Mr. Morgan. When he'd get tired of beatin' on Ma, then he'd turn on me. I run off when I was just thirteen years old."

"How many years ago was that?"

Danny thought for a moment. "Six years ago, near as I can figure. I heard from some movers last year that Pa died. I been thinkin' of headin' back up that way to see if maybe Ma would take me back in. I could help her on the farm."

"Your ma would take you back in, Danny," Julie assured him. "You can count on that, believe me."

"Going to give up on a life of crime, boy?" Frank asked.

Danny smiled, and the smile made him look even younger than he was. "I wasn't much of a criminal, Mr. Morgan. First time I ever tired to steal anything I got caught. I didn't know what them men was doin' when I agreed to come along with them. And I didn't do no kidnappin', neither. I was back with the horses and the wagon when they attacked the wagon train."

"That's true," Susan said, verifying his statement. "Danny talked to me whenever he got the chance. I didn't tell him I was going to run away the last time because I didn't know when I was going to do it. When my chance came, I just took off."

Frank nodded his head. "You ride with us for a time, Danny." Frank got to his feet and went to the pile of supplies, most of them still packed up in canvas. When he returned, he handed Danny a gun belt with holster and a .45. "Susan says you'll do to ride the high country with, boy. And from what I've seen, I have to agree. You can get you a rifle for your saddle boot when you've a mind to. You know where they are."

Danny looked at the pistol for a moment, then stood up and buckled it around him. "I won't let you down, Mr. Morgan. I promise you that."

"You can use that pistol, can't you?"

"I can shoot, sir. Yes, sir."

Frank nodded his head and leaned forward, hottening up his coffee from the big pot. He added a dab of sugar and stirred it. "Danny, you think those men I cut loose back yonder will rejoin the group?"

"Yes, sir, I sure do. Most of them will anyway. They're a sorry lot. The whole bunch of them."

"I figure they will too. But I don't think they'll be stupid enough to try to ambush us on the trail."

"I wouldn't put anything past them, sir. I think we'd better keep a close eye on our back trail."

"Oh, I plan to do just that, Danny," Frank said with a smile. "I sure plan to do that."

Frank hung back, watching their back trail. On the second day out from the outlaw camp, his hunch paid off. He spotted four men dogging their trail. He rode up and told the others to hunt cover in the brush and stay put. He left Stormy and Dog with the group and taking his rifle, climbed up a small knoll and got into position. Frank waited.

Since he had not gotten a good enough look at those who had pulled out from the outlaw camp to identify any of them, he didn't want to start blowing some innocent riders out of the saddle. He waited until the four men were only about a dozen yards from his location, then stood up and called, "Hold it, boys. Right there."

The quartet reined up abruptly. "Morgan?" one asked.

"You got it. I warned you boys about following me."

"Now hold on, Morgan," another said. "We wasn't gonna cause you no trouble. We was headin' down to Tucson, that's all."

"Right," Frank said dryly. "And if I hang my socks out on Christmas Eve, Santa Claus will come down the chimney and fill them up with goodies."

"So what now, Morgan?" another asked.

"I see you boys got hold of some guns. Where'd you get them?"

"That ain't none of your damn business, Morgan," the fourth one said, a very surly note to his voice.

Frank pointed the muzzle of the .44-40 at the man's chest. "This says I'm making it my business, hombre."

"We had them hid out," one of the men said quickly.

"You're a damn liar!" Frank said. "So shuck them, boys. Right now."

"The hell we will!" the surly one snapped. "You go right straight to hell, Drifter."

Frank shot him. The .44-40 slug lifted the man out of the saddle and dumped him in a heap on the ground.

Frank shifted the muzzle to the first man. "Now you tell me: Where did you get those guns?"

"A couple of mover families and two driftin' cowboys, Morgan. We kilt them cowpokes when they made a fuss over givin' up their guns. But we didn't hurt them movers none."

"Except for their women maybe," Frank said, a very cold note to the statement.

"Well . . . one of them had a right good-lookin' daughter, and she was loath to lift them petticoats so we sorta lifted 'em for her."

"How old was she?"

"Oh . . . I reckon twelve or thirteen. She wasn't built up good at-all. Just had a couple of little knobs, that's all."

Frank's hands tightened on the rifle and he came very close to killing the man on the spot. Frank took a couple of breaths and forced himself to relax.

"Shut up, Al," one of the others said. "Shut your damn stupid mouth."

"What's your problem, Waddy?" Al asked. "I was just answering a question, that's all. That's all I was doin', wasn't it, Jeb?"

Jeb sighed. "Hush up, Al. Just hush up."

"Was the girl alive when you left?" Frank asked, his voice tight.

"Oh, sure she were," Al said. "Squallin' and bawlin' a bit. But she was alive."

"And the girl's mother?"

Al grinned nastily. "We done her too. That was fun. Me and Waddy held her down and Jeb—"

"Shut up!" Frank snapped. "I've heard enough. Just shut your mouths."

"Hell with your orders!" Al yelled, and grabbed for his pistol.

Frank blew him out of the saddle, then shifted the muzzle of the .44-40 just as the other two were dragging iron. Their horses were rearing and bucking in panic, preventing either of them from drawing smoothly. That was all the time Frank needed.

He shot Waddy in the head, and the man fell out of the saddle as lifeless and boneless as a rag doll. Jeb cussed Frank and managed to get his pistol out of leather and trigger off one shot. His shot missed. Frank's didn't.

Frank's bullet struck Jeb in the chest and that was it for Jeb.

Julie, Susan, and Danny came riding up just as Frank was climbing down from the knoll.

"Are you all right, sir?" Danny called.

"I'm a damn sight better than those four on the ground," Frank said. "Gather up their guns and get those horses calmed down."

"We're going to have enough guns to equip an army," Julie remarked.

"It might just come to that," Frank replied. "You never know."

Eleven

"Gone," Frank said, looking around the deserted camp. He had checked the long-cold ashes of several campfires, and then inspected the horse droppings in what had been a makeshift corral. "Several days, at least. Maybe longer."

"They didn't leave nothin' behind neither," Danny said. "This place has been stripped plumb bare."

"It's a hard ride to the next camp," Frank said. "We'll follow the East Verde down to the tip of the Tonto Basin. Half a day's ride past that there's an old trading post. I told you about it, Julie."

"The one owned by your friend, Dewey?"

"That's it. He'll tell us if any outlaws are within a hundred miles of there."

"How would he know?" Susan asked.

"Indians tell him. He gets along with Indians. One of the

few whites that do get along with the Apaches. He doesn't bother them, they don't bother him.''

"You want to make camp here, Frank?" Julie asked.

"No. We'll ride a few miles farther. But fill up the water bags and the canteens from the creek yonder . . . just in case.''

"In case of what?" Julie asked.

"In case the spring I've got in mind has somehow dried up." And he would say no more on the subject.

Relaxing and drinking coffee at the campsite late that afternoon, Frank jerked his thumb and said, ''There's a stage road over to the east about twenty-five miles from here. But there isn't but one town: Payson. Gold-mining town. No more towns on that road that I know of anyway. And the stage don't run on a regular schedule. We're going to stay on this route for a time. Even though the 'Paches—some of them—are on a rampage through this part of the country. We'll provision up with some potatoes and onions and the like at Dewey's trading post.''

"Is there a faster route?" Susan asked.

"Yes. But it's desert a lot of the way. And water is scarce. This way is better.''

"Sure is a lot different from where I was born," Danny said, a wistful note to his statement.

"I've never been to Iowa, Danny," Frank said. "What's it like?''

"Pretty and green," the young man replied. "Corn and wheat country. And you can grow a garden near'bouts any-where. Ma and me has us a garden. Potatoes and green beans and peas and such as that. We'd have us some corn on the cob and new potatoes and green beans, cooked with a big hunk of sowbelly for flavoring." He smiled. "That and some corn bread sure was some good eatin'.''

"I'd like to have me a big platter of that right now,"

Frank said. "Tomorrow I'll try to bring down a deer. We'll have us a feast on venison steaks from the back strap."

Danny grinned. "You kill it, Mr. Morgan, I'll clean it and skin it."

"You got a deal, boy. But for right now, those beans in the pot and that bacon in the skillet smell pretty damn good."

"Another few minutes for the beans," Julie said. "The biscuits are ready now."

"We had butter too," Danny said softly. "I used to help Mama churn." He shook his head. "That sure seems likes a long time ago." He looked at Frank. "I just recalled something, Mr. Morgan. Do you know a man named Cory Raven?"

"Heard of him. He's a hired gun. Why do you ask?"

"He's after you."

Frank set his coffee cup on the ground and looked at the young man. "How do you know that?"

"I heard some of the men talkin' about it. They said this Raven fellow had been hired to kill you."

"Did they say who hired him?"

"No, sir. I don't think they knew. Just that he was after you. And that he always got who he was huntin'."

"He's a bad one, for a fact. Last I heard tell of him he was up in Montana."

"Faster than you, Mr. Morgan?" Susan asked.

"I've heard he's quick, honey," Frank said. "But I've never seen him work, so I don't know for sure. He's gone up against some fast guns in his time, though. And he's always walked away. That tells me he's real good."

"Who would hire someone to kill you, Frank?" Julie asked.

Frank smiled. "Any number of people, Julie. The families of men I've killed. Stockholders in the many companies I have a piece of . . ."

"You have stock in big companies, Mr. Morgan?" Danny asked, a startled look on his face.

This time Frank laughed. "My ex-wife saw to that, boy. I hold stock in banks, factories, mines, railroads, land . . . Hell, I don't know exactly what all I own. I have lawyers taking care of all that."

"But . . . you're out here roaming around like . . ." Danny paused and nodded his head. "Now I get your nickname, sir. The Drifter."

"Well," Frank replied, "that was hung on me a long time ago, Danny. Long before it became known I have some money. Truth of the matter is, I just like to wander. I enjoy drifting. Me and Dog."

"How old is Dog, sir?" Susan asked.

"He's not very old. About three or four, I'd guess. He's a loyal friend, though."

"What kind of dog is he?" Danny asked.

"He's just plain dog, Danny. A mixed breed."

Dog wandered over and lay down beside Frank. Frank put a big hand on Dog's head. "He's a lot of company on the trail."

"Beans are ready," Julie said, smiling at the closeness between Frank and Dog. "Come and get it before I throw it away."

"Well, roll me in buffler crap and call me stinky!" the old man hollered. "If it ain't Frank Morgan in person. Light and sit, Drifter."

Frank dismounted and shook hands with the grizzled old man. "Dewey, you get uglier every time I see you."

"How long's it been, Drifter, five, six years?"

"At least that many." Frank introduced everybody, and quickly explained what had happened.

Dewey shook his head. "Pitiful, Drifter. The country's goin' to hell, for a fact. I know they's a group of no-'counts camped over west of here, 'tween the Tonto and the Spring. But they fight shy of me. Injuns told me 'bout 'em."

"How many, Dewey?"

"Pretty good-sized bunch, 'cordin' to the Injuns. Three double hands."

"Thirty or so."

"Yep."

"Any women in the bunch?"

"Injuns didn't mention none."

"And they would have."

"I reckon so."

"Mr. Dewey?" Susan said.

"Yes, child?"

"Is there a place where my ma and me could take a hot bath?"

"Shore is. It's out back. I'll stoke up the fire and get the water started heatin' up. Be about a half hour or so."

"Wonderful," Julie said with a sigh. "I have longed for a hot bath."

"Comin' right up, missy. Come on, Drifter, make yourself useful. You can help me tote the firewood."

Danny saw to the horses, Julie and Susan rummaged through the packs looking for clean clothes, and Frank helped Dewey get the fire started to heat the water. The bathwater heating, Frank went inside the old trading post in search of a cup of coffee.

"You've been here a long time, Dewey," Frank remarked.

"Damn near thirty years, Drifter."

"Just letting the world go by," Frank said with a smile.

Dewey cut his eyes to Frank. "Each of us, boy, in our own way."

"I reckon so," Frank admitted.

"Heard about you and your ex-wife gettin' back together couple years past. Heard about her dyin'. Shame. You reckon she could have settled you down?"

"I believe so. I like to think so."

"The Good Lord has a reason for ever'thin' that happens, Drifter. I reckon He had a reason for that too."

Frank nodded his head. Thinking about Vivian wasn't something he did very often. She was dead; no point in dwelling on that. "I reckon. You got anything good to eat around this place, Dewey?"

"Always. But game's been scarce the past few months."

"Tell me. I was going to kill a deer; had me a hankering for some back strap. Hell, I didn't see one."

"I got me a few head of cattle 'bout a mile east of here. Have me a few hogs for bacon. I like to take pork and venison and mix it up with some spices for my sausage." He rolled his eyes. "That there is good eatin', boy. Lip-smackin' good."

"Got any left?"

"In an ice cave not too far from here. I'll ride over and fetch us some. Matter of fact, I think I'll do that now. You keep an eye on the post for me."

"I'll do it."

Dewey rode off on a mule to get the meat, and Frank walked inside for a drink. He wasn't much of a drinking man, but he did enjoy a drink of whiskey occasionally. He took bottle and glass over to a table in a corner of the big room, which was filled with all sorts of merchandise a traveler might need, and sat down, pouring a drink. He rolled a smoke and relaxed, listening to the sound of the women in the back of the trading post as they filled up huge tubs with hot water. Danny came in and walked over.

"The women told me to get lost," the young man said.

His eyes wide, he added. "Them ladies is gonna strip plumb nekkid!"

Frank smiled. "Don't you, when you take a bath?"

"Well, sure. But . . . well . . . anyway, can I have me a drink of that whiskey? The thought of them women back yonder with no clothes on makes me all discombobulated."

"Help yourself. Glasses back of the bar."

Danny poured himself a shot glass of whiskey and sipped at it.

"You and Susan been sorta making eyes at each other," Frank said.

Danny blushed. "I didn't know it was that plain."

"Nothing wrong with it. You're a boy and she's a mighty pretty girl. Boys and girls been doing that for a long time."

"Me and her been talkin' some too."

"Oh?"

"Nothin' serious, mind you. Just jawin' is all."

"If you've a mind to tell me, I'm a good listener."

"I wouldn't know where to start."

"At the beginning, Danny."

The young man hesitated. "I reckon that would be when me and her first looked at each other."

"You kind of took a shine to each other right then, is that it?"

"Yes, sir."

"It happens."

"You believe in love at first sight, sir?"

"Well, I believe there can sure be a strong attraction the first time people meet. Love is not a subject I'm an expert on."

"You ever been in love, sir?"

Frank chuckled. "Oh, yes. That I can say for sure."

"Ever time I look at Susan I get a funny feelin' in the pit of my stomach."

"I'd say that was love then. Either that or a bad case of indigestion," Frank said with a straight face.

"You're makin' a joke out of this, sir."

"Not really, Danny. I'd have to say it appears like you're smitten, for a fact. But how does Susan feel about it?"

"The same way."

Frank hesitated for a moment. "Is this leading up to you wanting me to speak to Julie about you two?"

"Oh, would you?"

Frank cut his eyes to the young man. "You're sharper than I suspected, boy. But I don't think now is the time for me to be speaking to Julie about young love."

"Why not, sir? Miss Julie's all the time makin' eyes at you."

Frank set his whiskey glass on the table and stared at Danny. "You're mistaken, Danny."

"No, sir, I ain't neither. Susan's seen it too. We done talked about it."

Before Frank could respond to that, four men rode up to the trading post and swung down from the saddle. Frank stared at them for a few seconds. "Get out back and look after the women, Danny. We've got trouble."

Twelve

Frank stood up and slipped his Peacemaker in and out of leather a couple of times, making certain it was clear and slid easily. He walked over to the rough plank bar and waited. He knew two of the four men, Bad Eye Morris and Slim Dickson, and they were both trouble-hunting no-'counts. He did not recognize the other two.

The four men crowded in and stopped cold when they spotted Frank, leaning up against the bar. Bad Eye was the first to speak.

"Morgan," he said coldly. "Of all the people in the world I didn't want to see, you top the list."

"I'm not happy to see you either, Bad Eye," Frank replied. "You beat up any women or robbed any old people lately."

"You go straight to hell, Morgan!" Bad Eye snapped.

"Or raped any little girls, I might add." Frank didn't let up.

"Nobody ever proved I done that, Morgan!"

"You made your brags about it later, Bad Eye. Remember? You seemed really proud about doing it."

"Is that Frank Morgan?" one of the men Frank didn't know asked.

"Yeah, that's him, Brady," Slim said. "And I ain't got no more use for him than he does for Bad Eye."

"You gonna try to take all four of us, Morgan?" Bad Eye asked with a sneer.

"If it comes to that, yes. What are you doing in this part of the country?"

"That's none of your affair, Morgan," Slim said. "We ride where we want to ride. We don't need your damn permission."

"Looking for Val Dooley maybe?"

"How in the hell did he know that?" the other stranger asked.

"Shut up, Pike!" Bad Eye said.

"I ain't real sure I want to tangle with Frank Morgan," Brady said. "Four of us or not."

"He ain't nothin' no more," Bad Eye said. "Morgan's gettin' a little long in the tooth. 'Sides, I hear tell he's lost his nerve."

"You want to find out right now, Bad Eye?" Frank asked.

"I might, after I have me a drink."

"The bar's closed," Frank told him.

"Who says?"

"I say."

"Whose bottle is that over yonder on the table?" Bad Eye asked, pointing.

"Mine," Frank told him.

"Where's the barkeep?" Slim asked.

"He went for a ride. He felt an urge to commune with nature."

"He felt a what?" Brady asked.

"Hey," Pike said, glancing out an open side window. "I hear women chatterin' out back."

"Women?" Bad Eye questioned. "You're crazy, Pike."

"I ain't neither. I heared 'em."

"I smell soap for a fact," Slim said. "You got women washin' out back, Morgan?"

"There are two ladies bathing, yes. And they don't want to be disturbed."

"Says who?" Bad Eye asked.

"Me," Frank replied tersely.

"I'd like to gleam me some female skin," Pike said with a very nasty grin. "It's been a long time."

"So is being dead," Frank told him. "I'd give that a lot of thought were I you."

"Them women belong to you, Morgan?" Bad Eye questioned.

"They don't *belong* to anyone, Bad Eye. But they do want to be left alone while they enjoy their bath."

"I think I'll just have me a look-see," Bad Eye said, half turning toward the open door.

"Hold it, Bad Eye!" Frank told him.

But Bad Eye was already committed in his draw. When he turned to face Frank, his Colt was in his hand and he was smiling. "Now die, you son of a bitch!" he yelled.

Frank's Peacemaker leaped into his hand. He drilled Bad Eye in the belly, and the outlaw's boots flew out from under him and he went down on his back on the floor. His friends either jumped out the window or ran out the door . . . straight into the guns of Julie, Susan, and Danny.

Julie's Greener roared, and Slim Dickson was literally cut in half by the buckshot. Susan's rifle bullet tore into

Brady's chest and shattered his heart. Danny's bullet caught Pike in the belly, and the outlaw was doubled over on his knees in the dirt. Dewey galloped up just as Pike fell face-forward.

"Damn!" the old man said. "I always miss the fun." He looked up as Frank stepped out onto the porch. "Friends of yourn, Drifter?"

"Let's say I knew them." Frank named the outlaws.

"Heared of Pike and Bad Eye," Dewey said. "They was bad ones, for a fact. Prob'ly on their way to join up with that pack of trash Val Dooley runs."

"I 'spect so," Frank agreed. He looked at Julie, Susan, and Danny. "Y'all done well. I'm proud of you."

"I got an old horse I thought was dyin'," Dewey said, dismounting. "I dug a pit for her out back. Hep me with this sack of vittles and we'll drag these no-'counts out back and drop 'em in the hole."

"I ain't dead," Pike said. "Don't you be tossin' me in no death pit."

"Did your horse get all right, Mr. Dewey?" Susan asked.

"The horse come out just fine," Dewey replied. "She had the colic, I reckon."

"I said I ain't dead!" Pike protested.

"You will be soon enough," Dewey told him. "You got the look on you. Now shut up while I'm talkin' to this young woman 'bout my good old mare."

"This ain't decent," Pike said, watching as Frank dragged Bad Eye out of the trading post and stretched him out on the ground.

"Bunch of ugly bastards, for certain," Dewey said, after eyeing the dead and dying. He handed the sack of food to Danny. "Take that inside, will you, son? Thankee." Dewey squatted down beside Pike. "You're talkin' 'bout bein' decent? That's sorta like a skunk complainin' about somethin' smellin' bad.''

"You go to hell, you old coot!" Pike groaned.

"You'll be rotatin' on the spit long 'fore I ever get there, you ugly bufflar turd. Now hurry up and pass on so's I can get busy fixin' supper. I'm gettin' sorta hongry around my mouth.''

"You're a heartless, godless old bastard, you are!" Pike hissed at Dewey.

"I was gonna say a few words from the Good Book over you scum," Dewey told him. "Now I ain't gonna say nothin'. I'm just gonna shovel the dirt over you and good riddance.''

"You'll give me a proper Christian send-off, won't you, missy?" Pike asked, looking at Susan.

"You were going to join up with Val Dooley and you want a Christian burial?" Susan asked. "Go to hell!"

"Susan!" her mother admonished.

"That seems like a right good thing to say to me," Dewey said. " 'Cause hell is shore where he's a headin'."

"But she's only fourteen!" Julie protested.

"Ripe marryin' age, you ax me," Dewey opined. He looked at Danny, standing on the porch. "You, boy!"

"Yes, sir?"

"You axed this here comely lass to hitch up with you yet?"

"Now see here!" Julie said.

"I took me a squaw when she was fourteen. She was Blackfoot. Bore me three fine kids, she did.''

"My Susan is not a squaw!" Julie said sharply.

"But she's built up right good," Dewey said. "Time for her to git married. You axed her yet, boy?"

Frank was leaning up against a porch support post, and smiled at the exchange.

"I'm in pain!" Pike hollered. "Somebody get me a drink of whiskey."

"You got a belly wound," Dewey said. "You can't have no Who Hit John. That'd be bad for you."

"You old bastard!" Pike moaned.

"What happened to your children, Mr. Dewey?" Susan asked.

"The ones from the furst wife is all dead. I got kids from my second and third wife still around somewheres. I been a grandfather for years. Don't never see my grandkids, though. They all up in Canada."

"I want some whiskey to hep ease this pain!" Pike hollered.

"I told you," Dewey said, "you got a belly wound. I can't give you no whiskey. It's bad for your health."

Pike cussed him.

Bad Eye broke wind in death, and Pike jumped.

"We better get him in the ground," Dewey said. "He didn't smell good when he was alive. Dead, he's gonna be a real stinker."

"God, I might linger for days!" Pike said.

"I shore hope not," Dewey said. "You do that, I'll be sorely tempted to shoot you myself and put you out of my misery."

"*Your* misery?" Pike said.

"Grab Bad Eye's feet there, Danny," Dewey said. "Drag him around back. You're young and strong. Me and Drifter will tend to Slim."

"You ladies keep an eye on Pike," Frank suggested. "He might try to pull something."

"Ain't you gonna get a Good Book and read over 'em?" Pike questioned.

"We'll wait till you kick the bucket," Dewey told him. "Read over you all at once. It'll be easier that way."

"Easier for who?" Pike asked.

"For us," Dewey replied.

"Damned old coot!" Pike said.

When the men returned from dropping the dead into the pit, Julie pointed to Pike. "He's unconscious."

"Won't be long now, I reckon," Dewey said. "How-somever, I have seen 'em linger for two, three days. Git to be a real bother after a while."

"Bother?" Susan questioned.

"Oh, yeah, missy. They git to talkin' in their dark sleep. They'll start confessin' all their sins and Lord have mercy, that can take days. Gits plumb nerve-rackin'. I 'member one old mountain man name of Big Foot Fontaine. A Frenchy from up Canada way. He took him a Pawnee arrow in the belly and lingered around 'tween livin' and dead for days. Talked all the damn time. Like to have wore us all out. He talked about all the women he said he'd known. I don't think he realized he was jawin' with Saint Peter. And lyin' too. If Saint Peter didn't know nothin' 'bout women at the beginnin', he damn shore did when Big Foot got done."

Danny was laughing at the old man. "Is that the truth, Mr. Dewey?"

"I'm here to tell you it is, boy. I mean, I cleaned it up a mite on 'count of the females present."

Pike suddenly groaned, stiffened, and then relaxed.

"That's all for him," Frank said. "Grab his feet, Danny. It's time for a funeral."

Julie was in the living quarters of the trading post, reading a book. Danny and Susan were sitting out back on a bench, doing what kids in their teens have been doing for centuries: gazing into each other's eyes and breathing heavily. Frank and Dewey were sitting on the front porch, talking quietly.

''You done set yourself a near'bouts impossible task, Drifter,'' Dewey said.

''I know it.''

''But you're gonna see it through, right?''

''I sure am, Dewey. Val Dooley has to be stopped.''

''And you think you're the man to do it.''

''I reckon so.''

''Texas Rangers couldn't catch him. Mexican army couldn't stop him. Two dozen or more sheriffs' posses couldn't catch him. You takin' that into consideration?''

''I've thought about it.''

''You been real lucky so far.''

''I know that far better than you, Dewey.''

''You want another gun to ride with you?''

''You?''

''Yep.''

''I thought you'd never ask.''

Thirteen

"Are you just going to ride off and leave your store unlocked, Mr. Dewey?" Susan asked.

The first shards of silver were beginning to cut at the eastern sky.

"They'll be a couple of Hopis along soon as we pull out, child," Dewey replied. "They'll look after the place till I git back."

"How will they know you're gone?" Danny asked. "I ain't seen no Indians about since we got here."

Dewey smiled. "They'll know, boy. They been watchin' the place ever since y'all rode in."

"Will bad-acting whites pay an Indian, sir?" Susan asked. "Or just take what they want and harm the Indians?"

"They'll pay. And they won't harm these Hopis. They're breeds and they're big. Mean as hell if they're pushed. They been lookin' after this place for me for years. Don't you worry none about them. I sure don't.''

"I'd like to see them," Susan said.

"You might," the old mountain man said. "If they want you to see them.''

Frank watched as Dewey lashed down two boxes on one of the packhorses. He'd helped him inspect the contents the night before. The high-grade dynamite was in fine condition, carefully packed, and good to travel.

When Frank had spotted Dewey inspecting the high explosive, he had smiled and said, "You're not going to play around, are you, Dewey?"

"Too damn old for games, Drifter. We find these scum, I aim to send as many of them to hell as I can.'' He cut his eyes to Frank. "And the way I heared it, you ain't too shy when it comes to usin' dynamite yourself.''

Frank smiled. "I been known to toss a few sticks from time to time."

"Uh-huh," the mountain man grunted.

"Missy," Dewey said to Susan, "you be a dear girl and fetch that coffeepot off the far in the post. Bring it out here so's me and the Drifter can have us another cup and we can wash it up. You be kerful now, baby. That pot'll be some hot." He smiled and winked at Frank. "Danny, why don't you go with her and hep her?" He winked at Frank and whispered, "And you can steal another kiss or two.''

Frank chuckled softly. "You're either a matchmaker or a troublemaker, Dewey," he whispered.

"What are you two giggling about over there?" Julie demanded.

"We telling dirty jokes," Frank said.

"No, you're not. Don't you think I haven't noticed the looks between Susan and Danny? I know they've been sparkin' every chance they get.''

"I think I got an old bundlin' board in the post somewheres," Dewey said with a laugh. "You want me to go fetch it?"

"I most certainly do not!"

The men laughed, and Julie stalked off.

Frank watched as Dewey stuck a lever-action rifle into his saddle boot. "Where's your old Spencer, Dewey?"

"I give it up, son. This here Winchester suits me just fine now."

"You seen those new bolt-action rifles?"

"I seen a few of them. I don't figure they'll ever catch on, though. Too cumbersome, you ax me."

"Dewey, are you sure you want to come along with us?"

The old mountain man looked at Frank. "Why the hell wouldn't I?"

"How old are you, Dewey?"

The older man frowned. "That there, Drifter, is a damn good question. Tell you the truth, I don't rightly know. Near as I can figure it, I'm about seventy. Give or take a couple of years here and there." He smiled. "But I can still pleasure a woman. A much younger woman, I might add. That answer your hidden question?"

"I wasn't doubting your virility, Dewey."

"My what?"

"Here's your coffeepot, Mr. Dewey," Susan said as she walked up with Danny. "And some cups."

"Thank you, missy."

Frank and the old mountain man filled their cups, and walked over to sit under the shade of a tree and sip coffee and smoke.

"You got any kind of plan, Drifter?" Dewey asked.

"Not even the ghost of one," Frank admitted.

"Sometimes that's best, I think. We'll just make one up

as we go. You ain't got no idee how many hostages is in this camp, right?''

"That's right. Or even if there are any there.''

"Well, even if they ain't none, we can 'complish somethin'.''

"Oh? What?''

"We can kill a whole chamber pot full of worthless, no-'count rapin', murderin', kidnappin' bastards.''

"Great gobs of bufflar turds,'' Dewey whispered, handing Frank's field glasses back to him. "There must be a good fifty or sixty of them sorry bastards down yonder.''

"Yeah,'' Frank said, lifting the glasses and adjusting them to his eyes. "But I don't see any signs of hostages.''

"They might be in that big tent in the center of the camp.''

"If they're there, that's where they'd be.''

"Gettin' them out won't be easy.''

Frank grunted his response. Then an idea came to him, and he lowered the glasses and smiled.

"Uh-oh,'' Dewey said. "That grin tells me you got you a plan.''

"You brought your bow and a quiver of arrows, right?''

"I damn shore did. I'm better with that than with a rifle, and I'm an expert with a rifle,'' he said with a grin that matched Frank's.

"Don't start lyin', Dewey.''

"Now you've done gone and injured my feelin's. That ain't no way to talk to an old man who's on his last legs.''

"Oh, horse crap! You're healthy as a bear and you know it.''

"Damn, boy! I can't get no sympathy outta you a-tall. What about me and my expert ability with a bow and arrey?''

"Dynamite.''

Dewey blinked. "Say again?"

Frank laughed softly. "Oh, I think you're going to love it, Dewey. I really do."

"I ain't real sure I like that look in your eyes, Drifter."

"Come on, let's get back to the camp and talk this out."

"The five of us are going to attack fifty or so?" Danny asked after listening to Frank's plan.

"You have a better plan?" Frank asked. "If so, I'll be happy to hear it."

"I don't have any plan, Mr. Morgan," the young man replied. "I just don't see how the five of us have a chance of pulling this off."

"If I can drop some dynamite in the middle of a crowd," Dewey said, "I can take out eight or ten first off."

"At supper time," Julie suggested. "When they all gather around the cooking area."

"Sounds good to me," Frank said. "Dewey?"

"Where me and you was spyin' on them is a good spot. It's within range, I figure. Sure. I can drop an arrey right amongst them from there."

"The fuses you brought?" Frank asked, looking at the old mountain man.

"Don't worry 'bout that. I got quick-burnin' fuses and slow-burnin' ones. The force of the blast will knock some of them flyin' . . . if it's close enough. I've seen men addled for hours from the concussion."

"How many arrows can you let fly in, say . . . oh, a minute's time, Dewey?" Frank asked.

The older man smiled. "Enough, boy. Enough."

"When do we attack, Mr. Morgan?" Susan asked.

Frank looked at the girl. *What an army,* he thought. *A boy in his teens still part wet behind the ears. A young snip of a girl not long from playing with dolls. A mother of two girls who still carries the faded bruises of beatings and rapes. An old man who should be passing his remaining years in a rocking chair.*

Dog nudged his arm with a cold nose.

And a dog, Frank added, petting the big cur.

"Sir?" Danny pressed Frank for an answer.

"In about an hour," Frank replied. "No point in putting it off."

"I bes' git them arreys ready," Dewey said.

Frank had sent Danny around to the east side of the outlaw camp, as close to the corral as he dared to get. When the first explosion went off, Danny was to turn the horses loose by breaking down part of the rickety corral, made of brush. The horses would be ready to run in a panic after the dynamite blast.

Julie was with Susan on the north edge of the camp, on a slight rise behind some rocks. Frank was with Dewey on the west side. That left the south side open for the outlaws to run, which was what Frank hoped they would do.

Dewey had rigged up a dozen arrows with dynamite . . . with very short fuses, Frank noted. He had mentioned that to Dewey.

"Ain't no point in messin' around about it, Drifter," the mountain man had replied. "I don't want them outlaws to be able to pick up the arreys and chuck 'em back at us."

"Good point," Frank had admitted.

"They's about eight or ten or 'em all gathered 'round the big coffeepot," Dewey whispered. "You ready to open this dance?"

"You got the fiddle," Frank told him. "Get to sawin'."

"You bring the matches?"

Frank held up a lighted cigar.

Dewey fitted an arrow. "I hope ever'one's in place."

"Too late to worry about that now." Frank touched the lighted end of the cigar to a fuse, and it started sputtering. "Let 'er rip."

Dewey sent the arrow into the air, and it landed in the middle of the men gathered around the coffeepot.

"Good God!" one of the outlaws hollered.

The charge blew with enormous force, killing several of the men instantly. Bits of the big coffeepot, skillets, and cook pots were like shrapnel, bits and pieces flying in all directions and crippling several other men. The force of the explosion sent all the men, dead, dying, and merely confused, to the ground, those left alive momentarily deafened and completely addled.

Dewey let another arrow fly, being careful to keep it away from the big tent in the center of the camp where they suspected the hostages were being held. The charge blew and the force knocked down several tents, adding more confusion to the already chaotic situation.

Frank could hear Danny yelling at the horses.

"Get the horses," a man yelled. Those were the last words he ever spoke as both Susan and Julie fired, the bullets ripping into the man and slamming him dying to the ground.

Dewey spied a knot of men running toward the south, and let an arrow fly. It was perfectly timed. The arrow landed a few feet in front of the running men, and blew just as a couple of men attempted to jump over it. Really bad timing for those men. The dynamite blew and splattered the men all over the place. The concussion knocked the other men down, and Frank fired as rapidly as he could lever the empty brass out and close the breech on a fresh round.

The horses were galloping away in all directions, and Danny was firing from his position, as were Julie and Susan.

Everyone was firing with astonishing accuracy. There were dead and dying men now lying all over the place. Dewey didn't let up with his explosive arrows, but this time he was putting them *behind* the men who were running south, away from the hail of lead. The explosions were driving the men south, away from the camp.

Frank laid his rifle aside and filled his hands with Colts. "Keep it up, Dewey. I'm going into the camp."

"Don't be a fool, Frank!" the mountain man yelled. But it was a useless warning, for Frank was off and running into the campsite, heading straight for the tent in the center of the camp.

Fourteen

An outlaw staggered to his feet, saw Frank running toward him, and grabbed for his pistol. Frank shot him and kept on running toward the tent.

Dewey let loose with another dynamite-tipped arrow, and the explosion shook the ground beneath Frank's boots. Frank reached the tent and ripped open the closed flaps. In the dimness he could see two young girls, maybe twelve at the most, and a young boy about the same age. He didn't recognize any of the three.

"Come on, kids," Frank said. "Stay close to me and I'll get you clear of this camp."

When Frank stepped out the torn front of the tent, the ground was littered with dead and wounded outlaws. But nowhere was an outlaw standing. "Run for those rocks, kids," Frank said, pointing to where Dewey was stationed.

One of the young girls pointed to a dead outlaw. "He made me take off my clothes," was all she said.

It was enough. Frank knew what she meant.

"He'll never bother you again, honey. He's dead."

"Good," the girl said. "I hope he burns in the hellfires." Then she took off running toward the rocks, the other two right behind her.

Frank made the rocks right behind the kids. "Them scum that was able to headed south, Frank," Dewey said. "But I don't know how long we got till they take a notion to come back."

Frank nodded. "Watch the kids. I've got to help Danny get some horses for the kids to ride."

"Will do."

Frank circled around until he came to Julie and Susan's position. "Get over with Dewey and help him with the kids."

"I saw them, Frank," Julie said. "Did they say anything about any of the others?"

"I didn't have time to ask them, Julie. Go on now. I've got to help Danny."

But Danny was thinking ahead of Frank. The young man had saddled up four fine-looking horses, and was holding them when Frank reached him. "Damn good work, Danny. We only need three, but we'll take the fourth as a spare. Let's go, son."

Dewey had left the kids with Julie and Susan and slipped into the death camp, picking up some guns and ammunition. "Figured we might need them," he told Frank.

"Probably. Let's get the hell gone from here, Dewey."

"Grand idee, old son. Move!"

* * *

"We heard men talking about a place near Tucson," Tess told the group over supper that evening.

The rescued girls were Tess and Sarah. The boy's name was Jerry. They had been kidnapped from a small settlement in the northern part of Arizona. Their parents had been murdered in front of them.

"What about this place near Tucson?" Frank asked.

"That's where the kids are held until they're sent to Mexico," Sarah said.

"And other places," Jerry added.

"What other places?" Julie asked.

"All over," the boy replied. "We heard men talking about New York City."

"Sweet Jesus," Dewey muttered.

"It's a big operation," Frank said. "Somebody is making a lot of money."

"Are we safe now?" Tess asked. "Those men won't never have us again, will they?"

"No, child," Dewey said, putting an arm around the girl's shoulders. "The bad men won't never touch you no more. I promise you that."

They had ridden for several hours after the attack on the outlaw camp, gotten a few hours of sleep, then ridden on for ten miles. They were now camped by a tiny creek, resting.

"Where is the nearest settlement?" Julie asked.

"Phoenix," Dewey said. "Soon as we cross the Mazatzal Mountains we can follow the stage road right down to the town."

"You kids have any relatives?" Frank asked.

"Back in Missouri," Tess replied. "At least I do. My uncle and aunt."

"I got kin in Kansas," Jerry said. "But I don't like them and they don't like me."

"Why not?" Julie asked.

The boy shrugged his shoulders. "Way I heard it, they didn't like Mama marryin' up with Pa. They said Pa was a no-'count mover. Mama married him anyway. Then I come along. They said I'd probably turn out just like Pa—no good. Every time we'd visit, they'd lock up the egg money; said to my face they didn't want me stealin' it. I ain't goin' back to them folks."

"I got kin back East," Sarah said.

"Where back East?"

"Ohio."

"Well . . ." Frank said, taking off his hat and scratching his head. "We'll work all this out when we get to town. And town's a good four or five days away. We've got lots of time to talk it over."

"My belly's a-grumblin'," Dewey said. "Let's us think about rustlin' up some food. You kids hongry?"

They were.

"The beans are cooking," Julie said. "And the biscuits are in the camp oven. All that's left to do is for one of you men to slice up the bacon."

Frank took out his knife. "I can sure get to doing that."

"Mr. Morgan?" Tess asked.

"Yes, baby?"

"All them men that was on the ground back at the camp—was they all dead?"

"No, baby. Most of them were knocked unconscious by the blasts. They've all got bad headaches, I can tell you that. But they're still alive."

"Too bad," the girl said. "I was hoping they were all dead."

"Me too," Sarah said.

Julie and Frank exchanged glances and remained silent.

Dewey looked at Jerry. "How do you feel about them outlaws, boy?"

"They beat me several times," the boy replied. Then he got to his feet and walked away from the group, Tess and Sarah with him.

Susan stood up and said, "I think I'll join them. Unless you need me to help you with supper, Mother."

"No, you go ahead, Susan. I think being with someone their own age is just what those kids need right now."

When the kids were out of earshot, Dewey asked, "You don't reckon the boy was, well . . . messed with, do you?"

"Wouldn't surprise me none," Frank said. "There are some mighty strange people in this world."

"Disgusting," Julie said, placing the bacon Frank had sliced into the big skillet.

"It happened quite often back in ancient times," Frank replied.

"Still disgusting," Julie said.

"Don't start nothin' you cain't finish, Drifter," Dewey warned.

"I'm just stating something I've read."

"Keep on, you're gonna git you a skillet upside your punkin head," Dewey told him. "Words you read in a book won't mean a hill of beans then. 'Sides, here come the children. That ain't fittin' talk for them to hear."

"It is if it happened to them."

"Frank . . ." Julie warned. "Hush up."

"Mr. Morgan," Tess said, "we want to know what you plan on doing with us."

"Well . . ." Frank paused in his attempt to steal a biscuit from the camp oven. Julie spotted him, and almost took his hand off with a ladle. Frank barely jerked his hand back in time. "Well," he said, inspecting his hand to see if any fingers were missing, "when we get to town, I'll start sending out telegrams to your relatives."

"Why can't we stay with you and Miss Julie?"

"Ah . . . well . . ." Frank stammered, thinking fast. Then he said, "Why don't you ask Miss Julie?"

"Because Mr. Morgan and I aren't married, Tess," Julie replied.

Frank sneaked a hot biscuit, and smiled at Julie when she cut her eyes at him.

"You could have snagged me one too," Dewey fussed.

"You want to risk losing a hand, snag your own biscuit," Frank told him.

"But you're going to get married, aren't you?" Sarah asked. "That's what Susan says anyway."

Frank had just taken a bite of biscuit, and he started coughing at that.

"Susan!" Julie said.

"Well, if you're not," the girl responded, "how come you're always making moo-moo eyes at him?"

"Moo-moo eyes?" Julie put her hands on her hips.

"I think I'll go see about the horses," Frank said, getting up.

"I think I'll join you," Dewey said.

"*Sit down!*" Julie snapped.

Frank and Dewey hit the ground.

"Young lady." Julie directed the words at her daughter. "You're really a fine one to be talking about making eyes at someone. Don't you think I've seen how you and Danny look at each other?"

"They're going to get married too?" Tess inquired.

"Certainly not!" Julie said.

"Oh, yes, we are," Susan said.

"Lord, have mercy," Dewey moaned. "We ain't never gonna git to eat."

"You are not going to get married, young lady!"

"Oh, yes, we are too!"

Frank began placing the slices of bacon in the big skillet.

"You!" Julie said, whirling around to face Danny. "I blame you for this."

"I swear to you, Miss Julie," the young man said, "this is the first I heard any talk about us gettin' married. We been holdin' hands and kissin' some, yes, ma'am. But . . ."

"You've been smooching with my daughter?" Julie yelled.

"Quick, gimmie one of them biscuits," Dewey whispered.

"Yes, ma'am. We have." Danny stood taller. "And as far as us gettin' married. Well . . . I think that's a grand idea."

"Oh, you do, do you?" the mother challenged.

"I do too," Frank mumbled, his mouth full of biscuit. "I thought we had some jam around here someplace. This biscuit's sorta dry."

"You don't like my biscuits?" Julie yelled.

"I didn't say that," Frank declared. "I just said . . ."

"And I think Susan and Danny getting married is a dreadful idea," Julie said, cutting him off.

"Well, I just thought—"

"Who asked you to think?" Julie again cut him off.

"Now you done it," Dewey said. "This is shapin' up to be a real stem-winder."

"I love him!" Susan said, moving close to Danny.

"You're too young to know what love is," her mother replied. "My God, child! How will he support you?"

"By farming," Danny told her.

"These here biscuits is a tad on the dry side," Dewey said.

"Then *you* make the biscuits from now on!" Julie yelled at him.

"Now whose butt is overloading his mouth?" Frank questioned, looking at the old mountain man.

"When we get to a town, Danny and me are getting married," Susan announced, taking Danny's hand.

"The hell you are!" Julie said. "You don't have my permission."

"Then we'll just live together in sin and tell everybody we're married," the girl defiantly told her mother.

"If you want my opinion . . ." Frank said.

"I don't!" Julie told him.

"Then I'll be quiet," Frank said.

"Good!" Julie said. She looked at Dewey, who was walking toward the supplies. "Where are you going?"

"To find that jar of jam. These biscuits need some improvement."

Julie told him what he could do with the jar of jam.

"Whoa!" Dewey said. "That would be plumb uncomfortable."

"Not to mention that you would ruin the jam," Frank added.

"It's settled," Susan said. "Danny and me are getting married."

"Good," Dewey said. "Now can we eat?"

Fifteen

Long after the others had rolled up in their blankets and gone to sleep—or so he thought—Frank sat back a few yards from a dying campfire, drinking coffee. Julie and Susan had stomped around in anger for a time; then both had sat down and had a bite to eat. They were not speaking to each other when they went to their blankets.

Frank had poured another cup of coffee and leaned back against his saddle when he heard Julie heave a great sigh and toss back her blankets. She walked over to him and sat down.

"Coffee?" Frank asked.

"Please."

Coffee cup in hand, Julie said, "I certainly made a fool of myself this evening, didn't I, Frank?"

Frank chuckled softly. If he answered truthfully, he'd be

in more trouble with the woman. "Well, not really," he finally said. "I'd say you were reacting like a mother."

"Thank you for lying so tactfully, Frank. I really don't have anything against Danny. He's a good boy, I think."

"So do I, Julie. But a boy? Well . . . he's about nineteen. That's a man out here."

"How old were you when you got married, Frank?"

"Not much older than Danny."

She sighed heavily. "What am I going to do, Frank?"

"Let them get hitched, I reckon."

"I knew you were going to say that."

"It's either that or they'll run off and get married and you might never see Susan again. You want it that way?"

"Lord, no."

"We'll talk with them. See if they'll agree to hold off until this hunt for Becky is over. Want to try that?"

"That might be a good idea. That would give them time to really get to know each other."

"Yes. And one or both of them might decide they don't want any part of marriage. But don't count on that."

"Oh, I know, Frank. Susan can be a very determined little lady when she sets her mind to it."

"Sort of like her mother, hey?"

Julie smiled in the faint light from the fire. "I suppose you might say that."

"What about the other kids?" Frank asked.

"We send them back to their relatives."

"Suppose they don't want to go."

"They won't have a choice, Frank. They're just children."

"And if we can't find any relatives that will take them?"

"I guess then they'll have to be placed in an orphanage."

Frank sighed audibly. "Have you ever seen, been in one of those places?"

"No."

"I have. Dismal places. I wouldn't want to be responsible for sending any kid to one of those places."

"Do you speak from experience, Frank?" she asked softly.

"Oh, no. I ran away from home on my own accord. But I've seen orphanages aplenty in my time."

"I guess we'll settle it when we get to town."

"I reckon so."

Julie finished her coffee, yawned, and said good night, returning to her blankets. Frank glanced over to where Dewey was sleeping. "Did you get all that conversation, you snoop?" Frank whispered.

"I ain't a-snoopin'. I just ain't a-sleepin'," Dewey replied in a whisper. " 'Sides, it wasn't much of an interestin' talk you two had. Matter of fact, it was plumb borin'."

"What were you expecting?"

"Some sparkin', maybe. Anything 'ceptin' what I heard. Damn near come close to puttin' me to sleep."

"Did you agree with what I said?"

" 'Bout the orphanages?"

"Yes."

"Shore did. I seen them places time to time. I wouldn't want to send no kid to one. But, Frank, mayhaps you ain't gonna have no choice. You give that any thought?"

"No. Not much."

"Then you better put on your thinkin' cap and ruminate that thought around in your noggin a time or two."

"I'll do that. When I wake up."

"That's a right good idea. Now why in the hell don't you shut up and let an old man get his rest?"

"Good night, Dewey."

"Night, Drifter."

"*Good night.* Both of you," Julie called from across the camp.

"That woman shore has sharp hearin'. Don't she, Frank?"

Frank did not reply. He knew better. He simply pulled his blanket over him, lay back against his saddle, and closed his eyes.

A few yards away, Dewey chuckled.

"Last time I was here," Dewey said, "I bet you there wasn't fifty people in the en-tar damn town. Now just look at 'em. Must be two, three thousand. What a mess. Don't know what the hell they all do to make a dollar."

"Phoenix is growing, no doubt about that," Frank replied.

"I want a long, hot soapy bath," Julie said. "And some clean clothes. Then I might start feeling human again."

"You just had a bath a couple of weeks ago," Dewey said. "All of you. Too many baths ain't good for a person."

"I want a bath too," Susan said.

"Me too," Tess and Sarah said.

"Lord have mercy," Dewey said. "Y'all gonna use up the town's en-tar supply of soap."

"I believe I'll have me a good wash too," Frank declared.

"I think I'll have me a drink," Dewy decided. "Bathe later. I'll just keep my ears open and try to larn somethin'."

"How can you expect to hear anything with two weeks of trail dust clogging up your ears?" Frank asked with a grin.

Dewey gave him a dirty look and lifted the reins. "Let's find us a livery," he suggested. "Then y'all can go splash around in tubs and get soap in your eyes."

When the horses were stabled and everyone was settled into a hotel, Julie said, "Danny, you and Jerry go with Frank. We'll see you all in a couple of hours."

"Yes, ma'am."

"And we're taking Dog with us," Susan said. "For protection."

"Spoiling him rotten is what you're doing," Frank said. "You're going to make him more worthless than he already is." He took Julie to one side. "I'll set up a line of credit for you at that general store over yonder." He pointed. "You can outfit the girls there. Get them outfitted with clothes for the trail."

"We're not going to see about getting them back to relatives?"

"Maybe. I don't know yet. I'm about halfway decided to take them with us. I'm not putting any of the kids into an orphanage."

She touched his arm. "I knew you wouldn't, Frank."

"Yeah? Well . . . I told you how I feel about those places. We'll think of something in due time."

"Certainly we will. Frank? You keep an eye on Danny. Try to steer him away from preachers. I don't want those two sneaking off and getting married while we're in town."

"I thought they agreed to hold off for a time."

"They did. I just want some insurance, that's all."

Frank smiled and nodded his head. "I'll keep an eye on Danny."

"Thank you."

Frank set up a line a credit for Julie at the store, and let Danny and Jerry pick out a couple of sets of clothing to put on after their baths. He bought both the boys a bottle of sarsaparilla, and sat them down on a bench while he picked out a new shirt and some britches. Then he got the boys and the three of them went walking around the fast-growing town.

"Reckon where Mr. Dewey is?" Jerry asked.

"Having him a beer in a saloon," Frank replied. "He'll find out what's going on and report to us later."

"Two men are following us, Mr. Morgan," Danny whispered.

"I see them. I've had my eye on them for a while now. They picked us up as soon as we left the store."

"You know them?"

"I know they're trouble-hunters," Frank said. "If they brace me, you get Jerry out of the way, understand?"

"Yes, sir. Those men behind us, you reckon they're lookin' to make themselves a reputation by callin' you out?"

"Might be. Might be they're part of the Dooley gang."

"What are you gonna do, Mr. Morgan?"

"Get off this main street for one thing."

"And then?"

"Get you and Jerry away from me for another."

"I've got my gun, Mr. Morgan," Danny said. "I can help you."

"You keep that hogleg in leather, boy. Those men following us are skilled gun-handlers. I don't want to see you shot." He managed a smile despite the tense situation. "Susan would never forgive me or you."

"What do you want us to do, sir?" Jerry asked.

"Keep walking. Stay with me until we round that corner yonder. Then you duck into the first store we come to."

"Yes, sir," they both said.

The trio rounded the corner, and Danny and Jerry slipped into a saddle shop. The man sitting on a bench and working on a saddle looked up and his mouth dropped open when he recognized Frank. "My God!" he blurted out. "It's really you. I saw your picture in a magazine just the other day."

"Watch out for these two, will you?" Frank asked.

"Sure thing, Mr. Morgan. You know, sir, you look a lot like the outlaw Val Dooley. You know that?"

"So I've been told. Stay inside, mister. The lead is about to fly, I'm thinking."

The man rose from the bench, walked to the door, and looked out. "Those are the Tremaine brothers, Mr. Morgan. Ike and Neville. They're hired guns."

"I figured they were. Tremaine brothers. I've heard of them."

"I'm told they're pretty good."

"I'll soon find out, I'm thinking." Frank stepped away from the store and turned, facing the stalking gunmen. "You boys looking for me?" he called.

Ike and Neville stopped about forty feet from Frank. "You're Frank Morgan, ain't you?" Ike said.

"I sure am."

"Then we're lookin' for you."

"You found me. Now what the hell do you think you're going to do with me?"

"Kill you, Morgan," Neville said bluntly.

"It's been tried before, boys. I've left a few graveyards behind me."

"But this time you're gonna be in the graveyard," Ike informed him.

"Who hired you?" Frank asked.

"John Huddleston."

"I know that name. From New York City?"

"His man said he was from there," Neville said.

"His man?"

"The man who hired us."

"Did he have a name?"

"Douglas Sinclair," Ike said. "Least that's the name he give us."

"What difference do it make?" Neville questioned. "You ain't gonna be able to do nothin' 'bout it. In a few minutes you gonna be dead."

"Don't count on that, boys. I'm going to give you time to change your minds about this business arrangement."

"Cain't," Ike said. 'We done took part payment for seein' you dead."

"I'll call the marshal!" the saddle shop owner shouted.

"He's out of town and so is his deputies," Neville said. "And you know it. So you just mind your own knittin' in there."

"Stay out of this," Frank warned the local in low tones. "And get away from the storefront window."

"I wouldn't miss this for the world," the man replied.

Frank did not reply. He kept his eyes on the Tremaine brothers.

"Why did Huddleston want me dead?" Frank questioned.

"Sinclair didn't tell us," Ike replied. "And we didn't ask. 'Sides, this will be a feather in our hats, killin' you, Morgan."

"Yeah," Neville said with a sneer. "You 'posed to be such a hotshot fast gun and all that coyote crap. Personal, I think it's all talk."

"Yeah, me too," brother Ike said.

"You ready to find out?" Frank's question was offered in a low, menacing tone.

"Any time, Morgan," Neville said.

"Yeah," Ike said. "It's up to you, Morgan."

"No, boys," Frank said. "You started this, so you pull on me."

"How 'bout now!" Neville yelled, and started his draw.

Sixteen

Neville was quick, clearing leather and firing. But he missed his first shot, the slug whining harmlessly off into the hot air. Frank didn't miss. His bullet hit Neville in the belly and doubled the man over, dropping him to his knees on the boardwalk.

Ike hesitated, and that short pause cost him dearly: Frank shot him in the stomach, the force of the .45 slug knocking the hired gun off the boardwalk and into the street. Ike struggled to get to his feet, and succeeded only in falling into a watering trough.

Neville hollered in pain and anger at seeing his brother in a horse trough, and lifted his pistol. Frank put another slug into the man. The second bullet from Frank's Peacemaker stretched the Tremaine brother out on the boardwalk, badly hurt but still game.

"You bastard!" Neville shouted.

"Git me outta this here trough!" Ike hollered.

Gun smoke hung thick in the hot air, and a crowd had begun to gather on the boardwalk across the street, the men and women talking and pointing.

"I'll kill you, Morgan!" Ike yelled, trying to stand up in the watering trough. His boots slipped, and Ike was out of the trough, landing head-first in the dirt and horse crap in the street. He lost his pistol.

"You men stop this immediately," a woman yelled from across the dusty street. "Stop this barbaric behavior."

"Oh, shut up, you old bag!" Ike hollered, crawling around on his hands and knees in the dirt and horse droppings, trying to find his six-shooter.

"Old bag!" the citizen yelled. "Wilbur, that ruffian called me an old bag. Do something!"

Wilbur did nothing, and the woman began yelling in anger.

Neville sat up on the boardwalk, bloody but still willing to make a fight of it. He lifted his pistol, and Frank put another round into the man. That one did it. Neville slammed back onto the boards and expired.

"Where's my damn gun?" Ike hollered. "Neville, give me a gun so's I can kill that bastard. You hear me, Neville?"

"Neville's dead," Frank told the man as he rapidly reloaded. "Give it up, man."

"Hell with you," Ike yelled. "You're a dead man, Morgan."

"Not likely," Frank replied.

Ike's hand closed around the butt of his pistol and he hollered his satisfaction. He lifted and cocked the six-gun. "Got you, Morgan!" he yelled.

Frank shot him right between the eyes.

Ike fell back against the horse trough, dead as a rock, his

eyes wide open and seeing nothing on the living side of the veil.

"By golly!" the saddle maker yelled, stepping out of his shop. "That there was one hell of a gunfight. Best I ever seen."

"Somebody get the undertaker," a man shouted.

"Get Reverend Phillips too," a woman yelled.

"Why?" a man questioned.

"Because it's the Christian thing to do!" the woman shouted.

"Are you all right, sir?" Danny asked, walking out of the shop to stand beside Frank on the boards.

"I'm not hit," Frank told him.

"Reckon they got any money?" a man said, walking up. "I'll give them a nice funeral if they do. Mourners and shouters and wailers and a band too."

"I don't care if you drop them both into a privy pit," Frank told the man.

"Now that's not very charitable of you, sir," the undertaker admonished Frank.

"You weren't the one getting shot at," Frank replied.

"Well . . . that's true. Who are they, sir?"

"Ike and Neville Tremaine."

"The notorious gunmen?"

"That's them."

"Which is which?"

"I have no idea."

"Oh, my! That won't do."

"Have fun deciding who goes in what hole in the ground," Frank told him. He motioned for Danny and Jerry to join him and walked on up the boardwalk.

"I never seen a stand-up hook-and-draw gunfight," Jerry said. "But I've read about aplenty of them in penny dreadfuls."

"I hope you never have to see another, Jerry," Frank told him.

"I didn't mind it, Mr. Morgan. Long as the good man lives. And I'm sure glad you did."

Frank smiled. "I am too, Jerry."

"Who is this Huddleston man, Mr. Morgan?" Danny asked.

"He's a lawyer from New York City."

"You know him?"

"No. I've never met him."

"Why would he want to hire people to kill you?"

"I suspect he was acting on behalf of someone else, Danny." For that matter, who hired Cory Raven to kill him? Frank had been wondering about that ever since Danny had told him about it.

Huddleston? Maybe. Frank was damn sure going to find out. Even if he had to take a train to New York City and confront Huddleston.

"I'm hungry," Jerry said.

"Well, let's find us a café and chow down," Frank said. "I could use some coffee myself."

"Wonder how the ladies are getting along," Danny said, sort of a wistful note in his voice.

"They're getting along just fine without us," Frank told him. "And getting clean. Relax, boy, your girl isn't going to run off and leave you behind."

Danny grinned and blushed.

"Damn, I wish I'd been there to see that fight," Dewey said.

The old mountain man had found a horse trough and a bar of strong soap, and given himself a good wash, then dressed in clean clothes. He had caught up with Frank and the boys after Jerry and Danny had a bite to eat.

"You shaved, Mr. Dewey," Jerry said. "You look 'bout a hundred years younger."

"I reckon that's a compliment," Dewey said. "I'll take it as sich. The Tremaine brothers, you say, Drifter?"

"Ike and Neville."

"I knew 'em both. Bad ones. The world's a better place without them two. Say a man hired them to kill you, Drifter?"

"A New York City man. I don't know him personally, but I have heard of him. He's a lawyer."

"I don't like lawyers. Crooks, ever one of 'em."

Frank laughed at the mountain man. "Some good, some bad, Dewey. Just like any other profession."

"Crooks," the mountain man insisted.

"You seen the ladies?" Frank asked.

"Nope. They're probably still splashin' around in soapy water."

"Well, it's time for us to pick up our new clothes and take a bath. You can keep watch for us."

"I'll do it," Dewey said, walking along beside Frank. Danny and Jerry were loafing along a few steps behind the gunfighter and the mountain man. "You plannin' on takin' the kids along on the hunt, Drifter?"

"I'm not putting them in a damn orphanage."

"Good for you. I 'spect if we look hard enough, we can find some nice families who'll take the kids in."

"That's my thought."

"Lord have mercy," Dewey blurted out, as they rounded a corner. "Lookie yonder, will you? There's the ladies all spiffed up in dresses. They're lookin' like they want a night on the town."

"You like, Frank?" Julie said, doing a slow turn on the boardwalk.

"I certainly do," Frank said. "You ladies look very nice." For a fact, Julie was a very good-looking woman . . . and very shapely.

Danny's eyes were all bugged out, looking at Susan.

"What was all that shooting about?" Julie asked.

"Little trouble down thataway," Frank said matter-of-factly, pointing. "It's over. Nothing to worry about."

"Did it involve you, Frank?" she asked.

"Sort of. I'll tell you about it later."

"All right. What about the kids?"

"We're taking them with us."

"Thank you, Frank." Julie raised up on tiptoes and kissed Frank on the cheek.

"She done smooched him right here in front of God and ever'body," Dewey said. "Lord, what's this world comin' to?"

"Did you buy some new britches for the girls?" Frank asked, feeling a slight flush of embarrassment heat up his face.

"Yes. Several sets. I'm afraid I left you quite a bill at the store."

"Don't worry about that. I assure you, it's not going to break me. We're really going to have to stock up on supplies before we head south. It's a long, hot, dry trip down to Tucson."

"And dangerous?" Julie asked.

"That too."

"Indians?"

"If they're on the prowl, yes. And bandits."

"And people who for whatever reason want to kill you, Frank?"

"There is always that, Julie."

"Mr. Morgan?" Sarah called. "Here comes a man with a badge. And he's carrying a shotgun."

Frank turned, being careful to keep his hands away from his pistol, and watched as the marshal walked up to him.

"Frank Morgan?"

"That's me."

"Did you just kill the Tremaine brothers?"

"They were trying to kill me, Marshal."

"I don't doubt that. Way I hear tell it, you got about a hundred or so people tryin' to kill you."

"Have you heard why, Marshal?"

"No. That don't concern me. What concerns me is keepin' the peace in this town. How long are you goin' to be in town?"

"Probably leave day after tomorrow. We've got to let our horses rest a bit and then provision up." He turned to look at Julie. "Where's Dog?"

"At the stable with the horses. He's in the stall with Stormy."

Frank nodded and turned back to the marshal. "Day after tomorrow all right with you?"

"Suits me. I ain't tryin' to be pushy, Morgan. But trouble seems to follow you." He held up a hand. "I know, I know. You don't start it. But people still get killed."

"They usually deserve it, Marshal."

"I won't argue that neither." He looked at Julie. "You and these kids with Morgan, ma'am?"

"Yes, we are."

The marshal nodded his head. "I hope to see y'all pullin' out of town day after tomorrow, Morgan."

"You will, Marshal."

The marshal turned and walked away.

"Nice feller," Dewey remarked, only slightly sarcastically.

Frank put a big hand on Jerry's shoulder. "You ready for a bath, boy?"

"No, sir."

Frank laughed. "You're going to get one anyway. You ladies have a nice walk. We'll see you in an hour or so."

"Try to stay out of trouble, Frank," Julie said dryly.

"I always do that."

She rolled her eyes at that.

"Come on, boys. It's time to get some of this trail dust off us."

"I done took my wash," Dewey said proudly.

"And you look very nice, Dewey," Julie told him. "Doesn't he, girls?"

"Yes, ma'am," the girls said in unison.

"Shaved too," Dewey said, rubbing his face.

"I noticed," Julie said.

"Took years off me," Dewey said, grinning.

"Yeah," Frank said. "Now you only look ninety."

"Excuse us, ladies," Dewey said, taking Frank's arm. They walked off toward the bathhouse, Dewey cussing Frank every step of the way, and Frank laughing at the mountain man.

Seventeen

"It's about a hundred miles," Dewey told the group. "And it ain't no easy ride. Danny, you be shore them water bags ain't leakin' none."

"They're all right, Mr. Dewey," the young man said.

"Check 'em again, son. And top off all the canteens. A body can go a long time without no food, but you'll die quick without water."

Frank made sure the packsaddles were secure and balanced, then checked the leather booties he'd had specially made for Dog. The booties would protect Dog's paws from the hot desert sands and from thorns. He'd had several sets made.

It was not yet dawn and the kids were yawning, rubbing sleep out of their eyes, but they were game and ready to go.

"You ever find out the name of the rancher who's 'posed to be involved in these kidnappin's, Drifter?" Dewey asked.

"Collins," Frank said. "Big Max Collins. Heard his name mentioned several times last night in the saloon."

Dewey looked at Frank for a long moment in the lantern light. "You shore?"

"I'm sure."

"He's a bad one, Drifter."

"I've heard."

"He hightailed it out of Wyoming several years back with a posse hard after him. They was gonna hang him."

"I wish they had."

"He's a woman-abuser and a murderin' son of a bitch," Dewey said. "But he ain't never been convicted of nothin'. Don't ax me why that is."

"Because he stays one jump ahead of the law," Frank replied. "And he doesn't leave any witnesses alive."

Dewey moved closer to Frank, out of earshot of the others. "And he's 'posed to have Julie's daughter?" he whispered.

"That's the word I get."

"If he does, the girl's better off dead."

"I heard that too."

"Lord have mercy," Dewey whispered.

"If Big Max gets any mercy, it'll be from the Lord," Frank said grimly. " 'Cause he damn sure won't get any from me."

"Let's not shoot him," Dewey said.

"Why not?"

" 'Cause I want to hang him. Slow."

"Good idea," Frank agreed. "But I can't promise a thing."

"Just keep it in mind, will you?"

"You bet." He looked back at the others. "You folks ready to ride?"

They nodded their heads and all mounted up.

"Lead the way, Dewey," said Frank.

* * *

They were two days out of Phoenix and it was hot. Not a cloud in the sky and not a shade tree in sight anywhere.

"Land of the Hohokum," Dewey said.

"The what?" Julie asked.

"The people who lived here before," the old mountain man said.

"Before what, sir?" Tess asked.

"Before the Pima and the Navajo and the Zuni and the Apache and all the other Injuns around here today."

"What does Hohokum mean?" Sarah asked.

"Well, child . . . that's a right good question. Most of the Injuns I talked to about it say it means all played out or all used up. I don't think they really know. I don't think anybody really knows."

"What happened to these Hohokums?" Julie asked.

"Nobody knows that neither. They just up and disappeared hundreds of years ago. Back a few miles and a tad to the east of this road is some ruins folks say was built by the Hohokum. I wouldn't rightly know. They's also all sorts of ditches and canals folks say was built by them. I wouldn't rightly know about that neither." He cut his eyes to Frank. "What I do know is that we're bein' followed."

"I see them," Frank said. "They've been tagging along behind us for a couple of hours now."

"Indians?" Danny asked.

"No. Half a dozen white men."

"If memory serves me right," Dewey said, "they's some ruins of an old army fort about a mile ahead and off to the west. There ain't nothin' left 'ceptin' the walls, but they's water from a little spring and the walls is good cover."

"We can rig up a tarp for some shade and see what those hombres behind us want," Frank suggested.

"We shore got plenty of ammunition for a long siege," Dewey said. "And this is the stage road."

"There'll be travelers along from time to time," Frank said. "If y'all look hard off to the southwest, you can just begin to make out the ruins of the old fort."

"I see it," Sarah said.

"When we get even with the ruins, cut west and ride hard," Dewey said. "Them men behind us is closin' on us."

"And a half-dozen more are coming up fast from the south," Frank said after a quick visual sweep of the terrain in front of them. "Head for the ruins . . . now!"

The group made the ruins of the old fort with about five hundred yards to spare. Frank left the saddle, jerked his .44-40 from the boot, and ran to the wall facing east. The pursuers were closing rapidly, spread out in two long lines. One line coming from the east, the other line coming from the south.

"Jerry," Frank called, "you and Tess and Sarah rig up a tarp by that high wall yonder." He pointed. "Danny, get the horses behind that wall over there." Again, he pointed. "Secure a rope across the opening. That will keep them inside the area." *I hope,* he thought.

The dozen or so men who were spread out around the ruins had dismounted and taken to the ground, seeking cover behind the ancient, many-armed saguaro, some of the cactus standing forty feet tall.

"We got plenty of food and water with us," Dewey called. "And the water from the old spring is cold and sweet. I done took me a taste."

"Tess," Frank called, "when you and Sarah get done with that tarp, get a little fire going and make us some coffee, please."

"Yes, sir."

Frank looked over at Julie. The woman had her rifle and

her shotgun and had taken up position to Frank's right. She caught him looking at her and smiled.

One tough lady, Frank thought. *She'll damn sure do to ride the high country with. Easy on the eyes too.*

"Frank," Julie called softly, "I'll make you a bet those men out there are part of the Val Dooley gang."

"You're probably right, Julie."

"I was thinkin' the same thing," Dewey called. "I think they've been doggin' us for days, trackin' our every move and reportin' back to Dooley by wire."

"I'm sure you're right," Frank said. "And they're determined to stop us right here and now."

"Well, they ain't a-gonna do it," the mountain man said. Then he smiled and lifted his rifle. "Well, well," he muttered. "Would you just look at that?"

"What?" Frank called.

"A leg," Dewey said. "Watch this." He sighted in and squeezed the trigger.

"Ooowww!" a man hollered from the desert floor. "My leg. They done shot me in the leg. Ooohhh . . . it's broke!"

"You want us to call a doctor for you?" Dewey hollered.

"You old son of a bitch!" a man hollered. "I'm gonna stake you out over an anthill and listen to you beg for mercy."

"Come on and try, outlaw!" Dewey yelled.

"Hey, Morgan?" another man yelled.

"Right here," Frank shouted. "What do you want?"

"Them women!"

"Forget it."

"And them young boys too."

"Scum," Julie said.

"Them boys will bring a pretty penny. They can be trained as house servants . . . among other things."

Laughter rang out from the desert floor; unseen, obscene laughter.

Frank said nothing.

"There'll be more of us along in a few hours, Morgan," an outlaw called. "Then we'll rush you."

"That's a stage road behind you," Frank called. "There'll be travelers along."

"No, they won't, Morgan. Stage and freight wagons ain't movin'. Injun trouble. Everything is halted both directions."

"Well, that answers the question about why we ain't seen nobody for a couple of days," Dewey said. "Damn!"

"You still got some dynamite, don't you?" Frank asked.

"Shore. I stocked up back in town." Dewey laughed. "And yeah, I got my bow and plenty of arrows. You have a real vicious mind, Drifter, you know that?"

"So I've been told. More than once."

"For a fact."

"Get busy rigging up some arrows, Dewey."

"I'm on it."

"Morgan?" The call came from the desert.

"I'm still here."

"Give us the females and them young boys, and you and that damned old useless coot can ride out."

"Damned old useless coot!" Dewey fumed. "I'll show them no-goods about worthless. Damn their eyes."

Frank smiled. He knew that it wasn't a very smart move to make Dewey angry. The mountain man had some years on him, but he was still very spry and as strong as an enraged grizzly bear.

"My leg's broke, I tell you," the wounded outlaw hollered. "Somebody come hep me."

He was ignored by his comrades in crime.

"Damn it, Pennyworth," the wounded man called. "Didn't I hep you when you was pinned under that hoss?"

The outlaw named Pennyworth did not reply.

"Come hep me, Pennyworth!"

"Yeah, Pennyworth," Frank yelled. "Go on and help your friend. I won't fire on you. Go on and help him."

"You give me your word, Morgan?" Pennyworth yelled.

"I give you my word that *I* won't fire on you," Frank yelled.

A man jumped up and Julie nailed him, putting a rifle slug in his chest and dropping him like a hot rock.

"Damn you, Morgan!" another outlaw yelled. "You give your word."

"I said I wouldn't fire on him," Frank called. "I can't speak for everybody else."

"You're all a bunch of sorry no-'counts," another outlaw hollered. "Can't none of you be trusted."

"Now, that there is plumb pitiful," Dewey said, speaking as he rigged a stick of dynamite onto an arrow. "Them talkin' 'bout someone else not bein' trustworthy."

"You'll pay for that, Morgan," another voice added. It was a voice that was familiar to Frank.

"Zeke Farrow?" Frank called.

"That's right, Morgan."

"I thought that was you. You got Ben Bright with you?"

"Shore do, Morgan. And this time, you ain't gonna get out of this alive. We gonna kill you, Morgan, and cut your damned head off and put it in a bag and show it off."

"You will excuse me if I don't wish you luck in your endeavors."

"You funny, Morgan. I got to give you that. You can be real comical."

"You have my permission to laugh yourselves to death."

"I'm sorta sorry we have to kill you, Morgan," Zeke yelled. "You do make me laugh."

"You know them fellers, Drifter?" Dewey asked.

"Yes. Two hired guns out of Texas. They've been around for years."

"They good?"

"No. They've botched nearly every job they've ever been hired to do. But they're both cold-blooded killers."

"I got some arrows ready to go," Dewey said.

"Not yet," Frank cautioned. "If we got away from this mangy crew, we'd still have the second group to deal with."

"Let them all gather and bunch up, then deal with 'em?"

"Yes."

"Sounds good to me. We shore got the best position." He looked around. The girls had rigged the tarp, built a small fire, and were boiling water for coffee. "I'm salavatin' for a cup of strong coffee."

"Won't be long," Frank said.

"Somebody hep me!" the wounded outlaw moaned. "My leg's all swole up. I can't stop the bleedin'. I'm in real misery."

"Poor feller," Dewey said sarcastically. "He's gonna start hollerin' for his mommy any minute now."

"Hey, Morgan!" The shout wavered through the blisteringly hot air. "You hear me, Morgan?"

"I hear you, Ben." Frank looked at Dewey. "Zeke's buddy. Ben Bright."

"Is he?"

"Is he what?" Frank asked.

"Bright."

"Hell, no. He's as dumb as a sack of hair. What do you want, Ben?" Frank yelled.

"Them girls with you ain't worth dyin' over, Morgan."

"I have no plans for dying, Ben."

"You must be sweet on that woman, Morgan. She does look right tasty. Cain't blame you for that. I plan on havin' me a taste of her once we get shut of you and that old bastard.''

"You'll rot in hell before that happens, you pig!" Julie yelled.

"She's got spirit too," Ben hollered. "I like that in a woman. I like it when they fight."

Frank glanced over at Julie. She was grim-faced. He glanced at Susan. The girl-woman was holding her rifle at the ready. She caught Frank's gaze and smiled. Frank winked at her and she winked back. She was game, for sure.

"You and Zeke better call it quits and ride out of here, Ben," Frank called. "You can't win."

"How you figure that, Morgan?" another voice added.

"Because we're right and you're wrong, that's how I figure it."

"That don't mean horse crap, Morgan. We got you outnumbered right now and in a couple of hours, there'll be twice as many of us."

Frank laughed at him. "Smell that coffee boiling? Sure smells good to me. Pretty soon we're gonna have bacon frying and biscuits in the pan. What are you boys gonna eat?"

That got Frank a good cussing from several of the outlaws.

"I'll piss on your grave, Morgan!" an outlaw yelled. "I'll take that woman of yourn and hump her on your grave."

Julie had located the position of the man and fired. The bullet ripped into the saguaro, just missing the man's head. The outlaw fell back, unhit but hollering in fright from the close call.

"That's what you'll get from me!" Julie yelled.

"You boys relax for a while," Dewey yelled. "We're gonna have us some coffee. We'll think about you, all hot and bothered out there in the sand and rattlesnakes."

Eighteen

Those behind the walls of the old fort took shifts, drinking coffee and having something to eat, taking a few moments to relax in the shade of the canvas tarp. Frank petted Dog, silently reassuring the big cur that everything would be all right. Frank wasn't too sure the dog believed any of it, but after a few minutes Dog found a spot next to the wall, turned around in circles about half a dozen times, then lay down and went to sleep.

"Why do dogs do that?" Tess asked as she refilled Frank's coffee cup.

"I think it's just habit now, baby," Frank replied. "But some people who are a lot smarter than me say that a long time ago, before man domesticated dogs, they were looking for snakes before they lay down."

The girl thought about that for a moment. "Well, that makes sense."

"Hey, Morgan!" The shout came drifting over the walls.

"Right here. What do you want?"

"Last chance, Morgan."

"Last chance for what?"

"You and that old bastard ride out and leave us the females and the boys."

Frank took a deep breath and told him in no uncertain terms where he could stick his suggestion. Tess and Sarah giggled, and Julie frowned at Frank's language. Dewey made an obscene hand gesture toward the desert.

"I see the dust comin' up from the south, Morgan. That'd be our gang. It'll soon be all over for you."

"I reckon we'll see about that," Frank called. He looked over at Dewey. "You got lots of arrows ready to go?"

"Enough to blow that scummy bunch out yonder right straight to hell."

"Won't be long now." Frank looked around him at the defenders of the ruins. "Everybody get a good drink of water and check your weapons. Fill any empty loops with ammunition. This new bunch will probably circle wide around and come in from the rear. Everybody get set behind good cover and stay alert."

"I'm gonna have me another taste of that coffee," Dewey said. "Refill your cup for you, Drifter?"

"No, I'm good. But thanks."

Just as Frank had predicted, the new bunch, totaling a dozen or so, met with someone from the original gang out on the road, then began to circle wide to come up from the rear.

"You called that one, Drifter," Dewey said.

"I think I see a man's shoulder sticking out from behind one of those big plants out there," Susan said.

"Shoot it, child," Dewey told her.

Susan lifted her rifle and took aim, and her aim was solid.

The man hollered and fell back, kicking up sand and debris in his pain. "I'm hit, I'm hit!" he shouted. "My shoulder's broke. I cain't use my arm. Help!"

"Who is that?" a man yelled.

"Carter," another answered.

"Oh, God, I'm crippled for life," Carter moaned.

"Oh, shut up, Carter," someone called. "Crawl back to the road and die there. I'm tarred of listenin' to you."

"Johns, you 'bout as sorry as they come," Carter groaned. "If I git the chance I'm gonna gut-shoot you."

Johns cussed him.

"What a nice bunch of people," Julie opined.

"Salt of the earth," Dewey told her. "Drifter?" he shouted.

"Right here, Dewey."

"Are we gonna waste time buryin' these no-goods 'fore we pull out of here?"

"Hell, no."

"Just leave 'em for the buzzards, hey?"

"That's the plan."

The men shouted the brief conversation so the outlaws could hear it.

"That ain't decent," a man yelled from outside the ruins.

"You're not decent!" Julie joined in.

"I is too," the outlaw yelled. "My mama raised me right."

"Your mama was a whore," Dewey hollered.

"Goddamn you!" the outlaw screamed, momentarily forgetting where he was as he jumped out from behind a huge saguaro.

Frank was waiting for something like that. He nailed the man in the center of the chest. The outlaw stretched out on the hot desert floor and died without making another sound.

"This bunch ain't 'xactly eat up with smarts," Dewey observed.

"That's enough," another voice added, the shout coming from one of the new bunch behind the ruins of the fort. "Can't you see they're baiting you? Now calm down and don't pay any attention to those people."

"Charlie, he called Pete's mama a whore," a man yelled.

"Hell, Dave, she probably was," Charlie replied.

"Dave Moran," Dewey said. "Got to be. I heard he was ridin' with the Mason gang."

"He's a bad one," Frank said. "And he's got some smarts too."

"For a fact. He's been outlawin' for twenty-five years and ain't never served a day in prison."

"Smoke Jensen put lead in him about ten years back. So I heard."

"Yeah, he did. But Moran crawled off and recovered. Said he'd never go back to the Colorado high country."

"You know Smoke Jensen, Mr. Morgan?" Danny called.

"I've met him from time to time."

"He's almost as famous as you."

Frank smiled at that. He looked over at Dewey. The old mountain man was also smiling.

"You knew Preacher, didn't you, Dewey?" Frank asked.

"Shore did. Hell of a man, that Preacher. He could be as mean as a grizzly with a sore paw if you crowded him."

"I met him a couple of times."

"This ain't worth a tinker's damn, Dave!" a man yelled. "We got to do somethin' and do it pronto. It's hot out here and I'm hungry."

"I agree with you, Ned," Dave shouted. "I'm open for suggestions."

Ned did not reply.

"I reckon he ain't got no suggestions," Dewey said.

"Seems that way," Frank replied.

"Fix us another pot of coffee, girls," Dewey said to Tess and Sarah.

"Yes, sir," the girls echoed.

"Come nightfall we'll take them," another outlaw yelled.

"They got a point, Drifter," Dewey said.

"I know. But dark is hours away."

"Yeah, Jeff," Dave called. "Come the dark you can lead the charge."

"My en-tar chest is a-hurtin' and a-swellin' up," Carter moaned. "It's like somebody blowed me up with poison air. My head feels funny too. I got to have some relief."

"Oh, shut up, Carter!" someone hollered.

Carter cussed him.

Those behind the crumbling old walls waited in silence.

"They're beginnin' to creep up on us, Drifter," Dewey whispered. " 'Bout an hour 'fore full dark."

"I see them. Pass the word around: Pick a target. Whether it's a good shot or not, choose one. When I open fire, everyone open up."

"Will do."

Frank had already picked his first target. A man had been slowly crawling toward the old fort and had now paused, his lower body sticking out from behind a saguaro cactus. Frank lifted his rifle and sighted in.

"Ever'one's got a target," Dewey whispered.

Frank squeezed the trigger. His bullet tore into the man just a couple of inches above his belt buckle.

Everyone behind the walls who was armed fired. The man Frank shot in the belly began screaming in pain, thrashing around in the sand. Other outlaws yelled either in pain or surprise.

"On your feet!" Dave yelled. "Charge the ruins."

"Light 'em up, Dewey," Frank yelled. "And let 'em fly."

Dewey let fly three dynamite-tipped arrows as fast an any Indian could on his best day. There was silence on the desert floor for a few seconds. Then a man yelled, "Them arrows is dynamite-tipped. Good God, boys, run!"

But it was too late for several of the charging outlaws. The dynamite blew and the sound was enormous on the desert floor. Dewey let fly more arrows, with twelve-year-old Jerry lighting the fuses. One charge uprooted a huge old saguaro cactus, about fifty feet in height, probably between a hundred and a hundred and fifty years old, with several dozen arms and weighing probably five or six tons.

The huge old cactus fell on two outlaws, crushing and killing one instantly and breaking both legs of the second. The man with the badly broken legs began screaming in pain, both from his broken legs and from the dozens of needles penetrating his flesh.

"Back, back!" Dave shouted. "Get back!"

But while they were retreating, the defenders scored several more hits on the outlaws, their bodies joining the other dead and badly wounded outlaws littering the desert.

"Goddamn you all to hell!" one outlaw shouted. "You'll all pay for this. I promise you, you'll pay dearly."

"What are you gonna do?" Dewey hollered. "Talk us to death?"

The dusty sand was still swirling around from a west wind, and the wind was steadily picking up.

"Oh, God!" Julie breathed.

"What's wrong?" Frank called. "Are you hurt?"

"No. A big rattlesnake just crawled up."

"Let me have him," Dewey said. "I'll have some fun with him."

"You're certainly welcome to the damn thing!" Julie replied.

Dewey snatched up the big rattler, making it look easy. But Frank knew better, and told the boys that.

"What are you going to do with that damn snake, Dewey?" Frank asked.

"Watch, Drifter," the mountain man whispered. "See that big cactus with the broke-off lower arm about twenty-five feet away? Off to your left. 'Bout midway 'tween us."

"Yeah. So?"

"I think they's a man done crawled up that far and can't go no further, and he's a-feared to try to go back."

"All right. What about it?"

"I bet I can change his mind and make him move."

Frank chuckled. "You've got a real mean streak in you, Dewey."

"I shore do. I take great displeasure at folks tryin' to kill me. Watch this."

Dewey gave the snake a fling and it landed right where Dewey wanted it to land. The outlaw behind the cactus started hollering. "Oh, good Christ! A rattler done fell out of the cactus. He's a-strikin' at me. I'm bit, boys. I'm bit."

No one rushed to help the outlaw.

The snakebit man yelled once more, and then his screaming abruptly ceased.

"Must have got him in the neck," Dewey said. "It don't take long once that happens. I've seen that a couple of times."

Julie and the girls all shuddered at just the thought.

"I hate this country," Julie said. "I hate snakes."

"The country is neutral, Julie," Frank told her. "It's neither for you nor against you. A person has to learn to live with it. Try to fight it, and you're fighting yourself."

"You can have it," the woman said. "I don't want it."

"Me neither," Danny said. "I want grass and trees and water. I don't like this part of the country."

"The outlaws are running away," Tess said, peeping out through a hole in the old wall. "They're riding away."

Frank took a quick look. The desert floor was littered with dead and wounded men, many of them mangled from the dynamite blasts.

"Is it over?" Jerry asked.

"I think so, son," Dewey replied. "At least this fight is."

"What do you think, Dewey?" Frank questioned. "Ride out or stay put?"

"Why leave?" the mountain man asked. "We got good water and a good position."

"Suits me," Frank agreed. "Let's fix supper."

Out on the desert floor, several wounded outlaws moaned. The defenders of the old fort ignored them.

Nineteen

The victors of the fight at the ruins pulled out before dawn the next morning. They neither tended to the wounded nor buried the dead.

"I'll kill you someday, Morgan," one wounded man gasped as Frank led the party out at predawn. "I swear on my mother's eyes I'll kill you for this."

"We left you some food and coffee in the ruins," Frank told the man. "The girls' idea. Not mine. If you can drag yourself over there, you might make it. The water's cold and sweet. Personally, I hope you murdering, kidnapping, child-raping bastards all die and rot right where you fell."

"You're a mean, heartless son of a bitch, Frank Morgan!"

"I hope the ants get you all," Dewey told another wounded man.

"I hate you, you sorry old bastard!" the wounded outlaw hissed.

Dewey smiled at him, lifted the reins, and rode away.

"You gots to hep me!" the man who was still pinned under the giant saguaro cactus called feebly.

"I don't gots to do nothin'," Dewey told him.

"Val Dooley'll kill you all!" another man called.

Dewey answered that with an obscene hand gesture.

"Mr. Morgan," Tess said when they were on the road south, "you and Mr. Dewey are hard men."

"It's a hard land, Tess," Frank told the girl. "I have no sympathy for men like those we left back at the ruins."

"They're all going to die, aren't they?" Sarah asked.

"Probably."

"I hope so," Susan said. "I hope they die hard. They're cruel and evil people."

Frank cut his eyes to Julie, who was riding along beside him. The woman's expression did not change at her daughter's words.

"Well, I guess I do too," Tess said.

"Me too," Sarah said. "But us leaving them food just proves that we're better people than they are."

"You girls are good people," Dewey told them. "But if them men we left back yonder ever get another chance to do to you what they done before, they will. Don't never doubt that. Trash is trash. You can pour a bottle of perfume on garbage, but it's still garbage."

"Keep your eyes open for any dust," Frank told the group. "This is Apache country and we've still got a long way to go."

"Is Tucson a big city?" Tess asked.

"It ain't no little town," Dewey replied. "I 'spect they's probably six or eight thousand people all jammed up there."

"Why?" Sarah asked.

"Damned if I know, child," Dewey said. "I never have understood why people want to act like sheep and all crowd together. When was the last time you was in Tucson, Drifter?''

"It's been several years, Dewey. More years than I like to think about really.'' Frank took off his hat and used his bandanna to wipe the sweat from his face. "And it sure hasn't gotten any cooler.''

"Dust to the south of us,'' Dewey said, squinting against the fierce glare of the sun.

"A lot of it,'' Frank said. "I don't think it's Injuns.''

The column of dust drew closer and Dewey said, "Soldier boys. A whole mess of 'em.''

"They're a long way from Fort Huachuca,'' Frank said.

"Them ain't Buffalo Soldiers,'' Dewey said as the column of cavalry came into clear view. "Them boys is white. Must be a special detail sent out here to fight the 'Paches.''

The long column of cavalry, complete with supply and hospital wagons, stopped and waited for the slim line of riders to approach.

"Are you people aware this road has been closed to civilians?'' the officer at the head of the column said.

"If that's the case, how are we 'posed to get from one place to the other?'' Dewey asked. "Fly?''

The colonel gave the old mountain man a very jaundiced look. "You were supposed to stay put, old-timer. For your safety.''

"Well, we decided to take a little ride, General,'' Dewey told him. "We wanted to see the sights, I reckon you might say.''

"I don't care for your attitude,'' the colonel replied.

"Tough titty, as the kitty said. But the milk was good.''

Several junior officers smiled at that. One glance from the colonel wiped the smiles from their faces.

"It was very irresponsible on your part, bringing children

into a zone of hostility," the colonel told him, looking at Tess, Sarah, Susan, and Jerry.

"That's Frank Morgan!" one cavalaryman blurted out from the ranks.

The colonel looked at Frank. "Is that true, sir?"

"That's my name," Frank told him.

"The shootist?"

"I been called worse, I reckon."

"Where are you going, Morgan?"

"That's my business, Colonel."

"I'm making it my business, Morgan."

"I'm taking a pleasant ride through the cool countryside."

"Why are you so reluctant to answer a simple question?"

"I don't like the way you asked it, Colonel."

The colonel and Frank Morgan spent the next full minute staring at each other. The colonel blinked first.

"Very well, Morgan," the colonel said. "The well-being of these innocent children is in your hands. I'll hold you responsible for them."

"I been looking after them and Mrs. Barnes for the past month, Colonel."

The colonel shifted his gaze to Julie. "You are Mrs. Barnes?"

"I am. And what Mr. Morgan just told you is quite true."

"Are all these children yours?"

"Not hardly, sir. Only Susan."

Susan raised a hand. "I'm Susan."

"And the others, ma'am?"

"We rescued them from the Val Dooley gang north of here. The Val Dooley gang killed my husband and kidnapped me, Susan, and her sister, Rebecca. Frank Morgan single-handedly rescued Susan and me. We are looking for Rebecca."

"I . . . see," the colonel said hesitantly. He looked at

Frank. "You are to be commended, sir. You believe Rebecca is being held in the southern part of Arizona Territory?"

"I do, Colonel."

"And you intend to rescue Mrs. Barnes's other daughter?"

"I intend to rescue all the children who are being held at a certain spot not far from Tucson. Furthermore, I intend to kill every man who is a member of the Val Dooley gang and also those who buy, sell, or have a hand in the kidnapping."

The colonel blinked at the bluntness of Frank's words. "Well, sir, don't you think you should alert the authorities rather than take matters into your own hands?"

"No, I do not."

"May I ask why?"

"You're not from this part of the country, are you, Colonel?"

"No, Mr. Morgan, I am from New England."

"That explains it."

"Oh? What does it explain, sir?"

"You folks got rules and written codes and laws and police officers and the like. Don't no one where you come from tote a gun, do they?"

"No. Absolutely not. Only officers of the law are permitted to carry pistols."

"You'd have a damn sight less crime if everybody packed a pistol. Then if you saw someone breaking the law, you could just shoot them and be done with it."

"I . . . see. That's the way you handle it, sir?"

"That's about the size of it, Colonel."

The colonel of cavalry saw a very slight smile crease Frank's lips, and realized then that Frank was putting one over on him . . . at least to some degree, he thought. He nodded his head. "Very good, Mr. Morgan. You had me going there for a moment."

"If you say so, Colonel."

"If I might make a suggestion, Mr. Morgan?"

"Of course."

"It's time for us to rest our horses and perhaps make some coffee and have some hardtack. Would you and your party join us?"

"Coffee sounds good, Colonel. We'll pass on the hardtack."

"I can't blame you for that, Mr. Morgan." He pointed. "Over there, if you will."

As the fires were built for the soldiers' coffee, Frank squatted down and waited for the colonel, Dewey with him.

"What you reckon that stuffed shirt's got on his mind?" Dewey asked.

"No way of knowing, partner. Here he comes, so I reckon we'll soon know."

"Coffee will be ready in a few minutes, gentlemen," the officer said. "By the way, my name is Clayton. Thomas Clayton. Let's dispense with the formal titles, shall we?"

"I'm Frank and this here is Dewey. What's on your mind, Tom?"

"The safety of the females and the boy, Frank."

"Colonel," Dewey said, "back up this road a few miles you're gonna come to the ruins of an old army fort."

"I'm familiar with it, sir."

"I'm glad you is. Well, by now the buzzards is havin' a feast on the bodies of the outlaw scum that attacked us yesterday."

"I beg your pardon, sir?" Colonel Clayton said stiffly.

"Bodies, Colonel. All shot up . . . by us. They was about twenty-five or thirty of 'em when they attacked us. I reckon maybe a dozen rode out, and some of them was wounded.

Miss Julie and her daughter accounted for several of them dead and wounded. You get my drift?''

''I do, sir. You know who these men are . . . were?''

''Part of the Val Dooley gang,'' Frank said.

''You're sure of that?''

''They mentioned his name.''

A sergeant walked over with three cups of coffee and passed them around. Colonel Clayton thanked him and the sergeant backed off.

The coffee was hot and strong, and both Frank and Dewey sipped theirs gratefully.

''And you are going to attack the Val Dooley gang, Frank? You and Dewey and the lady and the girls?''

''And Danny and Jerry,'' Frank said with a smile.

''Of course,'' Clayton acknowledged. ''And Danny and Jerry.''

''That's the plan, Tom.'' Frank had decided not to tell the army officer anything about the rancher, Big Max Collins.

The colonel shook his head in disbelief. ''Well, I don't have the authority to stop you. All I can do is wish you good luck.''

''Thank you,'' Frank replied.

''I have tried to stay out of civilian affairs,'' Colonel Clayton said after a moment of silence. ''However, I can tell you this. I have heard that a rancher name of Max Collins is involved in the buying and selling of men and women. I do not know if there is any truth in the report.''

''We heard the same rumor,'' Frank said.

''I've met the man,'' Clayton continued. ''He is a very disagreeable sort. Very crude and obnoxious. Somewhat of a bully, I would say.''

''I've heard the same thing,'' Frank said.

The colonel stood up. ''I have to say that it is my belief the world would be a much better place without Max Collins." He smiled. "If you get my drift. Good day, gentlemen, and good luck to you all."

Orders were shouted and the cavalry rode off.

"Interestin' sort of feller, that colonel," Dewey remarked.

"Yes," Frank agreed. "He is that."

"You sort of have to think some on his words, don't you?"

"Being a military man and having to live under a hard set of rules and regulations, he has to be careful about what he says. But I do believe I got his message."

"We ought to go kill Max Collins."

"Somebody should."

"Well . . . I been sayin' that for years."

"So what are we waiting for?"

"For you to git up and let's ride."

Frank stood up. "I'm up."

"Let's ride."

Twenty

Tucson was crowded, busy, hot, and dusty. After they stabled the horses and Dog with them, then got rooms at a hotel, Julie and the girls called for a hot bath. Leaving Danny and Jerry to look after the privacy of the women, Frank and Dewey went in search of the seediest-looking saloon.

"When them females git nekkid, no peekin' now," Dewey told the young men, bringing a flush of color to their cheeks.

Frank laughed at the young men.

On a side street, Frank spotted a likely-looking watering hole. "That looks about right for a place to have some trouble."

"It shore do, Drifter. For a pure-dee fact. Wonder if that feller layin' out front is passed out drunk or dead."

Frank looked up into the sky and then pointed. "No buzzards."

"Hell, he might smell so bad even they don't want to have nothin' to do with him."

"That would be some powerful, Dewey. You ready to cut this dust from our throats?"

"I figure a bottle might do it."

"I'll leave the rotgut to you," Frank told him. "I'll settle for a couple of beers."

It was smoky but cool inside the dimly lighted saloon. About a third of the tables were occupied, with half a dozen men at the bar. Frank and Dewey took a spot at the end of the bar and waited for the barkeep.

"What'll it be, boys?" a big man in bad need of a shave and wearing a very dirty apron called from the other end of the bar.

"A bottle for my friend and a beer for me," Frank called. "You got anything to eat in this place?"

"Beans and tortillas."

"Bring a couple of plates, will you?"

"Comin' up." The barkeep paused and looked back at Frank. He frowned. "Don't I know you, Mister?"

"I don't think so."

"I think I do. It'll come to me in a little while. You sure look familiar."

Frank sipped his beer and Dewey knocked back a shot of red-eye while they waited for their food. When the food came, it was surprisingly good. The beans were spicy and the tortillas were hot and fresh.

Frank caught the bartender's eye. He motioned toward the food. "Good, real good."

The barkeep pulled a beer for himself and walked down to the end of the bar, leaning against it. "My old woman's a good cook."

"She shore is," Dewey mumbled around a mouthful of food. "This here is damn good grub."

"You boys look like you've come a piece."

"Phoenix."

"That road's closed," a young man standing a few yards away from Frank said. "Nothin' movin' north or south in days."

"Except for us," Frank said quietly. The man was hunting trouble; Frank picked up on that immediately. But Frank was not the sort to back down from anyone, much less a loudmouth.

"I say you didn't come from Phoenix."

"And I say I don't much give a damn what you say."

"Nobody talks to Ted Collins like that, mister," the young loudmouth said, pushing back from the bar to face Frank.

"I just did, Ted," Frank said softly, picking up on the name Collins.

"You ain't never heard of me?" Ted demanded.

"Can't say that I have."

"Then you ain't been around much, have you?"

Frank smiled and picked up his beer mug. With his left hand. A motion that did not escape the barkeep's eyes. "I've been here and there, Teddy."

"Don't call me Teddy!"

Frank carefully set the mug down on the bar. "That's your name, isn't it? I bet your mama called you Little Teddy, didn't she?"

"Damn you!" Ted hollered.

The patrons in the saloon fell silent.

"Ted's a bad one, mister," a cardplayer called. "He's fast."

"Some people say I am too," Frank replied, never taking his eyes off Teddy.

"You got a name?" Teddy demanded.

"Don't we all," Frank asked, adding, "Teddy?"

"I told you not to call me that, damn you!"

"All right, Teddy. I won't call you Teddy anymore. Does that suit you, Teddy? Oh, excuse me, *Ted*."

"Well?" Ted demanded.

"Well, what?" Frank asked.

"What's your damn name, mister?"

"Frank."

The bartender straightened up and blinked. "Oh, hell," he muttered.

"Frank don't tell me squat!" Ted almost shouted the words. "Frank what, damn you?"

"Morgan," the bartender said. "That there's Frank Morgan."

"These here beans are shore good," Dewey said. "You reckon your wife would tell me how she fixes 'em?"

"Man, this ain't no time to be discussin' beans," the barkeep said.

"I don't believe that there's Frank Morgan." Teddy said.

"Now you're calling the barkeep a liar, Ted," Frank said. "You really should watch your mouth."

"You ought to watch your own damn mouth," Ted snapped. "And you ain't Frank Morgan neither. Frank Morgan's old as dirt."

"Well, I'm glad that's settled, aren't you, Dewey?"

"What's been settled?" Dewey asked.

"I'm not Frank Morgan."

"You're not? You shore could have fooled me."

"Teddy says I'm not."

"What the hell does he know?"

"Don't call me Teddy!" Teddy hollered.

"Your wife's added a little something extry to these beans," Dewey said. "They's mighty tasty."

"I'll tell her you said so," the barkeep replied, looking nervously first at Ted and then at Frank.

"I'll have another mug of beer," Frank said.

"You'll talk to me!" Teddy almost yelled the words. "By God, I ain't used to people ignorin' me."

"What would you like to talk about?" Frank asked the trouble-hunter. "You just pick a topic and we'll have a good time discussing it."

"Huh?" Teddy blurted out.

"The boy ain't right in the head," Dewey said.

"What'd you say about me, you old coot!" Teddy yelled.

"I said you was crazy," Dewey told him.

"Crazy!" Teddy hollered. "You callin' me crazy?"

"I can't get over how good these beans is," Dewey said. "I can taste the onions and the peppers. But they's somethin' else."

"I'll ask my wife," the barkeep said.

"To hell with your damn beans!" Teddy said. "I ought to call both of you out."

"Out where?" Dewey asked. "I like it in here. If you want to go outside and play in the sand, boy, you go right ahead."

"Boy!" Teddy's eyes bugged out. "You callin' me a boy?"

"Not only is the boy ain't right in the head," Dewey remarked, "he can't hear worth a damn neither."

"I noticed that," Frank said.

"That's it!" Teddy said, stepping away from the bar. "By God, that does it."

"Settle down, Ted," the bartender warned.

"You shut up, Amos," Ted said. "This ain't none of your affair."

"The hell it ain't," Amos said. "This is my place."

"You any relation to Max Collins, Teddy?" Frank asked.

"That's my pa."

"Well, you come by the big mouth naturally then."

"What?" Teddy yelled.

"You heard me, Teddy."

"My pa'll kill you! Whoever you are."

"I told you who I am, Teddy. Now why don't you run along and go tattle to Daddy?"

"Goddamn you!"

"Now, that's no way for a nice young man to talk. Your daddy would be ashamed of you, Teddy." Frank was moving ever closer to the angry young man. Max Collins's son appeared not to notice.

"If my pa was here, he'd kill you!" Ted yelled.

"No, he wouldn't, Little Teddy. He's all mouth, just like you." Frank was just about within swinging distance of Teddy.

"My pa?" Teddy said. "All mouth? My pa's kilt dozens of men. And that ain't countin' Mexicans or Injuns."

"Did he shoot them in the back, Teddy baby?"

"Teddy baby! Damn you, Morgan!"

"Oh. Now you believe I'm Frank Morgan?"

"So what if I do? Your name don't mean crap to me."

"Tell me something, Teddy baby. You reckon that horse of yours could find his way home all by himself?"

"Hell, yes, he could. Why do you ask something stupid like that?"

"Just curious, Teddy baby. Haven't you ever been curious about anything?"

"Why are you crowdin' me, Morgan?" Teddy just then noticed how close Frank was to him. "Huh? Why are you crowdin' me?"

"So I can do this," Frank said.

"Huh? Do what?"

Frank hit the young man square on the side of the jaw with a short hard left, then followed that with a right cross. Ted Collins hit the floor, out cold.

Dewey looked over the side of the bar at Teddy. "Now what are you goin' to do with him?"

Frank smiled. "Oh, I think you'll like it, Dewey."

"You got that look in your eyes again, Drifter. That tell me you're about to be up to no good."

"I think Big Max is going to come to us. If I'm right, that will save us a lot of trouble."

"Oh? And how are you gonna arrange that?"

Frank pointed to a man sitting at a table. "You know young Ted's horse?"

"I sure do. Are you really Frank Morgan?"

"Yes. Go get his horse and bring it around back. Will you do that for me?"

"Sure. Right now."

"Help me carry him out back, Dewey. This is going to be funny."

"Might be to you. But I don't think young Collins here is gonna see the humor in it."

"I don't think his daddy will either," Frank replied.

"And you're countin' on that, right?"

Frank laughed. "You bet I am."

Twenty-one

When Ted regained consciousness, he had been stripped naked and tied in the saddle . . . backward.

"You can't do this to me!" Ted hollered.

"I just did it, Teddy," Frank told him.

"I'll be cooked time I get home!"

"You're going to be well done, for a fact."

"My pa will kill you for this!"

"Doubtful, Teddy baby. Real doubtful."

"This ain't decent!" Ted yelled.

"Neither is your pa," Frank said as he led the horse up the alleyway toward the street.

"You can't put me out on the street," Ted squalled. "I'm buck-ass nekked."

"You shore ain't no sight for women to see, for a fact," Dewey told him.

"You shut up, you damned old worthless coot!"

"Hey!" a citizen on the street yelled at glimpsing Ted. "Come see this, everybody."

"Stop gawkin' at me!" Ted hollered as a crowd began quickly gathering, the men and women laughing and pointing at him.

"That's disgraceful," a woman yelled.

"I think he's sorta cute," a soiled dove from a local sporting house remarked.

"You shut up, Maybelle!" Ted told the woman.

"You're not going to be doing much pokin' for a while," Maybelle replied. "That sun's gonna cook you . . . in places it ain't never touched before."

That brought a laugh from the crowd.

"That's disgusting," another local lady said.

"Here now!" a deputy yelled, pushing and shoving his way through the gathering crowd. "What the hell is going on here?" The sight of Ted Collins, buck-assed naked, tied backward in the saddle, brought the lawman up short. He stood for a few seconds, grinning. "Well, now, ain't that a sight?"

"You get me down from here, Will," Ted yelled.

"Who put you up there like that?" the deputy asked.

"I did," Frank said.

"And who are you?" the deputy asked.

"Frank Morgan."

The deputy opened his mouth, then abruptly closed it. He stared at Frank for a moment.

"Frank Morgan? *The* Frank Morgan?"

"I reckon so."

"In Tucson?"

"Here I am." Frank slapped the horse on the rump and said, "Go home, boy. Home!"

The horse galloped up the street. "Oh, hell!" Teddy hollered, swaying like a drunk man in the saddle.

"The deputy said it was an easy hour out to the ranch," Frank said. "Say an hour and a half with Ted riding backward." The men had bathed, Frank had gotten a haircut and shave, and both had changed into clean clothing. Frank looked at his watch. "He should be getting to the ranch about right now. Give Big Max an hour to look after his son and an hour to get into town. That should put him here about four-thirty."

"I axed around whilst you was splashin' in the tub and singing that song 'bout goin' swimmin' with bowlegged women," Dewey said. "Nobody knows whatever become of Ted's mother. She wasn't with Big Max when he come here and the boy don't seem to know nothin' 'bout her."

"She either left him or he killed her," Frank said.

"Either way, she's better off."

Julie and the girls were shopping, with Danny and Jerry in tow. Frank and Dewey were sitting in the shade on the boardwalk under the hotel awning. After his bath, Frank had carefully cleaned and oiled his Peacemaker.

"You gonna tote just that one gun?" Dewey asked.

"That's all I figure I'll need."

"Well, I'll be close by when Big Max shows up. Now, you know he ain't gonna ride in here all by his lonesome, don't you?"

"I figure he'll bring some company."

"Yeah," Dewey said dryly. "Like maybe a small army."

"I don't think so, Dewey. Way I hear it, Big Max is a proud man with a big reputation. He'll probably bring a few boys in with him for insurance, but he'll want to face me alone, either with fists or guns."

"He's a big man, Frank. And I'm told he's killed men with his fists."

Frank looked at the old mountain man. "So have I, Dewey."

It was a quarter of five when Big Max Collins rode into town, accompanied by six tough-looking men. One of the riders spotted Frank and Dewey sitting on the boardwalk and the group reined up in front of the hotel. Big Max sat his horse for a moment, staring at Frank.

"You Frank Morgan?" Max asked.

"That's me. And you must be the man who likes to kidnap and rape little girls, Max Collins."

"That's a damn dirty lie!" Max said.

"No, it isn't, Max. Some of the men who worked for Val Dooley told me all about your part in the kidnapping and raping of young girls and women."

"Then they lied!"

"I tell you what, Max. Why don't you and me go visit the county sheriff and then we'll all take a ride out to your ranch and look around? And when we go visit the sheriff, we'll take along some of the girls kidnapped during one of the raids up north of here. How about that?"

"I'll kill you, Morgan," Max hissed.

"Have at it, Big Mouth . . . ah . . . Big Max."

"Maybe I will."

Frank stood up. "Let's have it, Max."

"But I think I'll beat you to a bloody pulp and then kill you."

"You can try, Max."

Big Max Collins stepped down from the saddle. Frank took that opportunity to size him up.

Big Max was big, for a fact. A couple of inches taller than Frank and no fat on the man. All muscle and bone.

"You want your ass-whuppin' right here in the street, Morgan?"

"You want to try to do it right here in the street, Big Mouth?"

Big Max cussed Frank and charged up the steps to the boardwalk. Frank stepped forward and busted the bigger man right in the mouth with a hard right fist. Big Max sailed off the steps and landed in the street in the dirt, flat on his back. Frank was after him instantly. Max stumbled to his feet and Frank hit him again, this time on the side of the jaw. The blow knocked Max to his knees. Max grabbed up a handful of dirt and flung it at Frank. But Frank had anticipated that, and sidestepped the cloud of dust.

Max got to his feet, cussing Frank. Frank smiled at him and said, "What's the matter, Max? I thought you were a fighter."

Max cussed him again and came in swinging.

Frank stepped to one side and buried his right fist in the big man's belly. The air whooshed out of Max and he staggered backward, his face turning chalk white under his tan. Frank pressed him, swinging lefts and rights that connected and hurt Max. A trickle of blood leaked from Big Max's mouth and nose. Frank threw a short hard left that caught Max flush on the nose and flattered it. The blood began to pour out of Max's busted beak.

Enraged, Max charged Frank and caught him in a bear hug. "Kill you!" Max gasped. "Crush the life out of you."

Frank lashed back with a boot, sinking a spur into Max's leg. Max howled in pain, loosening his bear hug. Frank slipped away and turned. He busted Max on the side of the head with a right fist. Blood began leaking from a mangled ear. Frank didn't let up. He hit Max twice in the face, a left and right, the blows glazing Max's eyes. Frank slammed a hard fist to Max's mouth, pulping the man's lips.

Max backed up, shaking his head.

Out of the corner of his eye, Frank observed two lawmen standing in the crowd, watching and smiling as Max got the crap beat out of him. Obviously, Big Max Collins was not the best-liked man in town.

Max staggered toward Frank, swinging both fists that hurt when they connected with Frank's arms and shoulders. Hurt, but did no real damage.

Frank stepped back, planted his boots firmly in the dirt, and knocked Max down with a right to the bigger man's jaw. Max struggled to his feet and Frank hit him again. Big Max's eyes seemed to roll back in his head and the big man sighed and slumped to the street, out cold.

"Whooee!" a man yelled. "That there was some fight. Best I've seen in years."

"Damn sure was," another local said.

Frank reached down into a horse trough and splashed double handfuls of water on his face. Big Max wheezed into the dirt, out cold.

"Drag him over to my office," a man in a dark suit said. "I'll check him out and set that broken nose." He looked at Frank. "Are you hurt?"

"No," Frank said.

Well, you're either very good or very lucky," the doctor said. "As far as I know, that's the first time Max Collins has been bested in a bare-knuckle fight. What's your name, mister?"

"Frank Morgan."

The doctor stared. "Are you serious?" he asked.

"I reckon so."

The doctor stepped closer and peered at Frank. "By God, it is you. A friend of mine sent me a copy of a magazine a few months ago that had an article about you in it, along with a picture. The article wasn't very flattering."

"I stopped reading them a long time ago."

"Are you aware that you strongly resemble the outlaw Val Dooley?"

"So I've been told, Doc."

Big Max Collins groaned and broke wind.

"Charming fellow," the doctor said.

"Isn't he, though?"

"How are your hands, Mr. Morgan?"

Frank flexed his fingers a few times. "They're all right. I have good hands, Doc."

Big Max moaned again.

"I told some of you people to get him over to my office. Now do it!" the doctor snapped. "Right now."

Four of Big Max's hands picked him up and toted him off.

"I'm sure he isn't hurt too badly," the doctor said. "I don't think you could hurt that man with an ax."

"I'll probably have to kill him after this," Frank said.

"That will not be any great loss to society."

Frank smiled. "We sure agree on that."

"If your hands start bothering you, soak them in hot salt water. But I'm sure you already know that." The doctor smiled. "Quite an enjoyable fight, Mr. Morgan. I'll see you around town, I'm sure."

"See you, Doc."

The crowd broke up and Dewey walked over to Frank. "You've studied some boxing, my boy."

"Some, for a fact."

"I bet Big Max ain't had a whuppin' like that since he was a boy."

"Probably not. But killing comes next."

"That gonna bother you?"

"To put lead in someone like Big Max? No," Frank said flatly.

"Didn't figure it would. Where's Miss Julie and the girls?"

"Still resting, I guess. And you can bet Danny isn't too far away from Susan."

"That boy's in love, shore nuff. But so's Susan."

"They'll make it. I mentioned to Julie about them taking a train and getting clear of this situation."

"And her reply?"

"She told me what I could do with my suggestion."

"Wagh!" Dewey snorted. "I wish I could have been there to hear that."

"It was blunt," Frank admitted.

"I'm shore it was. So Miss Julie and the kids is in for the long haul?"

"Looks that way."

"Speakin' of looks, them hands of Collins is shore givin' us a hard look."

"I see them. But I don't think they're going to do anything. Max wants his revenge personally."

"I thought they was six of 'em rode in with Big Max?" Dewey questioned.

"There was."

"So where's the sixth man?"

"Probably hightailing it back to the ranch to warn the others."

"So . . . where does that leave us?"

"Following their trail, I reckon."

"You figured this would happen, didn't you?"

"Yes. I think Max was probably warned, by coded telegraph, when we pulled out of Phoenix. Certainly he was warned after the fight at the old fort."

"So you think the girls have already been moved 'crost the border?"

"I doubt it, Dewey. I've been mulling over what Colonel Clayton said to us. I think the army's had their eye on Big Max for some time. That's just a hunch, mind you, but it's a strong one."

"Makes sense to me."

"I think the girls are still on this side of the border. Maybe they've been moved north, maybe they've been moved over into New Mexico. I want to talk to the sheriff here; some of his deputies. I have to think they had at least a suspicion of what was going on."

"You'd think so."

Frank stood up from the chair and stretched.

"You goin' somewheres?" Dewey asked.

"I have to take care of some important business."

"Like what?"

Frank smiled. "Feeding Dog."

Twenty-two

Yes, the deputy had told Frank and Dewey. His office had been keeping as close an eye as they could on Max Collins for some time.

"And?" Frank had pressed him.

The deputy had shrugged his shoulders and replied, "It's hard to do anything when the subject under suspicion has a local judge in his pocket."

"I figured as much," Frank said.

"This judge won't be in office much longer," the deputy said. "He was appointed and his appointment is about to be jerked out from under him. He'll be damn lucky if he isn't run out of town on a rail. Or lynched," the deputy added. He looked at Frank. "You want to press some charges against Max Collins? I would just love to arrest that arrogant, bigmouthed bastard . . . and to have him resist would be the stuff dreams are made of."

Frank laughed at the wistful expression on the lawman's face. "It would be a waste of time. I whipped him, remember?"

"And did a damn good job of it too, so I heard. I wish I could have seen it. But Deputy Barnett filled me in."

"The sheriff won't move on Max on his own?"

"The sheriff's in Washington, D. C. He's getting himself appointed a deputy U. S. marshal. Then, by God, if Max is still around, we'll do something about him."

"If I have anything to say about it, he'll be six feet under."

The deputy smiled. "Send me an invite to the shootin', will you?"

Frank laughed at that. "It's probably going to be real suddenlike."

"Ain't they always?"

Outside the sheriff's office, Frank and Dewey watched as Big Max Collins and his men rode slowly out of town.

"The next time I see you, Morgan," Max hollered, "I'm gonna kill you."

"I'll keep that in mind, Big Mouth," Frank told him.

Max spat on the ground and kept on riding.

"We gonna hang around this city until Max comes a-lookin' for you?" Dewey asked.

"I hadn't planned on it. That'll give me time to go sneak around Max's spread."

"That'll give *us* time to go sneakin' around," Dewey corrected.

"I just can't get rid of you, can I?"

"Nope. Somebody's got to look after you."

Frank rolled his eyes at that. "Come on. Let's go get the ladies and have dinner."

* * *

For the next several days, the ladies rested and did a bit of shopping while Frank and Dewey prowled around, making several trips out to Max Collins's spread.

"The place sure ain't guarded," Dewey said. "We ain't seen nobody."

It was the third day of their prowling about.

"There is nobody to guard," Frank guessed. "They've all been moved."

"So now all we've got to do is figure out where," Dewey said. "How do you propose to do that?"

"I'm thinking on it."

"That means you ain't got a clue."

"Right."

"I got a plan."

"And that is?"

"We grab one of Max's hands, heat up a runnin' iron, and get the information from him. How 'bout that?"

"Suppose he doesn't know to begin with?"

"Then I reckon he's in for a lot of hurt."

"Max does run cattle out there. What if the man we grab is just a cowboy?"

"You got more what-ifs than a damn dictionary," Dewey said sourly.

"I just don't want to see any more innocents hurt."

"Anybody who throws in with the likes of Big Max Collins ain't innocent, Drifter. You know that as well as me."

"Maybe."

"Maybe, hell! Well, let's go grab up this judge that's in Big Max's pocket and go to work on *him*."

"And you talk about me having a mean streak. You're

getting plumb ornery in your declining years, you know that?''

"Declining years! You swing out of that saddle and I'll whup you right here in the middle of this damn road!''

"We don't have time for that right now. Riders heading our way. If you'd stop flapping your gums, you'd a-seen them before I did.''

"You don't have a lick of respect for your elders, do you, boy?''

"So you admit you're getting long in the tooth?''

Dewey had a number of words to say in response to that, coloring the hot air with profanity. Frank sat in his saddle and laughed at the old mountain man.

"Them's Big Max's hands," Dewey finally wound down and said.

"You want to run away and hide?" Frank asked with a smile.

Dewey withered him with a look.

The four hired guns stopped a few yards from Frank and Dewey.

"This was a right nice ride," Dewey said. " 'Fore we run into ugly.''

"You talkin' about us, old man?" one of the hands asked.

"Well, you in the middle of the road and you're sure as hell ugly," Dewey said. "You figure it out.''

"I ought to jerk your old ass outta that saddle and whup you right here and now," another of the hands said.

"I don't see no one stoppin' you from tryin' that," Dewey told him. "And I stress *tryin'* that.''

"Settle down," a hand said to his friend. He looked at Frank. "What are you doin' out this way, Morgan?''

"I don't figure that's any of your business.''

"I just made it my business.''

"Well, if you insist. We're out here countin' horny toads."

The hand frowned. "You got a real smart-aleck mouth in your face, Morgan."

"Ain't you got no interest in science and such, boy?" Dewey asked.

"Huh?"

"Horny toads," Dewey said. "Them folks who study nature commissioned us to count horny toads."

"You're full of crap!" the hand stated.

"The man's eat up with the dumb ass," Dewey said.

" 'Member what Big Max told us," another hired gun said. "No trouble. Let's go."

"I don't like that old coot."

"Too bad. He'll get his. All in due time." He looked at Frank. "And you'll get yours too, Morgan."

The four hands rode on after giving Frank and Dewey hard looks.

Dewey glanced at Frank. "Horny toads?" he questioned.

"Just popped into my mind."

"Well, pop it back out. Let's head to town. I need a drink."

Frank and Julie took a walk after dinner. Despite the time of the year, the night air was pleasantly cool.

"I'm going to tell you again, Julie," Frank said. "You and the kids need to get on a train and get out of here."

"Frank, the kids have had a terrible experience. They've lost their parents."

"I know that, Julie. But—"

"Let me finish, please."

Frank waited.

"We're all they have, Frank. I'm sure there is a medical

term for it, but it boils down to this: We are the parents in their lives now. You and I. They need us.''

''For how long?''

''Until the need passes.''

''That doesn't tell me much.''

''I'm not a doctor, Frank. And I'm sure not one of those fancy medical people who study the workings of a person's mind.''

''One of those what?''

''I forget what they're called. But I read an article about them once.''

''How can anyone study a person's mind? You can't see a person's mind.''

''I don't know, Frank. I just know I'm not one of those people.''

''Thank God for that.''

She laughed, took his arm, and they continued walking in silence for a time.

''Frank?''

''I'm right here.''

''If you insist upon us leaving, I'll take the kids and we'll go away . . . someplace.''

''I'm not going to insist, Julie. I enjoy your company.''

''I'm happy about that.''

''Julie, when this hunt is over, and we get Becky back, what are your plans?''

''You mean *if* we get Becky back, don't you?''

''I guess so.''

''I don't know, Frank. I try just to live one day at a time.''

''I do know that feeling.''

''What are *your* plans? Are you still thinking about buying that land in New Mexico?''

''I'm thinking about buying that valley, yes. Beyond that, I don't know.''

"The whole valley?"

"Yes."

"How big is it?"

"The valley is just part of it. There are grassy meadows and a couple of creeks, and there's a stone house that someone built many, many years ago."

"It sounds lovely."

"It is."

"I'd like to see it."

"Then you shall, Julie. When the hunt is over. If you still want to see it."

"What would change my mind?"

"I don't know. Don't women change their minds often?" She laughed softly. "That is our prerogative, Frank."

"Whatever that means."

"You know exactly what that means, Frank Morgan. Don't you try to play dumb with me. I know you too well for that."

"You don't know me at all, Julie."

She stopped, forcing Frank to stop, and looked up at him. "Now what in the world do you mean by that?"

"Just that, Julie. You know only what I've told you."

"And what I've observed."

"Maybe I've been on my best behavior?" he said with a quick smile.

"Oh, sure." She nudged him with an elbow, and they resumed their evening stroll through a quiet section of Tucson.

"I'm going to lose Susan when this hunt is over," Julie said softly.

"You'll be gaining a son when she marries Danny."

"Well, yes. But I'm certain they'll be going to Iowa. That's what I meant."

"You have any desire to go to Iowa?"

"No. Besides, I would never dream of interfering with their marriage. They've got their own lives to live."

"Good for you."

"What about Max Collins?" she said, abruptly changing the subject.

"He's a dead man," Frank said, his voice cold. "He just doesn't know it yet."

"Killing him won't bring Becky back any sooner."

"No. But it will stop him from being a part in any more kidnappings and rapes."

"He might try to grab Susan and Tess and Sarah, or even Jerry, while we're in town . . . or walking around out here."

"He's going to run up against a very tough old mountain man if he does. And a very determined young man who is very much in love with your daughter. You're all reasonably safe here in town. Max wasn't that bad hurt during the fight. A few more days and he'll come to town looking for me."

"And then?"

"Then we'll continue the hunt for Becky."

Twenty-three

"Big Max just rode into town," Dewey informed Frank. "Lookin' fit as a fiddle and mean as a bear."

It had been five days since the fight between Frank and Big Max.

"It's about time," Frank said. "I was beginning to have my doubts about his showing up at all."

"He's got some of his hired guns with him, Drifter."

"They'll stay out of it until Max goes down," Frank replied. "Then they'll either start shooting or pull out."

"You don't look like you're worried at all, Mr. Morgan," Tess said. "You look like you're really relaxed."

"No point in worrying about it, Tess. Worrying tenses a man all up." Frank stood and slipped his Peacemaker in and out of leather a couple of times. "Time to go and see which one of us sees the elephant today."

''Is there a circus in town?'' Sarah asked.

''No, child,'' Dewey told her. ''That's just an old expression.''

Frank stepped out of the hotel lobby onto the boardwalk and looked around. Big Max had dismounted and tied up at a hitch rail in front of a saloon across the street and a couple of doors down. The man was standing on the boardwalk, glaring at him.

''Big ugly bastard, ain't he?'' Dewey said.

Frank did not reply, knowing Dewey was not expecting one. Frank continued to stare across the street at Big Max.

Dewey stepped back to stand beside Julie and the young people.

''What are they doing?'' Julie asked in a whisper.

''Stare-down,'' Dewey told her. ''Seeing who will blink first.''

''And that will mean what, sir?'' Sarah asked.

''Means someone's nerve ain't as strong as it should be.''

''Men!'' Julie said, stamping a foot. ''I never heard of such a thing!''

''I've seen two bull buffar do it,'' Dewey said. ''Right 'fore they went after it, fightin' over a cow or territory.''

Julie muttered something under her breath. Susan was the only one who heard, and she giggled.

''But them buffar rarely fought to the death,'' Dewey said. ''When the two yonder get done, one of them is gonna be dead.''

Julie fell silent.

''This time there ain't gonna be no talk, Morgan,'' Max called.

''Suits me, Big Mouth.''

''So step out into the street,'' Big Max said.

''After you, Max. You're the one who wanted this.''

Max stepped out into the hot dusty street. Frank stepped

down from the boardwalk and faced him, the street's width between them.

"You gonna pull, Morgan?" Max said.

"After you, Max."

"You yellow bastard!"

Frank did not reply. He waited patiently.

"I'm better than you, Morgan."

"We'll see."

"Everybody says I am!"

"There was a time when most everybody thought the earth was flat. They were wrong."

"You're afraid of me, aren't you, Morgan?"

"I'm afraid you're going to put me to sleep with all your yakking."

"This one's gonna be for my son, Ted. He's still sick after all that sun."

"You have my most insincere condolences."

"Damn you, Morgan!"

"You're boring me, Big Mouth. Are you trying to talk me to death?"

"Now, Morgan!" Big Max hollered.

Max cleared leather, but Frank was an instant faster. Max's bullet slammed into the building behind Frank. Frank's bullet tore into Max's lower right side.

Max grunted and lifted his pistol, cocking it. Frank's second shot ripped into Max's guts, and put the big man down on his knees in the street.

But Max was a tough man and wasn't going to go out of this world easily. He struggled to his feet and stood swaying, blood leaking from his wounds. He laughed insanely and lifted his pistol. "Die, you son of a bitch!" he yelled at Frank.

Frank drilled him in the center of his big chest and Max went down again. This time he did not get up.

The deputy Frank had spoken with about Max and about the local judge stepped out of the crowd. "That's it, Frank. It's over. He's done."

"You saw it all?" Frank questioned.

"I seen it all. He drew first. He come into town lookin' for a killin'. And I reckon he damn sure found one."

The doctor Frank had talked with after the fistfight walked over to Max Collins and knelt down, quickly examining him. He stood up and shook his head. "He's alive, but fading fast. Somebody go get the undertaker. No point in trying to move this man."

"Damn you to hell!" Max said.

"You're on your way out of this world, Collins," the doctor said. "You best be asking the Good Lord for forgiveness."

"I ain't scared of Him either," Max gasped.

"Then you are a fool," the doctor replied.

Frank had walked over to stand a few yards away from Big Max Collins. Max cut his eyes to Frank and spat at him, the bloody spittle plopping into the dirt in front of Frank's boots.

"You missed again, Max," Frank told him.

"Damn you to the hellfires, Morgan!" Max said.

"Where are the kidnapped children, Max?" Frank asked. "Where were they taken?"

Max grinned at him. "A long ways from here, Morgan."

"Either you tell me, or I'll beat it out of your son."

"You leave Ted out of it. He don't know nothin'."

"I'll see about that, Max. I don't figure it'll take me long once I heat up a runnin' iron."

"Don't do that to my boy, Morgan. He can't stand pain."

"Then it won't take me long, will it?"

"Up in Northern New Mexico, Morgan. Val's got 'em. Now leave my boy alone."

Frank knelt down beside the dying man. "Where in Northern New Mexico, Max?"

"North and east of Santa Fe, Morgan. In the mountains. That's all I know. I swear to you it is."

"What's this about kidnapped children?" the doctor asked.

"Are there any kids left at your ranch?"

"No. They was moved out long before you got here. I can't see too good, Doc. But the pain is gone. What's happenin' to me?"

"You're dying, Max," the doctor told him.

Max closed his eyes and shivered.

"Correction on that, Doc," Frank said.

"What do you mean, Frank? Correction on what?"

"He isn't dying. He's *dead*."

Frank waited one more day before taking his group and pulling out of Tucson, giving the sheriff's deputies time to search Max Collins's ranch.

"There was kids there, all right, Mr. Morgan," one of the deputies told Frank. "We found plenty of evidence of that. But they're long gone."

"Max's son?"

"We got him in jail. He's singin' like a little birdie. He was involved in this up to his eyebrows."

"I thought he might be. He's admitted his guilt?"

"Oh, Lord, yes. The more he talks, the more charges we're filing against him. And the judge I told you about?"

Frank nodded.

"He's left town. Nobody knows where he went."

"What was his name?"

"Clay. Vernon Clay."

"I'll remember that in case I ever run into him."

The deputy smiled and took out a photograph and handed it to Frank. "You can have this. That's Vernon Clay. You going after those kidnapped kids, Mr. Morgan?"

"First thing in the morning."

"Good luck."

Frank and Dewey and their unlikely posse headed for Northern New Mexico before first light. Frank had provisioned up for the long haul the day before, and during his stay in Tucson had had several extra pairs of paw boots made for Dog.

"You take better care of that damn dog than you do for yourself," Dewey groused.

"He's a friend of mine."

"And I ain't?"

"You want me to have some booties made for you?" Frank asked with a grin.

Dewey uttered a few very choice words and walked away, muttering to himself.

"You got any idee at all where the kids is being held?" Dewey asked, riding alongside Frank.

"No. When we get to Santa Fe we'll hang around for a few days, listening. Maybe we'll pick up something."

"Could be Miss Julie's girl is a thousand miles away or dead," Dewey said. "Has she talked to you about that?"

"Not in great detail."

"Can't blame her, I reckon. Mother's got to cling to hope."

They rode in silence for a time, until Dewey finally asked, "You two gonna get hitched up, Drifter?"

"We have talked around that subject some . . . in a matter of speaking."

"You gun-shy 'bout that?"

"Dewey, I've been a gunfighter all my adult life. I've tried to hang up my guns several times. Didn't work. Won't work."

"That's the end of the subject, huh?"

"What kind of life would she have with me?"

"I used to say I'd never leave the mountains. But I did."

"That's different."

"No, it ain't. That way of life played out, that's all. Your way of life ain't got many more years 'fore it plays out. What then?"

"I don't know."

"Was I you, I'd be doin' some head ruminatin' on it." Dewey turned his horse's head and rode back to the rear, taking the drag, leaving Frank alone.

Julie rode up and asked, "Want some company?"

"Sure."

"I've been doing some thinking, Frank."

"Oh?"

"Becky may not be alive."

Frank said nothing.

"Is it wrong of me to think about that?"

"No, not really. I reckon a person has to consider all the options. But that doesn't mean you have to give up hope."

"But she could be almost anywhere, Frank."

"That's true. But more than likely she's right where we're heading."

"How can you be so certain?"

"I'm not sure about it, Julie. But look at all the camps and hideouts we've busted up and closed down. Now we've shut down Val's main accomplice in Southern Arizona. He's got to pull in the reins for a time and lay low. He's got no choice in the matter.''

"I'll never stop looking for her, Frank.''

"*We'll* never stop looking for her, Julie.''

She reached out and touched his arm.

No other word or gesture was needed.

Twenty-four

At a small community in the San Francisco Mountains, just west of the Continental Divide, and just inside the somewhat ill-defined boundaries of New Mexico Territory, Frank halted the group for supplies and for a meal not cooked over a campfire.

"You're Frank Morgan, ain't you?" a man in the general store asked.

"That's right."

"Thought so. Seen your picture in a magazine the other day. You resemble the outlaw Val Dooley, you know that?"

"So I've been told. Has he been through here?"

"Val? Naw. But there was some hard cases through here last week. Had some kids with 'em. I thought that was strange."

"Girls?"

"Girls and boys. None of 'em over, I'd say, oh, fifteen. Kids acted funny. Like they was half asleep. They was all sort of glassy-eyed."

"Drugged maybe?"

"Yeah! That's it. Opium or something. But why would kids be on opium? Was they all sick?"

"Did any of the men say where they were headed?"

"Naw. Not directly. But I overheared one of them talkin' 'bout Santa Fe."

Frank talked with the local for a few more minutes, then paid for his supplies and left. He found Dewey in the small town's only watering hole, having a drink.

"We're on the right track, Dewey." He brought the mountain man up to date, telling him what the local had told him.

"Well, they had to cross the mountains and fight shy of some Injun reservations," said Dewey. "They probably hit the main road north, don't you figure?"

"No. I'd say they kept to the less-traveled trails because of the kids. The only reason they stopped here was that they had to provision up."

"Then they went through some rough country," Dewey said.

"So will we. Let's chow down, get a good night's sleep, and head out first thing in the morning."

"You act like a wolf on a blood scent, Drifter."

"I aim to get those kids back, Dewey. And kill that damned Val Dooley."

"Settle down, boy," Dewey told him. "The kids was alive a few days ago. We know that."

He looked closely at Frank. "You gonna tell Miss Julie?"

"It wouldn't be fair not to tell her."

"I reckon not." He held up a newspaper. "I found me a newspaper to read. It's only a week old. There ain't nothin' in it 'bout any kidnapped kids."

"That doesn't surprise me a bit. There isn't anyone alive to present any solid evidence about the kidnappings ... except Julie and Danny and the kids. And they haven't spoken to anyone about the incident. Ted's information probably won't be released until the trial starts."

"I reckon it wouldn't help none if the kids did say somethin'. Hell, Drifter, it's like we're chasin' ghosts."

"Except these ghosts bleed, Dewey. And there's going to be a lot of bleeding when we catch up with them."

"That's Jim Lawson right over there, Mr. Morgan," Danny said, looking at a man standing on the other side of the street. "I remember him from the gang I was with. He's a bad one. His ridin' pard, Pat Gillian, should be close by."

Frank was standing close to Danny, both of them in the shade of the awning in front of a store. They would be no more than indistinguishable shadows to anyone across the street.

"I'm familiar with Pat's rep," Frank said. "He's quick, for a fact. I don't know a thing about Lawson."

"Likes a knife, so I'm told."

"He won't get that close to me ... not if I can help it. But I want to talk to at least one of them. Let's see if Pat shows up." Frank thought for a moment, then said, "No, let's don't. You stay put, Danny. If Pat shows up before I can work up behind Lawson, holler at me."

"I'll do it, sir."

Frank slipped into the alley and worked his way around to the other end of the street in one of Santa Fe's less-than-desirable sections, mainly frequented by men looking for a good time from the soiled doves who hung around the area's sporting houses and saloons.

Frank circled around and came up behind Lawson. He

stuck the muzzle of his Peacemaker in the man's back and said, "Stand loose and easy, Lawson. Make any moves toward a gun or that knife you carry, and I'll blow a hole in you big enough to drive a buckboard through. You understand all that?"

"I sure do. But who are you?"

"Frank Morgan."

"*Morgan!* Man, I ain't got no quarrel with you."

"Listen to me, you kidnapping baby-raping son of a bitch. You turn real easy and walk into that alley behind us. You got that?"

"Yes, sir. I'm movin' real easy-like."

At the rear of the alley, Frank jerked Lawson around and faced him. "Everything you know about Val Dooley's kidnapping operation, Lawson. Starting with the location of his hideout and how many kids are there."

"Why . . . I don't know what you're talkin' about, Morgan. I don't know nothin' 'bout Val Dooley or any kids. I—"

Frank put a hard left fist into the man's belly, doubling him over and dropping him to his knees, gagging and coughing.

"Lawson, I can drag you out of town and start carving on you. I can guarantee you so much pain you'll tell me things you wouldn't tell the devil . . . just to make the pain stop. How do you want it?"

Lawson knew all about Frank Morgan; knew the man did not make idle threats. The outlaw caught his breath and started talking so fast, Frank had to slow him down to be understood. Before he was through, Frank had learned more than he really needed or wanted to know about Val Dooley's plans.

"Is there a girl out there named Becky?" Frank asked.

Lawson nodded. "Becky Barnes, yessir. Real pretty girl.

She's a favorite of Val. He's been . . . well, you know, ever since she was grabbed.''

"Yeah, I know.'' Frank started naming other kids.

Lawson nodded his head. "All them kids is out at the ranch. They all fixin' to be sold real soon.''

"How soon?''

"Next week.''

"Who's the buyer?''

"I swear I don't know that.''

Frank shoved the muzzle of the Peacemaker harder against Lawson's belly and jacked the hammer back.

Lawson's sweaty face paled under his tan. "I swear on my mother's eyes, Morgan. I don't know. For God's sake, man! I don't run the outfit.''

Frank eased the hammer down on the .45, and Lawson visibly relaxed. "Tell me all about the ranch, Lawson. How many men?''

"They's 'bout thirty or so out there now.''

"Where are the kids being held?''

"The kids is held in a new bunkhouse just off from the main house. You can still smell the pine lumber. That's how new it is.''

"Windows, doors?''

"Windows is high up and barred. One door, and it's a heavy one with a padlock.''

"Does Val ever come to the ranch?''

"Yeah, but he ain't there now. He pulled out a couple of days ago. And I don't know where he went. He don't confide in me.''

"How long will he be gone?''

"That's anybody's guess. He might be back right now. He might stay gone for days or weeks. I just don't know.''

"Lawson, I'm going to give you a break. Was I you, I'd take it.''

"You ain't gonna kill me?"

"No."

"Oh, thank you, Jesus!"

"At least, not right now."

"What do you mean?"

"I want you to get on your horse and ride out of town."

"I can do that, Morgan," Lawson said quickly. "I shore can."

"And don't ever cross my trail again."

"If I do, it won't be on purpose. I can gar-untee you that."

"Don't tell your friend Gillian anything. Don't say good-bye, don't say anything. Just get the hell gone from my sight."

"I won't. I promise you, I won't. Can I git gone now, Morgan?"

"Yes. Move!"

Lawson hotfooted it out of the alley, heading for the livery and his horse. Frank didn't believe Lawson would stay gone. He figured Lawson would ride out of town for a mile or two, then circle back and try to warn Gillian. But it would be too late for that. Frank walked across the street to Danny.

"Find Dewey," he told the young man. "Tell him I'll be in that saloon across the street."

"You goin' after Gillian?"

"Yes."

"Alone?"

"Go tell Dewey what's happening, Danny. Then find the ladies and Jerry and stay with them. Go on, boy. I'm counting on you."

Frank walked across the street and into the small saloon. He'd seen the same scene hundreds of times in that many saloons all over the West. Half of the tables had men sitting at them, drinking and playing cards. Four men standing at the bar, one of them Pat Gillian. Frank recognized Pat by his gun belt: six cartridge loops, then a silver dollar, in that order, all the way around the belt.

Frank ordered a beer and leaned against the bar, keeping a steady gaze on Gillian, knowing that the man would pick up on the unwavering gaze quickly and have something to say about it.

It didn't take long. Pat turned his head and looked into the cold, hard eyes of Frank Morgan. He straightened up and Frank did the same. Both of them held their drinks in their left hands. Frank a beer, Pat a shot of whiskey.

"Morgan," Pat said. At the mention of the name Morgan all conversation in the saloon ceased and all eyes turned toward the long bar. "Haven't seen you in years. I heard you were dead."

"You heard wrong, Gillian."

"My ridin' partner will be comin' through them batwings any minute now. You aim to try to take both of us?"

"Wrong, Gillian."

"Huh? Wrong about what?"

"Doubtful your partner, Lawson, will be coming through the batwings."

"Why the hell not?"

"I ran him out of town about ten minutes ago."

"I don't believe that!"

"Then you're a damn fool," Frank told him. "Your partner told me all about the ranch. All about the new bunkhouse where the kids are being held. Said the bunkhouse was so new you can still smell the fresh-cut pine. Had bars on the windows and a heavy door with a sturdy lock. Sound familiar, Gillian?"

"I don't know nothin' 'bout no kids, Morgan."

"You're a goddamned lying son of a bitch, Gillian."

The hired gun flushed, the red creeping up slowly from his neck to his face. "No man talks to me like that, Morgan."

"I just did," Frank replied very matter-of-factly.

"You take it back, Morgan. You do it or, by God, I'll kill you!"

"You got the killing part to do, Gillian. That is, if you think you're the man who can do it. Personally, I don't think you've got the sand in you to pull on me."

"Goddamn you!" Gillian shouted, and stepped back from the bar.

Frank stepped around the corner curve of the bar and faced the man.

The men standing at the bar quickly got out of the line of fire.

"Is that really Frank Morgan?" a man whispered.

"Damn shore is," another man said.

"What's all that about kids bein' held?" The whisper reached Frank.

"I reckon we're 'bout to find out."

"I'll be known as the man who killed Frank Morgan," Gillian said.

"No, you won't," Frank contradicted.

"Why not?" Gillian demanded.

"Because you'll be dead!"

Pat Gillian's hand snaked toward his pistol.

Twenty-five

Frank's Peacemaker roared just as Pat's hand closed around the butt of his six-gun. The force of the bullet tearing into Pat's chest knocked the outlaw back, causing him to lose his grip on his pistol. The gun slipped back into leather. Pat grabbed for the edge of the bar and held on, a very confused look on his face.

"Good Lord Almighty!" a saloon patron said. "I never even seen the draw."

"Faster than a snake can strike," another said.

Blood began leaking from Pat's mouth, dripping down onto his shirt. He opened his mouth to speak; his lips moved, but no sound came out.

Frank slowly holstered his Peacemaker.

"Damn you!" Pat finally managed to gasp.

"Somebody git the doc," a man said.

"Somebody best fetch the undertaker," another said. "That ol' boy's had it."

"The hell you say," Pat whispered. "I ain't done yet. Not by a long shot. I'm a-gonna kill you, Morgan."

Frank said nothing to that, just stepped back around the curve of the bar and picked up his mug of beer . . . with his left hand. He took a sip and waited.

"Damn you, Morgan!" The shout came from behind the batwings. Lawson stepped into the saloon. "You've kilt my partner!"

Frank turned just as Lawson cussed and grabbed for his gun.

Frank's Peacemaker roared again. The slug ripped into Lawson's belly and the man grabbed for one of the batwings for support. He tore the batwing off its hinges as he fell to the barroom floor, his pistol still holstered. He had not cleared leather.

"Damn you to hell, Morgan!" Gillian said. "Lawson was a good man."

"I gave him a chance to clear town and live," Frank said. "He's got no one to blame but himself."

Lawson moaned and cussed Frank.

Gillian lost his grip on the bar and fell to the floor.

A man wearing a star on his chest stepped over Lawson and into the saloon. "What started all this?" he demanded. He looked at Frank. "Morgan? Frank Morgan?"

"That's me," Frank acknowledged.

"Did you start all this killing, Morgan?"

"No, he didn't," a local said. "He was just defending himself."

"I didn't ask you, Tom," the lawman said without taking his eyes off Frank. "I asked Morgan."

"Let's go somewhere and talk," Frank told the lawman. "I've got a lot to tell you."

Frank talked with the local law for over an hour, bringing them up to date on the activities of Val Dooley and his gang. The sheriff had a deputy go get Julie and the kids and Dewey. The lawmen listened intently as Julie quietly and calmly told them, in essence, what Frank had just told them. Then the kids told them their stories and the lawmen got mad.

"Those men will be brought to justice," the sheriff said after sending a deputy over to get a judge to sign some warrants. "And it'll be done damn quick. Like today." He looked at a deputy. "Round up a posse, Charlie. Good men all. Do it now."

"You want me to go along, Sheriff?" Frank asked.

"No, Morgan, I don't. You're too quick on the shoot to suit me. From this day on, the law will handle this."

Frank smiled at that.

"You find that amusing, Morgan?" the sheriff asked.

"Somewhat, yes. The law damn sure hasn't been much help up to now."

"That is about to change, Morgan. I want you to stay out of trouble while you're here. You hear me?"

"I hear you, Sheriff. But what am I to do if I'm braced by some gun hand looking for a reputation?"

"Defend yourself, Morgan. I wouldn't deny that right to any man. But you know what I meant."

Frank nodded his head. "What about the kids out at the ranch?"

"They'll become wards of the territory."

"A damned orphanage?"

"Probably."

Frank swore under his breath.

"They're not going to go traipsin' all over the damn country with you. I can tell you that for a fact." The sheriff stood up. "I've got to see about gettin' outfitted. It would pleasure me greatly if you were gone when I get back, Morgan.''

"I'll probably be right here, Sheriff."

"I can't begin to tell you how much that thrills me, Morgan."

"I've received warmer welcomes from hostiles on the rampage, Sheriff."

"I'm not a fan of yours, Morgan. Gunfighters don't impress me a damn bit."

Frank shrugged that off.

"Just stay out of trouble in this town, Morgan. And if you want to do me a big favor, get gone from here as quickly as possible."

The sheriff, his deputies, and the posse rode out, and Dewey came to stand by Frank's side outside the jail. "The folks I've talked to in town say the sheriff is a great feller. But right by the book all the time."

"I'm sure he's a good lawman. He just doesn't like gunplay in his town, that's all."

"Well, I think he's gonna be surprised when he gets back from this raid on the ranch."

Frank looked at his friend. "What do you mean?"

"They's a couple of hard cases in town askin'questions 'bout you."

"They have names?"

"Don't ever'body?" the mountain man asked with a smile. "Yeah. The Crow brothers. Do that name ring any bells in your noggin?"

"Seems to. Yes. Friends of Ray Hayden. Ray got crossways with me over in Wickenburg a couple of months ago."

"Where's this Hayden feller now?"

"Buried."

"Thought so. Them Crow boys is talkin' 'bout killin' you."

"All I need now is for the Bookbinder boys to show up," Frank said.

"The who?"

"Friends of a man named Mack something or another."

"This Mack feller . . . did he get crossways with you too?"

"As a matter of fact, he did."

"And now he's buried?"

"Yes."

"Are you tryin' to depopulate the earth all by your lonesome, Drifter?"

"Sometimes it sure looks that way. Is there anyone else with the Crow brothers?"

"I don't think so. Was you 'spectin' someone else?"

"Just wanted to make sure, that's all. The Crow brothers . . . two of them?"

"Yeah. They're hangin' tight with each other over the other side of town. Little saloon name of . . ." Dewey frowned. "Hell, I forgot the name."

Frank shrugged that off. "It isn't important. The Crow boys are Todd and Boyd. The Bookbinder brothers are Jules, Kenny, and Alvin."

"Now I know who you're talkin' 'bout. Jules changed his name to Books. Jules Books. He's a bad one, Frank. Hired gun and he's greased lightnin'. Been killin' sodbusters over in Colorado."

Julie walked up to the two men. She had enjoyed a long hot bath, and was now dressed in a simple but form-fitting calico dress.

"You look lovely," Frank told her.

"Thank you."

"I'm gonna go check on them damn Crow brothers," Dewey said. "Y'all behave. See you later."

"Frank," Julie said, touching his arm, "am I going to have trouble taking Becky with us?"

"No. I asked the sheriff about that."

"That is—" Julie frowned—"if she's out there."

"But the other children will go to orphanages."

"I feel sorry for them."

"So do I. But the sheriff made it plain that it's out of our hands. And this is a man who is not going to brook any interference."

"Do you have any plans for this afternoon, Frank?"

"No. You?"

"There is a small traveling show in town. I thought I might take the kids to see that. I think it would do them good."

"I'm sure. I'll meet you for dinner at the hotel this evening."

"It's a date." She smiled. "See you then."

Frank lounged away most of the afternoon, taking short walks and then sitting in a chair in front of the hotel, talking with Dewey. Just before six that afternoon, the sheriff and his posse returned to town. There were two wagons filled with kids, a half-dozen men with their hands handcuffed behind them, and seven horses with dead men roped down across the saddles.

Julie stepped out onto the boardwalk and looked intently at the wagons as they rumbled past. "Becky is not among them, Frank."

"There may be more wagons, Julie."

"You see any kids you recognize, Miss Julie?" Dewey asked.

"No. None of the Sutton kids, nor any of the Carter children." She turned slowly and went back into the hotel.

Frank walked down to the jail and waited for the sheriff to show up. He wasn't long in coming. The lawman looked at Morgan and grunted.

"Hello to you too," Frank said.

"Come on in, Morgan. I'll fill you in and maybe then you'll get out of my town."

"I can't tell you what a warm feeling your greetings give me, Sheriff."

Inside the large outer office, the sheriff pointed to a chair. Frank sat. The sheriff took a sheet of paper from his jacket. "The names of all the kids who were out at the ranch. There was no one named Becky Barnes."

"Julie saw the wagons as they went past the hotel."

"Now what, Morgan?"

"We keep looking."

"Let me question the prisoners. If they know anything about the Barnes girl, I'll tell you."

"Thank you, Sheriff. I'll be at the hotel. Oh, by the way. There are two brothers in town, Todd and Boyd Crow. They're gunning for me. I've done my best to avoid seeing them. Just thought you'd like to know." Frank walked to the door. The sheriff's voice stopped him.

"Maybe I've been wrong about you, Morgan. Stay around in town until I talk to the prisoners and send out some wires. I'll know something late tomorrow or the next day."

"Thanks, Sheriff. From both Julie and me."

"I've heard of the Crow Brothers. They're bad ones. If they brace you . . . ." He shrugged. "A man's got a right to protect himself."

Frank smiled and stepped out of the office.

"I'll never see my daughter again," Julie said. "I just know it."

"Don't say that," Frank gently admonished her. "You don't know any such thing."

"The kidnappers are staying one step ahead of us, Frank. And we don't have any idea where Val Dooley is or where Becky might be."

The two were sitting in the hotel's dining room, at a table in a far corner, away from other diners.

"Val isn't far away," Frank said. He held up a hand. "I don't know that for sure, Julie. It's just a feeling I have."

"Why do you feel that way?"

"He's running out of places to hide, that's why. He can't go to Texas. Folks over there will shoot him on sight. Every lawman in Arizona and New Mexico Territory is looking for him."

"You think he's close?"

"Yes. I think he's here in the northern part of New Mexico."

"And you're going to continue the hunt?"

"Of course. If the sheriff has any more information on the kids, he's going to let me know as soon as he finds out something . . . one way or the other. Then we'll provision up and move on. But I have one thing I'd like to request of you."

"You want to leave the kids here."

Frank smiled. "You have this knack of getting into my head, Julie. Yes."

"I spoke with some ladies from a local church group today about that very thing, Frank. They agreed to look after the children for as long as it takes."

"Danny and Susan too?"

She hesitated, then said, "Susan asked me today if she and Danny could be married."

"And you said?"

"I said I'd give it some serious thought."

"And have you?"

Julie nodded her head. "She's almost fifteen and it's very obvious to me that she and Danny are in love. I'm going to tell them tomorrow that they have my permission to marry. And I hope I'm doing the right thing."

"Do they have any plans?"

"They said they would stay here and wait for some word about Becky."

"And then?"

"They would go to Iowa and farm. I told them to go on to Iowa and get on with their lives."

Frank pushed back his chair and stood up, holding out his hand to Julie. "Then I guess we'd better get busy."

She looked up at him, her eyes wide. "Doing what, Frank?"

"Planning a wedding, my dear."

Twenty-six

Julie arranged with for the kids to stay in Santa Fe. Frank bought train tickets for Danny and Susan, and then laid in several weeks' provisions, then went to see the sheriff.

"Nothing new, Morgan," the sheriff told him. "But I did get the impression that Val Dooley, some of his gang, and some of the kids are still in this part of the country. They got them a hidey-hole somewhere. Probably up in the mountains."

"That's my thought, too, Sheriff. I'm thinking that is just might be in the general area where I'm planning on buying some land and settling down."

The sheriff gave Frank a very dark look. "Somewhere close to here, Morgan?"

Frank laughed at the expression on the man's face. "Several days' ride away, Sheriff. Does that make you feel better?"

"It helps. But just havin' you in the territory gives me a queasy feelin'. Exactly where is this land you're lookin' at, Morgan?"

Frank pointed. "Thataway, Sheriff."

The sheriff grunted. "That certainly helps a lot, Morgan." He leaned back in his chair. "Sorry I couldn't be more help to you and Mrs. Barnes. Are you leavin' town now?"

"Right after the wedding."

"What wedding?"

"Julie's daughter and the young man who rode in with us. You're invited, if you'd like to attend."

"Two things I hate, Morgan. Weddin's and funerals. But thanks for the invite."

"See you around, Sheriff."

"Not soon, I hope," the sheriff replied with a smile.

Danny and Susan were married in a church, with only a few tears shed, most of those coming from Julie.

Dewey told Frank just before the ceremony, "You look plumb nekked without your hogleg strapped on."

"I feel naked too," Frank replied.

"Be quiet, both of you," Julie told them.

"Be a hell of a time for the Crow brothers to come bustin' in here," Dewey whispered.

"Dewey," Julie said just as the piano player began playing, "if you don't be quiet, I swear I'll hit you with a church hymnal."

"I got my knife, though," Dewey whispered as soon as Julie had turned around.

"Frank," Julie said, "get up here. You've got to give the bride away."

"Oh, Lord," Dewey said. "Don't give her to the wrong person, Drifter."

* * *

Three days later, Frank, Julie, and Dewey had put the growing town of Santa Fe far behind them. They topped a rise, broke through the lush timber, and were looking down at a beautiful long valley sprawling below them.

"It's lovely," Julie whispered.

"That's my valley," Frank said.

"You done good, Drifter," Dewey said.

"There are passes that open to large grazing areas on both sides of the valley," Frank said. "The passes are open twelve months out of the year. It's got good water. Farther on up the valley, although you can't see it from here, there's a stone house built on a ridge."

"Why did we come here first, Frank?" Julie asked.

"I can answer that," Dewey said. " 'Cause like me, he smelled and then seen the little fingers of smoke yesterday, just off to the north of where we is now. And he's also been followin' sign that I admit I missed at first. Right, Drifter?"

"That's right." Frank dug in his jacket pocket and handed Julie several tiny pieces of cloth. "Look at these."

Julie fingered the cloth. "Two ribbons and half a dozen torn pieces of calico."

"One of the captive girls has some smarts," Frank said. "She's been marking the trail. I came upon the first one, that dark blue ribbon, by accident. Then I picked up a very distinctive hoofprint. I think Val and the kids he took from the ranch outside of Santa Fe are somewhere right over there." He pointed.

"But you didn't say anything about it," Julie chided mildly.

"I didn't want to get your hopes up and I didn't want to

get in a rush. I wanted to lie back and take it slow and easy.''

"How far away are they?" Julie asked.

"Five or six miles, maybe less. Right over those mountains." Again he pointed. "That's a guess, but I think it's a good one."

"So close," Julie said.

"We'll stay right at the timberline for the ride over to the house," Frank said. "Once there, we'll use dry wood to built a fire for supper. I don't want any more smoke than is absolutely necessary."

"And then?" Julie asked.

"I'll tell you later," Frank replied, avoiding Dewey's smile and his knowing glances.

"You want us to stay at the house while you go after Val Dooley alone," Julie said. "Right, Frank?"

"That's about it." Frank lifted the reins. "Let's go."

"You can't even hardly see the house!" Julie said.

"That's right," Frank said. "It's partly built into the mountain. Come on. You'll see."

The stone house had four rooms: a large kitchen and living room combined, two bedrooms, and a storeroom that actually was part of the mountain.

"I think the people who built this place used the storeroom as sort of a root cellar," Frank explained. "It stays mighty cool in there year-round."

"Damn fine field of fire too," Dewey said from the main room. "Whoever built this place had defense in mind."

"Probably from the Indians," Frank said.

"Nearest road is two days' ride away," Dewey said. "You'll have to pack in all supplies."

"But just look at that view," Julie said. "Are there any neighbors?"

"None that I know of," Frank said. "Probably will be in a few years, though. Country is filling up fast."

"Ain't that the God's truth," Dewey said. "Used to be a man could ride for days and days without seein' a livin' soul. Now all sorts of folks is a-crowdin' in. Country's gonna soon be like one of them damn cities. Won't be able to spit without it landin' on somebody. I think it's a damn shame myself. People ruin everything."

Julie laughed at him. "Dewey, if I didn't know you better, I'd think you're just an old curmudgeon."

"A what?" the mountain man said.

"A cantankerous old fart," Frank said with a laugh.

"Oh, well," Dewey said. "I know that. I thought you was really insultin' me."

Frank slipped out of the house while Julie was still sleeping, and made ready to ride out before dawn. Dewey was waiting for him at the small corral.

"You aim to take on the en-tar bunch all by your lonesome?" Dewey questioned.

"I don't think there will be that many, Dewey."

"How do you figure that?"

"Val's gang has scattered," Frank explained. "The sheriff got that information from some of the men he arrested out at the ranch. We've killed two dozen or more ourselves. Lawmen are looking for Val from Texas to California and from the border to Colorado. He's on the run, running for his life. Val's been forced to break up his gang."

"You hope," the mountain man added.

"I'm betting on it."

"You're betting your life, Drifter."

"I know. But somebody has to stay here with Julie."

"You know she ain't said a word about Susan since we pulled out."

"I know."

"Fast as them trains is, they ought to be in I-o-way 'bout now."

"I imagine they're close."

"Them two young'uns will be all right. They'll make it."

"That's what I keep telling Julie."

"Does she reply to that?"

"No. Not a word."

"She'll soon get over that, bein' a woman an' all. Y'all talked any more 'bout gettin' hitched up?"

"No. I think she may be having second thoughts about that."

" 'Cause of you bein' who you are?"

"Probably."

"You didn't make her no promises 'bout changin', did you?"

Frank smiled. "No. I'll never change, Dewey, you know that. I might want to, I *do* want to, but I never will and you know why I won't . . . why I can't."

"I reckon, so, Drifter. Your mind shore seems to be made up on that subject. And I know that once you git somethin' planted firm in that noggin of yourn, there ain't no changin' it. Might as well be tryin' to move a damn mountain."

"Am I that stubborn, Dewey?"

Dewey snorted in reply.

"I guess I am, for a fact."

"Least you know it and admit it. What happens if Val Dooley gets away from you this time?"

"If the kids are there, I'll bring them back here and you can escort Julie and the kids back to Santa Fe."

"And you'll go on the hunt. Is that what you're tryin' to tell me?"

"That's it."

"Alone?"

"Yes."

"Well, if that's the case, then I'm gonna tell you somethin'. I'm gonna say it just this one time and I'll never bring it up again. Here 'tis: Miss Julie got some mighty deep feelin's for you, Drifter. And you feel somethin' for her too. Y'all could probably work it out if you tried. But if you bring them young'uns back here and then ride off alone after this damn Val Dooley scum, that'll be the end of it for you and her. Miss Julie will go off and eventually find her a man that'll care for her, and you'll spend the rest of your days alone, closin' your eyes to sleep in some damn hotel room or rolled up in your blankets on some lonesome trail with a saddle for a pillow and the smell of gun smoke all around you. Now, do you want to argue that?"

Frank shook his head. "No, Dewey, I don't."

"Well, glory be."

"But I won't be alone."

"The hell you say!"

"That's right. I won't."

"Who you gonna have along?"

"Dog."

Dewey threw up his hands. "Oh, for God's sake. *Dog!*" He walked away, muttering and cussing.

Frank stepped into the saddle and rode off into the predawn.

Alone.

Except for Dog.

Wearing brand-new paw booties.

Twenty-seven

Frank picked up the hoofprint of the horse that had led them to the valley, and followed it into the range of mountains. Within an hour, he'd found two more pieces of calico, torn from a dress. An hour later, he began to smell wood smoke. He swung down from the saddle and quickly rigged a picket line for Stormy.

"You stay," he told Dog. "Guard."

The big cur immediately dropped down beside Stormy. Dog would stay put until Frank's return. Frank had no worries about that.

Removing his spurs and taking his rifle, Frank followed the smoke scent on foot. It didn't take him long to reach the camp of the kidnappers. There were no guards patrolling the outer perimeters of the camp. A tribute to the outlaws' stupidity . . . or arrogance, Frank thought. Probably a combination of both, he mentally added.

There were a half-dozen kids in the camp, all tied together with a long length of rope. Frank recognized Becky immediately. The Sutton kids, Gene and Claire, were there, as were Kathy and Debra Carter. Cindy Carter was not among the group. There were two other girls Frank did not recognize.

Frank carefully made his way around the half acre or so of clearing, keeping in the timber and brush, until he was directly behind the captives. As he worked his way around the camp, he counted the outlaws. Seven of them. Val was not among them. Frank had not expected him to be. Val had probably taken his best men and hightailed it out of this part of the country.

"Val ain't comin' back here, Johnny," a man said, his words clearly reaching Frank. "He said he'd be gone no more than a couple of days. He's been gone a damn week. Him and them that went with him has deserted us."

"I do believe you're right, Walt," Johnny said, walking up to his friend. "So what's your plan 'bout the girls?"

"Let's do 'em again and then kill 'em and get the hell gone from here. I'm tarred of listenin' to 'em whine and bawl."

The other outlaws had gathered around Johnny and Walt, all of them nodding their heads in agreement.

Frank couldn't wait much longer. The time to act was now, while the outlaws were all bunched up. He eared back the hammer on his rifle.

"I want that little one," an outlaw said. "I like her a lot."

Frank ground his teeth together. The little one had to be Claire Sutton. She was ten years old. Claire began crying as the burly outlaw looked at her and grinned, exposing a mouthful of decaying teeth.

"You and me, sweet thing," he said. "We'll have us a good time."

"Doubtful," Frank said. He stood up and began firing into the knot of outlaws and rapists, working the lever of his .44-40 as fast as he could.

The .44-40 slugs knocked outlaws spinning to the ground. When his rifle was empty, Frank jerked his Peacemaker from leather and finished what the rifle had started. When the gun smoke cleared, not one of Val's gang remained standing. But not all were dead.

Frank quickly pulled his short-barreled Peacemaker from behind his belt and stepped into the clearing. One of the wounded outlaws managed to get his pistol from leather and point it at Frank. Frank shot him between the eyes.

Kneeling down beside Becky, Frank pulled his knife from its sheath and cut the ropes that bound the girl. He laid the knife down in front of her. "Cut the others loose, Becky. Quickly now, girl."

While Becky worked at freeing the others, Frank walked over to the outlaws, sprawled on the ground, and looked at them. Four were still alive, two of them mortally wounded. One of them died while Frank stood over them.

"You bastard!" one outlaw cussed at Frank.

"You best make your last words directed toward God," Frank told him. " 'Cause you sure are gonna die."

The outlaw cussed Frank.

Frank gathered up all the weapons from the outlaws and dumped them in a pile. "Get a sack, Becky. Put the guns in it. Gene, you and a couple of the girls go saddle up horses. The rest of you prowl the camp and get all the food and blankets you can quickly pack up."

The kids went to work, and Frank turned back toward the outlaws. Another child-raper had died while Frank was speaking to the kids.

"You're Frank Morgan, ain't you?" an outlaw gasped.

"That's right."

"Damn your eyes!"

"Kill him, Mr. Morgan," Becky called. "Shoot him!"

"No need for that, Becky," Frank said. "He's hard gut-shot. He's not long for this world."

"Let me shoot Ike," little Claire called. "I will. Give me one of those guns."

"No, child," Frank told her. "You don't want to live with that. Besides, Ike's dying as we speak."

"Where I want to shoot him won't kill him," the little girl said. "But he'll sure feel it, I bet you that."

Frank let that alone. He had a pretty good idea where the girl wanted to shoot her rapist, and he damn sure didn't blame her a bit.

"You keep that girl away from me," Ike said.

"Shut your mouth," Frank told him. "Or I'll give her a pistol and let her shoot you where she wants to shoot you."

Ike closed his mouth.

"You gonna leave us here to die, Morgan?" a badly wounded outlaw questioned.

"I'm going to leave you, yes," Frank replied. "Whether you die or not is no concern of mine."

"You a coldhearted son of a bitch, Morgan!" another outlaw said.

Gene Sutton led three saddled horses into the clearing, then went back to saddle more.

"I hope you and all them brats git tooken by the Injuns and die hard," another outlaw gasped. "I hope they skin you alive, Morgan."

"I wish you the best too," Frank responded. "Now shut up."

"Marty just died," an outlaw said. "Me and him rode many a trail together. You gonna bury him, Morgan?"

"Not a chance."

"Damn you! You better hope I die, Morgan. 'Cause if I live through this I'm comin' after you."

"I'm so frightened I'll probably faint from the fear," Frank told him.

Across the clearing, Becky laughed at that.

"Bitch!" an outlaw said. "You wasn't no good nohow. You wouldn't even make a good whore."

"We have the food and the blankets, Mr. Morgan," a girl called. "We rolled the blankets and stuffed the saddlebags."

"Leave us a bottle of whiskey," an outlaw pleaded. "It'll help ease the pain from our wounds."

"I broke the bottles of whiskey," Debra Carter said, walking up to stand beside Frank.

The outlaw cussed her.

"Where is your older sister, Cindy?" Frank asked.

"She was sold to a man from back East," Debra said. "Right after the wagon train was attacked. I don't have any idea where she is."

"I know," a man with a belly wound said. "I'll tell you if you'll get me to a doctor."

"He's lying," Debra said. "He wasn't there. He just joined this gang."

"You miserable little bitch!" the outlaw said.

Debra shrugged that off and went to help her sister.

"They's wolves and pumas and bears in this area, Morgan," Ike said. "We'll be helpless agin them. It ain't right you leavin' us here like this."

"You forgot to mention the buzzards," Frank reminded him. "They'll be gathering in a few minutes."

"We're ready to go, Mr. Morgan," Gene called, leading more saddled horses into the clearing. Bedrolls were tied behind the saddles, saddlebags stuffed with food.

"Mount up," Frank told the group.

"Morgan, for God's sake!" a man called. "We'll die

hard like this. You can't just ride off and leave us. It ain't right.''

''Don't talk to me about right and wrong,'' Frank told the man. ''Those words have no meaning coming out of your mouth.'' Frank looked around. The kids were all mounted up and ready to ride. He looked at the outlaws, sprawled on the ground. ''You boys have a real nice day now, you hear?''

Frank stopped at a small creek about two miles from his valley and told the kids, ''Wash up as best you can.''

''I brought some soap,'' Claire said. ''Three bars. Those filthy outlaws never bathed or nothing.''

''We'll get your clothes all washed up and patched when we get to my valley,'' Frank told them. What he hadn't told Julie or Dewey was that he had bought the land while in Santa Fe. It was *his* valley.

''Get to scrubbing,'' Frank told the kids. ''Gene, you wait until the girls are done with their bathing. I'm going to make a pot of coffee.''

While the coffee water was heating up, with the girls giggling in and out of the cold waters of the creek, Frank looked up at the sky over the outlaw camp. The buzzards had begun to gather, slowly circling high in the blue sky.

Gene had followed Frank's eyes. ''I hope the buzzards don't get sick,'' the boy said.

''You got anything you want to talk about, Gene? Man-to-man.''

''No, sir. I reckon I'll just live with what they done to me.'' The boy paused. ''Maybe I'll forget in time.''

''Maybe so, boy. I hope so.''

''Is it all right if I pet your dog? He don't bite, does he?''

''I don't think he'll bite you, Gene. Go ahead. I'll holler at you when it's time for you to wash up.''

Gene called to Dog and the big cur walked over, allowing the boy to pet him. Frank busied himself dumping in the coffee and then adding a bit of cold water to settle the grounds. After a moment he poured a cup, then rolled a cigarette and settled back to enjoy both. It was both his first cup of coffee and first smoke since leaving his valley early that morning.

Frank thought briefly about the outlaws-kidnappers-rapists he'd left back at the campsite. He felt no sympathy for any of them. They had chosen their way of life; no one had forced them into it. They had no one to blame but themselves. To hell with them.

Becky walked up, her hair still damp from the bath. Frank poured her a cup of coffee and she sat down on the ground.

"No point in worrying about this dress getting dirty," she said. "It can't get any dirtier than it already is. But I do feel better after that bath."

"I think your mother brought you some britches to wear."

"Is Mama wearing men's pants?"

"Yes, she is."

Becky smiled. "I can't wait to see her." Her smile faded. "But I wonder how much I should tell her . . . about what happened, I mean."

"I think you should be honest with her. However, I don't believe your mother will pry too deeply."

"I hope she doesn't," the girl said. "I'd hate to have to lie to her."

Frank did not push that issue.

"There are just some things I think it's best to keep to myself," Becky said. She sipped her coffee and then sighed. "But I wish I could have been there to see Susan get married. Is Danny a nice boy?"

"I believe he's a fine young man. I think they're going to be all right."

The other girls began coming back to the campsite from the creek. Frank called to Gene and motioned toward the creek. "Time to wash the dirt and bugs off, boy," he said. "You can take Dog with you if you like. He needs a bath too."

"What happens to us now, Mr. Morgan?" Debra Carter asked, sitting down and pouring a cup of coffee.

"I take you all back to Santa Fe and the authorities will handle it from there. After that, I don't know."

"I'm just glad to be free from those men," another girl said. Frank did not know her name. She looked at Becky. "I thought sure Val Dooley was goin' to take you with him. He talked like he was."

Frank stood up and walked away, letting the girls talk. He felt they would talk more freely and openly without him present. In Santa Fe all the newly freed hostages would be questioned extensively by the law, telling their stories over and over. It would be a long time before the girls would ever feel safe again.

The sounds of many horses coming closer broke into Frank's thoughts.

"Riders coming, Mr. Morgan," a girl called.

It was the sheriff from Santa Fe, leading a large posse. The chief lawman of the county swung down from the saddle and walked up to Frank.

"I got to thinking about the situation, Morgan," he said after shaking hands with Frank. "Figured I'd get some men together and follow you. Looks like you done all right."

"You saw Julie and Dewey?" Frank asked.

"We did. I left some men with them at your house. Yes, I did some checking back at the land office. Saw where you'd bought the whole damn valley. You got you a real nice place there, Morgan."

"I think so, Sheriff."

"Let's get these kids rounded up and head on back," the sherif said. "Miss Julie is on pins and needles about her daughter."

"I'm sure."

"I need to talk to these kids about Val Dooley."

"You don't have to worry about Dooley, Sheriff."

"Oh?" The sheriff arched one eyebrow. "Why is that, Morgan?"

"Because I'm going after him, I'm going to find him, and then I'll kill him."

Twenty-eight

Frank hung back as Julie and Becky embraced. He watched as Julie led her daughter off a ways and sat down on the ground. Dewey walked over to stand beside Frank.

"I put on water for coffee soon as I heard y'all comin,' " the mountain man said. "Figured you could use a couple cups."

"You sure figured right," Frank replied.

"Be ready in a few minutes. You gonna tell me what happened or do I have to guess?"

"There were only seven or eight of them. Val deserted this bunch. They were about to rape and kill the kids. I stopped them."

"You damn shore ain't much of a storyteller, Drifter. But I guess that'll have to do. Since you didn't bring back no prisoners, I reckon they wasn't none alive to bring back."

"A couple. I left them for the buzzards."

Dewey grunted. "Serves them right."

"Now I'm going to find Val Dooley."

"What about Miss Julie?"

"She can go back to Santa Fe with the posse. I imagine she and Becky have a lot of catching up to do."

"And me, Drifter?"

"You have a store to run, Dewey."

"That's a fact, for shore. Be fall 'fore long. I best be makin' me a list about what I need to stock up on and get it ordered."

Frank knew Dewey was just saying that to let him off the hook. The old mountain man knew Frank wanted to go on alone.

"Miss Julie will be all right, I'm sure," Dewey said. "She told me she had some family she could visit for a time, and she has some funds to tide her over."

"I'll see that she has money, Dewey."

"Figured you would. Coffee ready. Let's have us a cup or two."

The men of the sheriff's posse were busy making their own camp, off from Frank's stone house. Frank got a pencil and a piece of paper from his saddlebags and wrote out his lawyers' addresses, one in Denver, one in San Francisco, and another in New York City. The New York City firm took care of all Frank's business dealings east of the Mississippi River. One of the three firms almost always could get in touch with him. He also wrote out a note instructing any bank to give Julie Barnes money if she requested it.

But he doubted she ever would ask for any money. She was a very proud woman. She was also a frontier woman, tough and resourceful. Also very pretty, Frank thought with a sigh, the sigh touched with just a bit of regret. But he was better off alone. And in the long run, Julie would be much better off without him. He was sure of that.

Dewey returned with two cups of fresh-made coffee. Frank rolled a cigarette and sat back to enjoy his coffee and his smoke.

"You know how old I am, Drifter?" Dewey suddenly asked.

Frank looked at him. "No, I don't, Dewey. Why do you ask?"

"Well, I don't know neither," the mountain man replied. "I think I'm near'bouts seventy. Near as I can figure it."

"You've lived a good life."

"Yeah, I have." Dewey put wise old eyes on Frank. "Have you?"

"I've played the cards fate dealt me. And I think I've played them well. I know where you're going with this, Dewey. And I recall you saying you weren't going to bring it up again."

"I changed my mind, Drifter. When Miss Julie heads back to Santa Fe, you ain't never goin' to see her again, right?"

"That's probably correct, Dewey."

"You got a real pretty valley here, Drifter. Nice house too. Man could run some cattle and horses here. Make himself a good life. If'n that man had some stick-to-it-ness in him."

"Maybe someday, Dewey."

"Your wife, the one who was kilt a couple of years back . . . you really cared for her, didn't you?"

"Yes, I did."

"A dead woman's memory ain't worth a damn on a cold night, Drifter."

Frank chuckled. "You just won't give up, will you, Dewey?"

"Your son . . . you ever see him?"

"Not in a while. We don't get along very well."

"I ain't gonna say no more about you and Miss Julie, Drifter. I'll be pullin' out with the posse and the kids come the dawnin'. This here little hoohaw we been on has been right enjoyable. But you're right, it's time for me to git on with my life. I'm gonna leave some supplies with you. You might find a need for them." He stood up. "I'll see you at first light, Drifter."

"Good night, Dewey."

Frank stood in front of his house and watched the posse ride out just as first light was filtering over the mountains. Julie had waved good-bye to him and Frank had returned the wave. The morning was cool and pleasant as Frank sipped his coffee. The silence settling around him was comfortable.

Dog padded over to him, and Frank laid a hand on the cur's big head. Frank and Dog watched the sun burst forth over the mountains. "We'll come back here one of these days, Dog," Frank said. "I like it here."

Dog looked up at him. If an animal could wear a skeptical expression, Dog did.

Frank went on the hunt. He took his time, never getting into a rush. He stopped at every little town and every country trading post and every lonely farmhouse and asked questions. For a time, it appeared that Val Dooley and his gang had dropped off the face of the earth.

About twenty miles south of the Colorado line, in the San Juan Mountains, in a small town where Frank had stopped for a meal at the town's only café, Frank noticed a couple of trail-worn horses tied up outside the saloon. Frank decided to postpone his meal for a few minutes and have him a beer and check out the riders of those tired horses.

Frank was rough-looking. He hadn't shaved in more than a week, and his was naturally a heavy beard. His clothing was dusty and he looked like an out-of-work cowhand, just drifting around looking for a job.

He left Dog with the horses and stepped into the saloon. He stood near the batwings for a moment, letting his eyes adjust to the relative dimness of the interior. Two men at the bar seemed to tense at his appearance. They ducked their heads and began speaking in whispers. The bartender picked up on that immediately and looked over at Frank.

Frank walked to the bar and ordered a beer.

The barkeep set the beer down in front of Frank and said, "Haven't seen you around here before, friend. You just passin' through?"

Frank took a swallow of beer. "I'm looking for a piece of coyote crap name of Val Dooley, and any low-down buzzard puke who ever rode with him."

The two men at the bar stiffened at that.

"That's strong talk, mister," the barkeep said. "This Val Dooley, he's bad medicine, so I hear."

"He's a kidnapping, child-raping coward," Frank said, raising his voice so the men seated at the tables in the large room could clearly hear. "And so is any man who ever rode with him. Pure scum, that's all they are."

The two men at the bar stepped back, tossed some coins on the bar, and started to walk out. Frank stepped away from the bar and faced the men, blocking their way.

"We don't want no trouble, mister," one of the men said. "But if you're a mind to have some, we'll oblige."

"You got a name?" Frank asked.

"Yeah, I got a name. Do you?"

"Yeah. Frank."

"Frank what?" the second man asked.

"Morgan."

"Oh, hell," the barkeep muttered.

"Frank Morgan?" a man at the table said. "Here?"

Frank ignored the barkeep and the local, keeping his eyes on the two hard cases in front of him. "You boys have names?"

"I'm Mel and this here is Cec. If it's any of your damn business."

"Raped any children lately, boys?" Frank asked.

"Done what?" another local asked. "Rape?"

"I ain't never raped no child!" Mel blurted out, his face suddenly sweaty.

"Me neither," Cec said, his right hand hovering near the butt of his pistol.

"You're both liars," Frank said. "Man I left to die down in Arizona mentioned two men name of Mel and Cec."

"What was his name?" Cec asked.

"Carter."

The two men exchanged quick glances but said nothing.

"Is Mel and Cec all you want on your headstones?" Frank asked.

"We ain't planned on dyin', Morgan," Mel said.

"You better change your plans, boys. 'Cause you're dead. You just don't know it yet."

"We left Dooley's gang, Morgan," Cec said. "We ain't no part of it no more."

"Where is he?" Frank asked.

"I don't know," Mel said after a quick look at his partner.

"You're lying again," Frank said coldly.

"You got to understand, Morgan," Mel pleaded. "No one rats out Val and lives very long. That's the way it is."

"You have a chance of living if you answer my question,

boys. Lie to me and you die right here on this barroom floor.''

"That ain't fair, Morgan," Cec said. "We ain't got nothin' to do with Val no more."

"Where is he?" Frank asked, his voice filled with impatience.

"You go to hell, Morgan!" Mel yelled. "I ain't squealin' on Val. That's the way it is. If you don't like it, that's tough."

Frank took a step toward the two outlaws, and Mel and Cec took a step backward. Cec held out a hand.

"We don't want no trouble with you, Morgan. Just leave us be."

"Val Dooley," Frank persisted. "Where is he?"

"Damn you!" Mel yelled. "Damn you to the pits of hell!" He grabbed for his six-gun.

Frank's Peacemaker roared. His draw was so smooth, so fast, if anyone in the saloon had blinked, they would have missed it. Mel's pistol slipped back into leather as he slumped against the bar.

"Good God!" a local said in hushed and reverent tones. "I ain't never seen nothin' so fast."

Mel lost his grip on the bar and fell to the floor, one hand holding his punctured belly. "Kill him, Cec," he said.

"I don't think so," his partner replied.

"He shot me!" Mel gasped. "You got to avenge me, Cec."

"Val Dooley," Frank said. "Where is he, Cec?"

"I don't know for shore," the outlaw said quickly. "And that's the truth, Morgan. He moves around a lot. He's runnin', tryin' to build up his gang."

"The last time you saw him?"

"He was camped over on the Vermejo. Near the headwaters. I swear to you, that's the truth, Morgan."

"Kill him, Cec," Mel begged, his voice growing weaker as his life blood leaked out of him. "Do it for me."

"Not a chance, partner," Cec said, looking down at Mel.

"Then get me a doctor," Mel said. "I'm beginnin' to hurt something awful. My guts is on fire."

"There ain't no doctor here," a local said. "Nearest one is fifty miles away."

"And he's drunk near'bouts all the time," another local said.

"How many men does Val have with him?" Frank asked.

"Not many," Cec said. "Most of his gang quit him."

Mel stretched out on the floor, his head resting on a cuspidor. His face had turned ghostly white.

"How many is many?" Frank asked.

"Maybe ten," Cec said.

"Get me a preacher," Mel said.

"We ain't got one of them either," a local said. "Not since he run off with Otis Farnworth's wife, Mavis."

Mel cussed, then closed his eyes and died.

Twenty-nine

"You ride," Frank told Cec. "And don't ever run into me again."

Cec didn't need a second invitation. He walked out of the saloon without looking back and rode away.

Frank had no idea whether Cec would try to warn Val, and he didn't much care one way or the other.

"Whoever wants to plant this one," Frank said, pointing to Mel, "can have what's in his pockets and his guns and horse and saddle."

Two locals stood up and without a word began dragging the body of the outlaw out the back door.

"Those two old rummies just might drop him down a privy pit," the bartender said.

Frank shrugged his total indifference and picked up his mug of beer, taking a swallow. "The café serve good food?"

"It's been shut down for six months," the barkeep said. "This town is dryin' up and blowin' away. But I got some pretty good stew on the stove and the wife just made some bread. And she's a good cook."

"Dish it up," Frank said. "And bring me some coffee." He looked around and found a good spot near the front window with his back to a wall. "I'll be sitting over there."

The two old drunks were outside in the street, arguing over who would get the horse and who would get the saddle.

Frank relaxed in the chair. He was tired. He'd been on the trail now for three weeks. His horses were tired and Dog was tired. "Is the livery open?" he called to the bartender.

"Oh, yeah, it's still in business. I own it."

"I'm going to stable my horses there. You got a man to rub them down and feed them?"

"Sure do. Ol' Bob is there now. He's a good man. Treat you right. You can pay him."

Frank ate two bowls of the stew and polished off a loaf of hot bread smeared with butter. Then he sat and drank coffee and smoked and relaxed. Dog had caught and killed and eaten two rabbits that day, so Frank wasn't worried about him. He was full of fresh rabbit meat.

"If you need a place to bunk tonight, Mr. Morgan," the barkeep called, "you can sleep in the loft of the stable. There ain't no hotel nor boardin'house no more."

"Thanks. I'll take you up on that."

"Nights gettin' cool this time of year, but the hay is fresh and comfortable."

"No barbershop or bathhouse?" Frank asked.

"Not since the barber died last year. I figure a couple more years this town will be nothin' but a memory."

Frank finished his coffee and saw to his horses. Then he bought a few supplies and returned to the stable. He filled a pail with fresh water for Dog. Before the sun went down,

Frank was rolled up in his blankets, asleep in the hay in the loft.

Dog's low growling awakened Frank. Dog had been sleeping in Stormy's stall. Frank's hand closed around the butt of his Peacemaker and he silently slipped out of his blankets. In his stocking feet, he made his way to the edge of the loft and peered over the side. He could see two shadowy figures standing just inside the open front doors. Frank had no idea what the time was, but he had awakened alert and feeling very refreshed, so he figured it must be sometime in the very early morning. He felt he had slept seven or eight hours.

Dog had sensed Frank was awake and had ceased his growling.

Using his left hand to cover the sound, Frank eared back the hammer of his .45. "Stand easy, boys," he said.

A roar and a flash of flame tore the darkness as one of the men below fired in the direction of Frank's voice. The bullet hit the edge of the loft, sending splinters flying. Frank returned the fire. His bullet hit human flesh and brought a grunt of pain. Frank rolled to one side, away from his original position, just as the second man fired.

Frank's .45 slug knocked the second man sprawling to the floor just as the first assailant fired again. The bullet grazed Frank's upper left arm, and Frank felt the warm flow of blood leaking down his arm, the wound stinging.

Frank fired, and heard the thud of a body hitting the ground. He groped around in the darkness and found his boots, tugging them on. Then he went down the short ladder to the ground floor and quickly slipped to one side.

One of the fallen men groaned and moved, the movement just visible in the dim light through the huge open doors. The other man neither groaned nor moved.

Frank waited, doing a slow silent sixty count, just in case there might be a third man lurking in the darkness.

Nothing. Only silence greeted him. No lights in the tiny town flickered on.

Frank walked up to the fallen men and kicked their guns away. Then he prodded the men. One made no sound or movement. He was either unconscious or dead. The second man moaned and stirred.

"Your partner's dead," Frank said. "You feel any urge to join him?"

"No," the man said.

"Can you get up?"

"I'm belly-hit. I hurt bad."

"No doctor in this town. If you got anything to say, you'd better say it now."

"I ain't got a damn thing to say to you, Morgan."

"Then lie there and die, partner. As for me, I'm going to find a coffeepot and make some coffee."

Frank lit a lantern hanging from a nail on the post, turning the wick down. Then he gathered up the gunmen's pistols and laid them on a small table near the front of the livery. Then he stoked up a stove in the tiny office and filled a pot with water, setting it on the stove to boil. Frank returned to the fallen gunman and rolled him over on his back, taking a look at the wound.

"I hurt real bad, Morgan," the outlaw groaned.

"You won't hurt for very long," Frank told him. "If you've got anything to say to me, you better get it said."

"You messed up a real good thing we had goin', Morgan."

"You call kidnapping and raping children a good thing?"

The dying outlaw had no reply to that.

"Where's Val Dooley?"

"He'll kill you, Morgan. He's the fastest gun I ever seen."

"We'll see about that. Where is he?"

The outlaw laughed, and blood sprayed from his mouth.

Lung shot, Frank thought. The bullet must have angled up after tearing up his innards and nicked a lung.

"Where is Dooley?"

"He'll find you, Morgan. Or some of his gang will. You got a bunch of hard ol' boys on your trail."

"If they're like you and your partner, I don't have much to worry about, do I?"

The outlaw moaned his reply.

"You got a name you want on your marker?" Frank asked.

The outlaw cussed him.

"I don't think all that will fit," Frank said, squatting down and rolling a cigarette.

"Dave Morris," the man said. "My partner's name is Dallas."

"Just Dallas?"

"That's all I ever heard him called. Can I have a smoke, Morgan?"

Frank struck a match and lit up, then placed the cigarette between the man's lips.

"Thanks. Dooley changes camps every two, three days. He's always on the move. Has maybe five or six men with him all the time."

"Any hostages?"

"No. They done all been sold. Is Dallas really dead?"

"Cold as a hammer in January."

"You'll see that we're buried proper, Morgan?"

"I'll do that."

"I'm gettin' real cold, Morgan. It's close, ain't it? I mean, I'm bein' touched by the darkness, ain't I?"

"I reckon so, Dave."

"I think I'll . . ." Dave never finished whatever he was going to say. He closed his eyes and stiffened slightly; then life left him.

Frank took the cigarette from the man's lips and heeled it out.

Frank went into the office and fixed his coffee, then sat down in the only chair and smoked and drank a cup of the strong brew. He found a couple of horse blankets and covered the bodies of Dave and Dallas. He popped open the lid to his pocket watch and checked the time. Two o'clock. It was going to be a long wait until the dawning.

Four days later, Frank eased his way into brush on a slight rise and looked down at the outlaw camp. Or one of the outlaw camps, at least, he realized grimly.

A Mexican family had told him about the camp of some very bad men who had some children with them. The Mexican family could not understand why such evil-acting men would have such nice young girls with them.

"Anglo girls?" Frank had asked.

"*Sí, sí,*" the man had replied. "Very unhappy-looking Anglo girls."

And there the girls were, Frank saw after inspecting the camp more closely through field glasses. Three girls. Frank watched one of the men walk over to one of the girls, jerk her to her feet, and slap her. She fought back and he struck her with his fist, knocking her to the ground. She did not move.

"Damn little whoor!" the man shouted, his words reaching Frank clearly. "When I tell one of you to git nekked, I mean strip now!" He pointed at another young girl just as Frank was adjusting the sights on his .44-40. "Shuck them clothes!" he yelled.

Three other men were lounging around a fire, drinking coffee and laughing at the scene before them.

They stopped laughing when Frank's bullet knocked the

first man spinning to the ground. Five seconds later, only one man was left alive in the camp, and he was on his knees, his hands in the air, yelling for whoever it was on the ridge to stop shooting. He surrendered.

Frank stood up and walked to the camp. "One of you girls rinse out a coffeepot and make some coffee."

"Yes, sir," the three girls replied in unison.

"Frank Morgan?" the man on his knees asked. "Oh, God!"

"His name is Curly," one of the girls said. "And he's done some really terrible things to all of us."

"I didn't do nothin' them others didn't do!" Curly yelled.

"And they're dead," Frank reminded the man. "Or dying."

"Oh, Jesus!" Curly hollered. "Don't kill me, Morgan!"

"Give me one good reason why I shouldn't," Frank told him.

"I'll lead you to the other camps," Curly said. He cut his eyes as Dog walked up. "That's a mean-lookin' dog, Morgan. Don't sic him on me. I'll hep you find the camps. I swear I'll hep you. Just keep that dog away from me."

"He hates dogs," one of the girls said. "He kills every one he sees. I've seen him shoot dogs."

Frank lifted the muzzle of his rifle. "I like dogs," he said, a cold edge to his voice. "I *don't* like people who harm them."

"You gonna shoot me 'cause I don't like dogs?" Curly hollered the question. "Sweet Jesus, Morgan. That ain't no good reason."

Frank had watched the man edge one hand toward the back of his neck. He guessed the man had a knife there, the sheath suspended by a leather thong. It was a trick he'd seen more than once.

"No," Frank said. "I'm going to shoot you because you're a kidnapping, child-raping, low-down son of a bitch."

Curly jerked a knife out and drew back to throw it at Frank. Frank's bullet caught him in the neck, just under the jaw, and almost tore the man's head off. Curly fell back and kicked a couple of times as the blood gushed and squirted out of the gaping wound.

"I hope they all burn in the hellfires forever," one of the girls said, looking at the men sprawled in death.

"I suspect they will, girl," Frank said. "Get some blankets and toss them over them. Before they contaminate us all with ugly."

The girls smiled at that. Two of them went to fetch blankets while the third girl made coffee. "How long have you girls been captives?" Frank asked.

"I was taken two weeks ago," one of the girls called. "I'd been playin' at a friend's house and was walkin' back home when two men grabbed me. They done . . . things to me. We all got grabbed about the same time."

The other two girls nodded their heads in agreement as they tossed horse blankets over the dead men. All three girls exhibited no visible signs of sickness or shock at the bloody and very dead outlaws.

"You girls gather up whatever you want to take with you," Frank told them. "I'm going to have me a cup of coffee."

"Are we goin' home, sir?" one of the girls asked.

"Yes, child. I'll take you home."

Thirty

Frank took the girls back to Santa Fe and turned them over to the sheriff. Eastern newspapers had finally picked up on the story and reporters had converged on the town. Frank gave one short interview and then, after provisioning up, quietly rode out. He did not like reporters and made no effort to hide that dislike. Dog had picked up quickly on Frank's dislike of the press, and had taken to snarling every time a reporter got close.

One reporter had referred to Dog as "the beast from Hades." Dog certainly did his best to live up to that title.

Frank decided to pull out before Dog actually bit someone.

He made camp a few hours' ride outside of town and fixed coffee. Frank was bone-tired; tired of the chase. He'd been on the trail of Val Dooley and his gang for months and was weary of it all. Weary of the killing, weary of the plight of the girls, weary and sick at heart of hearing their stories of beatings and rapes.

Dog came to Frank and lay down beside the man. The summer had been rough on the big cur too. Frank and Dog both needed a long rest.

Frank put a hand on Dog's big head and petted him. "You want to stop the hunt, boy?"

Dog looked at him and growled low in his throat.

"Sure you don't want to provision up and winter in my valley?"

Dog growled again.

"All right, we'll spend a few more weeks on the trail. Val Dooley can't keep running from me forever."

Frank dozed for a few minutes under the shade of a small grove of trees not far from a tiny creek with only a faint trickle of water. He was awakened abruptly by the sounds of walking horses, and closed a hand around the butt of his Peacemaker.

"Hello, the camp," a man shouted. "I'm friendly and that coffee shore smells good."

"Come on in," Frank called. "Light and sit."

The rider was lean, bowlegged, and brown from years spent in the sun. Frank found a cup and poured the stranger a cup.

"Thanks much, mister. I'm Slim Rodgers."

"Frank. Frank Morgan."

Slim paused in his lifting of cup to mouth and stared at Frank. *"The Frank Morgan?"*

"I reckon so. I haven't run up on anybody else with that name."

"Everybody in the territory is talkin' 'bout you, Mr. Morgan. You savin' all them girls."

"I'm still looking."

Slim sipped his coffee and nodded his head. "Yeah, I reckon you are. You got the rep as a man who don't give up. You got any idea where this no-'count Val Dooley might be hidin' out?"

"Not a clue."

"I hear he's some south and east of Ute Peak. In the San Juans."

"You think that's good information?"

"I heard it three days ago. And the fellers who told me seemed to know what they was talkin' 'bout."

"Seems logical. That's rough country. Lots of places to hide. How about you, Slim?"

"Huh? What about me?"

"You drifting?"

"Oh. Yeah," the cowboy said with a smile. "I been workin' the high country in Colorado. Snow's gonna start flyin' in a few months. I ain't gonna spend another winter in a line shack, choppin' holes in the ice so's the critters can drink. Figured I'd head down into the southern part of the country and find some work where it's warm."

"Don't blame you a bit for that."

Slim drained his cup and stood up. "I best be movin' on. Got a few hours of daylight left. Thanks for the coffee, Morgan. See you."

"See you around, Slim. Hope you find some work."

Slim swung into the saddle and lifted a hand in farewell.

Frank finished the pot of coffee, and pondered for a few minutes whether he should put a few more miles behind him or stay put. He decided to stay put and get a good night's sleep. Start fresh in the morning. He'd head on up toward the San Juans come the dawning. Maybe he'd get lucky and find Val Dooley. Put an end to this hunt.

One way or the other.

* * *

At a tiny village right on the New Mexico-Colorado line, Frank dismounted and stretched tired muscles. He looked around at the single short street that made up the business district. A general store, a saloon, several buildings with boarded-up windows, a barbershop-bathhouse, a marshal's office with the front door missing, a livery that looked as though it had seen better times.

"A real bustling little town," Frank muttered. He walked his horses over to the livery and to his surprise, a man stepped out and greeted him.

"I didn't think you were open," Frank said.

"Oh, yeah," the man replied. "For a while, at least. Never was much to this town. Even less now."

"Take care of my horses?"

"You bet. Say, ain't I seen you around here before?"

"No. I don't think I've ever been through here."

"You got a brother livin' close by town?"

"No. Sorry."

"Man was in the saloon couple days ago sure resembled you. But now that I'm gettin' a close-up look, I reckon he was a few years younger than you. Yeah, this feller wore a two-gun rig. Fancy guns, they was, too. Had two really hard-lookin' men with him."

Val Dooley, Frank thought. *I'm getting close.* "Those men, they ranching around here?"

"I don't think so. They had them a couple of drinks, eyed some girls that walked into the general store."

"Young girls?"

"Twelve or so. The man that looked sorta like you, he had him a conversation with Sally Martin. She's twelve.

Made her laugh, he did. Then they pulled out. I heard him say he'd see her again. I figured that was just friendly talk. You know?"

"You know this Sally's folks?"

"Sure. Her pa owns the general store. Why?"

"That was not just friendly talk, mister. That man was Val Dooley. I've been on his trail for months."

"You got to be jokin'!"

"No. He's a murderer and kidnapper of young girls. You have a marshal in this town?"

"Now I know you're jokin'. In this town? Hell, no. Val Dooley? He's notorious."

"He's pure scum. Where's the nearest sheriff?"

"A good two days away."

"You got a mayor in this town?"

"Ed Martin. Owns the general store."

"You want a marshal?"

"Hell, we can't pay nothing. You want the job? What's your name anyway?"

"Frank Morgan."

"Frank Morgan?"

"Yes. You got a telegraph here?"

"No. You really Frank Morgan?"

"Yes. Do I get the job?"

"What do you think?"

Frank replaced the door to the marshal's office that afternoon; did the work himself. He aired out his blankets and made up the bunk in the small room off from the main office, then laid in some firewood for the potbellied stove. After that, he rubbed the silver badge Ed Martin had given him after swearing Frank in until it shone. Then he walked over to the saloon.

The bartender-owner gave him a nervous look as Frank walked up to the bar. "Evenin', Marshal Morgan."

"Evening. You got anything to eat here?"

"I can have a steak fixed for you. Steak and boiled taters and chess pie for dessert."

"Sounds good to me. Bring me a cup of coffee over there." He pointed to a table.

"Yes, sir."

Frank relaxed and drank his coffee while his steak was being cooked. A couple of farmers strolled in and took a table. Frank knew they were farmers by their clothing and footwear: one wore clodhopper shoes and the other wore low-heeled boots. Both wore strap overalls. The farmers glanced and nodded at Frank, but did not speak.

A few minutes later, two more men wandered in. They looked like cowboys —and one probably was—but the other one wore his guns tied down. That gave him away as something else. The one with the tied-down guns gave Frank a long once-over. Then he turned his back to him and ordered a drink.

"You the new marshal?" one of the farmers asked, speaking with a thick accent.

"Yes," Frank replied. "For a while."

"I didn't know we needed one," the other farmer said.

"You don't now," Frank told him.

"That's a good one," his partner said with a laugh. "He got you on that one, Amos."

Amos laughed and the men returned to their mugs of beer.

One of the men at the bar turned to stare at Frank. "You think you're man enough to wear that badge?"

"I reckon so," Frank told him, sugaring his second cup of coffee.

"Somebody might decide to take it off you," the man said.

"Somebody had better think twice before they try," Frank said softly.

"That's enough, Del," the other man said.

Del ignored that. "You look mighty familiar, Marshal. I think I seen you before. What happened, did you give up sodbustin' around here and turn to marshalin'?"

"No," Frank said, rolling a cigarette.

"I think you did."

Frank said nothing, just popped a match into flame and lit his smoke.

"You got anything to say about that?" Del persisted.

Frank sipped his coffee and smoked his cigarette.

"I axed you a damn question!" Del said, raising his voice.

"I heard it," Frank said. "I chose to ignore it. Now why don't you just enjoy your drink and leave me the hell alone?"

Del stepped away from the bar. "I don't like you, Marshal."

"I'm heartbroken about that," Frank said. "I can't tell you how much that upsets me. I'll probably lose hours of sleep just worrying about your dislike of me. Now I have a suggestion for you."

"What's that?" Del asked.

"Shut the hell up!"

"No man tells me that!" Del snapped the words at Frank. "Stand up, mister."

"I don't feel like standing," Frank told him. "I feel like eating. My steak should be out of the skillet any second now."

"You won't need food where I'm fixin' to send you. You'll need something to keep the chill of the grave off'n you."

"What's your problem with me, Del?" Frank asked. "How come you're on the prod?"

"I don't like two-bit deputy sheriffs."

"I'm not a deputy. I'm a town marshal."

"That's even worser. Stand up, damn you!"

Frank pushed back his chair and stood. "All right, Del. I'm standing."

"Del," the bartender said, "that's Frank Morgan."

Del caught his breath, and his shoulders slumped for just a moment. Then he took a deep breath and straightened up. "I don't believe that. What the hell would Frank Morgan be doin' in a two-bit crap-house town like this?"

"Believe it, Del," Frank told him.

"I don't give a damn who he is. Don't make no difference to me nohow. You apologize for tellin' me to shut the hell up."

"Turn around and drink your drink and leave me alone, Del," Frank told him.

"Come on, Del," his partner urged him. "Let's just forget this."

"You forget it, Roger," Del said. "And I don't believe that there's Frank Morgan."

"Your steak's ready, Marshal," the barkeep called.

"Hell with his damn steak!" Del yelled.

"Bring it on," Frank said. "I'm hungry."

"Huh?" Del shouted. "What's wrong with you, Marshal? I'm challengin' you. Ain't you got enough sense to see that?"

"I have enough sense to try and save your life, cowboy," Frank said as the barkeep walked toward him, a plate of food in one hand and a pot of coffee in the other. "Just set it right down, friend. And let me get to eating."

"I ain't believin' this," Del said, watching Frank sit down and pick up knife and fork.

"I'm a mite hungry myself," Roger said.

"You ..." Del pointed a finger at Frank. "You best enjoy that meal, Marshal. 'Cause when you're done stuffin' your face ... I'm gonna kill you!"

Thirty-one

Frank took his time eating. He was hungry and enjoyed every bite. The longer he took, the more agitated Del became. The man paced up and down in front of the bar, muttering curses under his breath.

A dozen more locals had entered the saloon as the word had spread through the tiny town. The men had trooped in and taken seats, being careful not to get between Del and Frank Morgan. Finally, Frank pushed his empty plate away and refilled his coffee cup. Then he leaned back and rolled himself a smoke.

"Now, by God!" Del shouted. "You'll stand up and fight!"

"After I finish my cigarette and coffee," Frank said.

"I ain't believin' this!" Del yelled. "I'm tellin' you to stand up and face me!"

"Why should I?" Frank questioned.

"Because I . . . because I told you to do it!"

"That's not good enough, Del," Frank said. He had been hoping his stalling would bring some sense to the frustrated man. It wasn't working . . . so far. "I got no reason to shoot you, and you don't have any legitimate reason to want to shoot me."

"You insulted me!"

"And you believe that's reason enough to risk death or serious injury?"

"Damn right! It's my honor we're talkin' 'bout."

"Del." Frank spoke softly, but loud enough for the man to hear. "Go home. Let's shake hands and put an end to this."

"That's one of the men who was with Val Dooley the other day," the man from the livery suddenly said. "Took me a while to recognize him. I don't think I've ever seen that other feller."

"You sure?" Frank asked.

"I'm sure."

A coldness spread over Frank. He slowly stood up and faced Del. "Now I'll face you, Del. Anyone who would ride with Val Dooley is scum."

Roger held up his hands. "I'm out of this. I just hooked up with Del yesterday. I don't know nothin' 'bout Val Dooley."

"You better be telling me the truth," Frank said.

"I swear to God I am," Roger said. "I been workin' up north of here. Just driftin' south when I come upon Del here."

"He's tellin' the truth," Del said. "I never seen him 'fore yesterday. He ain't nobody. Now, Marshal Morgan, or whoever you are, you get ready to die. 'Cause now you got me to deal with."

Frank's smile was very thin. "With a great deal of pleasure, Del."

Roger backed away. "Leave me out of this, boys. I punch cows. I ain't no gun hand."

"Stand clear then," Frank told him.

Roger backed farther away.

"Val Dooley is a great man," Del said.

"Val Dooley is a piece of coyote crap," Frank told him.

"Too bad you'll never live to say that to him in person," Del said with a sneer.

"Oh, I plan on telling him that," Frank replied. "Among other things. Just before I put lead in him."

"You got to get by me first."

"I don't see that as any great hill to climb."

"You 'bout a cocky bastard, ain't you? For a man with some gray in his hair and some years on his face."

"Experience, boy," Frank said. "Too bad you'll never live to gain that experience."

Del laughed. Frank waited. It was Del's play.

"Well, come on, old man," Del said. "Let's do it."

Frank slowly shook his head. "If you're that anxious to die, boy, you know where your gun is. Hook it."

The first little faint fingers of doubt crept into Del's eyes. And Frank saw it. He knew then Del was going to make a mistake. And that mistake was going to cost the young outlaw his life. Frank knew all the signs; had seen them many times over the years of his long, legendary career.

Del blinked his eyes a couple of times. "You want me to pull on you?" he questioned.

"That's right, Del. It's all your show."

"I'm better than you, Morgan."

"Prove it."

Del's hand dipped and his fingers closed around the butt of his pistol. He never managed to clear leather. He heard an enormous boom and felt a hammerlike blow slam him in the chest. The next thing he fully realized was his leaning against the bar for support and Frank Morgan walking slowly toward him.

"Where is Val Dooley?" Frank's words echoed in Del's head.

"He'll be into town in a couple days," Del said. His own words sounded very strange to him.

"I'll be here," Frank said.

"You look funny," Del said. "And you sound funny. What's the damn joke? I don't understand none of this. You're dead, Morgan. I shot you."

"No, you didn't, Del. And the joke's on you."

"How come? I don't like bein' the butt of jokes."

"Too bad. You thought you could take me."

"Next time, I will, Morgan. That's a promise."

"Sure, Del. Sure."

And just before Del closed his eyes for the last time, he heard Frank Morgan say, "Might as well make this legal. You're under arrest, Del."

Del hit the floor.

Four days after Del's shooting, two hard cases rode into town and tied up outside the saloon. Frank watched them from the general store across the street.

"That man dressed all in black is one of the men who was with the man who told me he'd be back," Sally Martin said.

"Did he have a name you recall?" Frank asked.

"I think the man you say is Val Dooley called him Lee."

"Lee Hart," Frank said. "No-good out of Arkansas. He's been staying one jump ahead of a rope for years. You ever see the other one?"

"No, sir."

"I think I'll walk over there and get acquainted," Frank said. "Sally, you stay here."

The early fall day had turned off cloudy and cool, a preview of the winter that was to come. Frank walked across the wide street, his boots kicking up little puffs of dust with each step. He stepped into the saloon and walked up to the end of the bar. The bartender cut his eyes to the two men standing at the far end of the bar. Frank nodded his head minutely.

"Let's have some service here," Lee's partner demanded in a gruff tone.

"Coming right up," the barkeep said, walking down to the end of the bar. "What'll it be, boys?"

"Whiskey," Lee said. "Leave the bottle."

With the outlaws served, the barkeep walked back to Frank. "Coffee," Frank said in low tones. "Then get out of the way."

"You don't have to tell me that twice," the barkeep replied. "That one dressed all in black was here with Dooley."

Frank nodded his head in understanding.

The barkeep placed a coffeepot and a cup in front of Frank and started to back off.

"The sugar bowl," Frank said, raising his voice so all in the saloon could hear. "When I can get it, I like my coffee with some sweetening."

"Well, you're a real girl, aren't you, Marshal?" Lee said with a laugh. "You maybe want a little lace napkin too?"

"What I want is none of your damn business," Frank told him.

Lee turned and gave Frank a hard look. "You best curb that tongue, Marshal."

"Or you'll do what?" Frank asked in a hard voice.

"You don't really want to know, sweetie," Lee said, placing special emphasis on the word *sweetie*.

Frank smiled at him. "I know what *I'll* do, Lee. Believe me, I do."

"You know my name, Marshal. How come that is?"

"Oh, you're a famous man, Lee. Lawmen all over the West know about you. As a matter of fact, they'd love to find you."

"And you think you're going to arrest me and collect the reward money, right?" Lee asked with a smile.

"I'm not interested in the reward money, Lee."

"Oh?"

"That's right. So . . . I think I'll just place you under arrest."

Lee laughed at that. "You hear that, Eddie?" he said to his partner. "Marshal Nobody is goin' to arrest me."

"That ain't nobody, Lee," Eddie said. "I just now figured out who he is. That's Frank Morgan."

Lee's smile faded. "You got to be wrong, Eddie. What the hell would Frank Morgan be doin' in a jerkwater town like this?"

"Totin' a badge is what he's doin'," Eddie replied. "And I ain't wrong neither. That there is Frank Morgan."

"You boys are under arrest," Frank said. "Keep your hands away from your guns and start walking toward the door."

"And if we don't?" Lee asked.

"I'll kill you both. Kill you just as dead as Del Davis. He's buried up on the hill."

"Del's dead?" Eddie asked.

"Cold and stiff in the ground," Frank said.

"I'm done," Eddie said. "I ain't goin' up agin Frank Morgan."

"They's two of us, Eddie," Lee reminded him.

"I don't give a damn if they's ten of us. I know men who've seen Morgan face four or five pretty good gun hands. They're all dead and he's standin' here lookin' at us. You want dead, you draw on him, not me. I'm unbucklin' my gun belt, Morgan. I'm out of it. Take me to jail if you want to. I ain't got no warrants out on me." Eddie laid his gun belt on a table and stepped back away from the bar.

"Sit down, Eddie," Frank told him. "Take your drink with you. Sit and relax and enjoy the show."

"This ain't no damn show, Morgan!" Lee blustered.

"It's going to be a short one, for a fact."

"Huh?"

"Won't take me but half a second to put lead in you."

"You got it to do, Morgan."

"You coming to jail peacefully, Lee?"

"Hell, no."

Frank cleared leather before Lee could blink. The outlaw stared in disbelief at the Peacemaker in Frank's hand. "Now are you coming along with me?" Frank asked.

"I reckon so," Lee said. "And I reckon you're as fast as rumor says you are." He stared at Frank for a moment. "You could have killed me, Morgan. Why didn't you?"

"I have something else in mind, Lee. Move it!"

The small jail had only two cells, each with two bunks. Frank put Lee Hart and Eddie in one cell.

"What happens now, Morgan?" Eddie asked.

"We wait for Val Dooley to show up."

"You figure on puttin' Val in jail?" Lee asked.

"No. I plan on killing him."

"You ain't gonna put him in jail or kill him," Lee said. "He's just as fast with a hogleg as you."

"And when you're dead," Eddie said, "we'll have our

way with the women in this town and then burn the damn place to the ground.''

"There's only one hitch to your plan," Frank told him.

"What's that?"

"Me. And I'm hard to kill."

"Val's smarter than you, Morgan," Lee informed Frank. "He's the smartest man I ever seen. He'll figure out a way to kill you and then bust us out of this jail."

"Keep dreaming, boys. I'll live to see both of you dance at the end of a rope."

"When do we get somethin' to eat?" Eddie asked. "I'm hongry."

"You'll get supper. Relax, boys. Enjoy your time left on earth. I figure in about two months you'll be looking at the hangman."

Both outlaws cussed Frank.

"I want somethin' to eat now, Morgan," Eddie said.

"Later, boys. Right now, I have something much more important to take care of."

"What?" Lee asked.

"Feed my dog."

Thirty-two

The general store served enough customers to stay in business, Frank noted, as did the saloon. There were probably a dozen or so small farms and ranches in the area, and it seemed as though each farmer had about six kids.

"Where do they go to school?" Frank asked Ed Martin the morning after placing Lee and his pal in jail.

"Used to have school over yonder in the church house. But the schoolmarm up and got married last year. Moved away. Now it's up to the parents." He looked up the street. "Riders coming, Marshal. Four of 'em. Can't make 'em out from here."

"I can," Sally Martin said, standing in the doorway to her father's store. "That man in the red shirt is the man who told me he was comin' back. Is that Val Dooley? He sorta resembles you, Mr. Morgan."

"That's him, Sally," Frank said, slipping the hammer thong off his Peacemaker.

"Flashy dresser, ain't he?" Ed said.

"More than that," Frank replied. "He's either got more nerve than a wolverine, or he's a damn fool, riding into town this way."

"He's challengin' you to arrest him, Marshal."

"I have no intention of arresting him, Ed."

"You don't?"

"No. I intend to kill him. I'm going to put an end to this once and for all. Close up your store, Ed. You and your family get into the back and stay there. And if you don't mind, take Dog with you."

"Consider it done," Ed said, and walked into his general store. Frank told Dog to follow, and the cur reluctantly followed Ed. The store owner shut the door and pulled the blinds.

Frank waited, fully exposed on the short boardwalk in front of the store. He didn't think Val would try to shoot him from ambush. Val was too vain for that. He wanted a rep: the man who killed Frank Morgan. It would be a stand-up, look-you-in-the-eyes, hook and draw. And that suited Frank just fine.

Val and the three men with him stopped at the far end of the short street, and sat their horses while they eyed Frank, standing on the boardwalk.

Frank waited alone.

After a moment, the four riders began walking their horses up the street, finally reining up in front of the saloon and dismounting. Val Dooley looked over at Frank, smiled, and then walked into the saloon, his men behind him.

Frank stepped off the boardwalk and walked across the street, stepping up onto the short boardwalk in front of the saloon. His holstered Peacemaker was loaded up full, as was his short-barreled Peacemaker, tucked behind his gun belt, worn butt-forward, covered by his coat. He pushed open the batwings and stepped inside.

Val was standing alone at the bar, a bottle of whiskey and a glass in front of him. His men were seated at a table near the rear of the saloon, off to Frank's right. Val looked at Frank and smiled. "Well, well, the famous Frank Morgan. Come in, Morgan, have a drink on me."

"It's a little early for me, Dooley," Frank replied, walking to the end of the bar nearest the entrance. "Bring me a cup of coffee," he said to the barkeep.

"Put it on my tab," Val said.

"I'll pay for my own," Frank said.

Val laughed. "What's the matter, Morgan? My money's no good?"

"Not for me, Dooley."

"Now why would that be?"

"I don't like the way you got it."

"Money's money, Morgan. But"—he sighed—"I'll respect your decision. A man who is about to die should have some rights, I suppose."

Frank smiled. "You planning on dying today, Val?"

Val's smile faded. "No," he said softly.

"Oh? That's very strange, Val."

"Why is that, Morgan?"

"Because I plan on doing the world a favor by killing you."

Val's smile again creased his lips. "And you think you're a fast enough gun to do that, Morgan?"

"Oh, yes, Val. I sure do."

"Funny thing, Morgan. I don't think you are."

"Then I guess that leaves us only one thing to do."

"I guess so, Morgan. But . . . for right now, I'm going

to enjoy a couple of drinks. It's awfully dry out, and I need something to cut the dust.''

"You go right ahead, Val. Enjoy your whiskey. I'm going to enjoy my cup of coffee.''

"I must say, Morgan, you're rather a friendly sort. Everyone else I talked to told me you were a surly sort.''

"They must have caught me in a bad mood.''

"I suppose that could be it. And you're in a good mood this morning?''

"Wonderful mood.''

"And why is that?''

"Because I'm finally going to rid society of you.''

"I don't find that particularly amusing, Morgan.''

"I don't give a damn how you find it.''

Val took a sip of whiskey. "You know, Morgan, you have been a real pain in the butt these past few months.''

"I'm glad to hear it.''

Val chuckled. "I had a real good thing going until you interfered.''

"Good thing? I wouldn't call raping children a good thing.''

"None of them died from it. As a matter of fact,'' he said smugly, "I would say that a great many of them enjoyed our, ah, dalliance.''

"Dooley,'' Frank replied, his tone filled with disgust, "you are indeed one sorry worthless son of a bitch.''

"I take great offense at that, Morgan.''

"Good.''

"You're pushing me hard. I thought you wanted to enjoy your last cup of coffee.''

It was an old game; one that Frank had played many times. Each man trying to rattle the nerves of the other.

"I am enjoying it, Val. And I plan on enjoying many

more cups over the course of my long life. Right now, though, I'm enjoying watching you sweat and squirm.''

"Huh? Me, sweat and squirm over facing the likes of you? You're dreaming, Morgan. Just dreaming.''

"Am I, Val?" Frank asked softly. "You've never seen me work. No man who ever seriously faced me has lived to tell about it. Not a one.''

Val carefully refilled his shot glass and knocked back the drink in one gulp. "I could say the same, Morgan.''

"Really, Val? Funny thing is, I've never seen any of your graveyards. Where are they?''

"All over the damn West, Morgan!" Val snapped.

"Filled with men you ambushed or shot in the back?''

"*Goddamn* you, Morgan!''

"What's the matter, Val? Getting itchy?''

Val didn't immediately reply. He carefully refilled his shot glass and stood for a moment, staring down at the whiskey. "It won't work, Morgan. I know what you're trying to do. You can't rattle me. But you're pretty good, I have to admit that. You came close.''

Frank took a sip of coffee. He offered no reply. He waited.

"You have a couple of my men in jail, Morgan," Val said. "I want them out.''

"How do you know I have them in jail?''

Val's only reply was a smile.

"They stay in jail until I hear back from the authorities in various states and territories.''

"I said I want them out, Morgan. Release them, and we ride out of here. Nothing happens to this village or its people.''

"And if I don't release them?''

"We take the town and kill everyone in it . . . after the more attractive women and girls entertain us.''

"Never happen, Val.''

"You going to stop us?"

"That's right."

Val turned to face Frank. "Well, Morgan, I guess you'd better get to stopping us. The time for conversation is over."

"Your play, Val."

Val and Frank pulled iron. Val was fast, getting off the first shot. But his bullet tore up the floor in front of Frank's boots. Frank was only the blink of an eye slower, but his bullet ripped into Val's belly and knocked him backward.

Frank didn't hesitate. He spun, drawing his second Peacemaker as he turned, and began putting lead into the three men seated at the table, just as they were jerking guns out of leather. The booming of Frank's guns was enormous, the sound rattling glasses behind the bar. Frank felt the sting of a bullet creasing the side of his head; another bullet drawing blood as it sliced through the fleshy part of his left thigh. Frank stayed on his boots, firing both .45s until they were empty.

"Marshal!" the barkeep yelled.

Frank turned in time to catch the Greener the barkeep tossed at him. He whirled around, cocking the sawed-off shotgun as he turned. Val had pulled his second .45, and was struggling to jack back the hammer when Frank pulled the triggers. Both barrels of the Greener spewed fire and smoke and buckshot.

The double load of buckshot caught Val Dooley in the belly and literally cut him in two.

What was left of Val Dooley fell to the floor with twin slopping sounds, making a big mess on the freshly mopped saloon floor.

Frank leaned against the bar for a moment as his own blood dripped onto the floor.

"You're hurt, Marshal!" the bartender said.

"Nothing serious," Frank told him as the batwings opened and a crowd of locals surged in.

"My God!" Ed Martin said, looking at the carnage that lay before him, all the outlaws in various postures of sudden death.

"Dear Lord, have mercy," another man said in hushed tones.

"Somebody haul off those bodies," Frank said, taking off his bandanna and using it to bind up the wound on his leg. "You can split the money in their pockets and their guns and horses for your trouble."

"Do you know who they are, Marshal Morgan?" another local asked.

"I don't have a clue as to their names. But I can tell you what they are: They're kidnapping, child-raping white slavers. Pure worthless scum. And that," he said, pointing to the twin mounds of glob on the floor, "is what is left of Val Dooley."

"That looks plumb awful," a man said. "I reckon we'll have to scoop him up with shovels."

"Hey," another local said, looking down at the bodies of the three outlaws. "I think one of these yahoos is alive."

The wounded and bloody outlaw was hauled into a chair. He was near death, but still able to speak. He groaned a couple of times.

"You got a name, feller?" he was asked. "I hate to bury a man not knowin' his name."

"Dick," the outlaw moaned. "Dick Bates. Them other two is Noble and Henry."

"Where is the gang's hideout?" Frank asked the man.

"Nowheres now. Val busted up the gang. We was all that was left."

"Don't lie, man," a local said. "It ain't good to meet the Lord with a lie on your lips."

"I ain't lyin', I swear it." Dick groaned, closed his eyes, and fell out of the chair dead.

"I wonder which one is Noble and which one is Henry," a man said.

"Hell, what difference does it make?" another said. "Put 'em in a big bag and shake 'em up and you won't be able to tell the difference nohow."

"I reckon so," the man said.

Frank walked slowly out of the saloon and over to his office. There he bathed his wounds with alcohol and bandaged his leg. He'd been hurt a lot worse during his long years.

He'd thought he'd feel happy when Val Dooley was finished on this earth. But instead he felt depressed; didn't understand why that was. He looked up as Ed Martin walked into the office.

"I guess you'll be moving on now," Ed said.

There was a hopeful note in the man's question that caused Frank to smile. Same old story. Gun-handlers were welcome in a town when the chips were down, but let the table get clear, with a new deck in the game, and men like Frank Morgan were sometimes not too politely asked to get out.

"I reckon so," Frank said after a moment of silence while he stared down the man. The merchant shuffled his brogans on the floor in quiet embarrassment.

"I want you to know we certainly appreciate what you've done, Marshal," Ed finally said.

"Right."

"And any provisions you need for your trip will be on the house."

"That's very kind of you."

"Well . . ." Ed said.

"I'll be pulling out about midmorning," Frank said. "I'll provision up at your store first thing."

"I'll be there, Marshal. Oh, and there won't be any charge for stabling your horses."

"Thanks."

The merchant quietly left the office. Frank looked down. Drops of his blood were leaking from his leg wound, puddling on the floor.

Thirty-three

Frank put the tiny town behind him and headed east, toward Texas. He was in no hurry, didn't even know why he was Texas-bound—he just was. He was drifting.

Frank had thought about wintering in his New Mexico valley, but he quickly changed his mind about that. Julie had loved that valley, and Frank had been quite fond of Julie.

"Drifting again," he muttered on his third day out. The weather was cool and very pleasant, the nights getting downright chilly. Frank had no intention of wintering in North Texas, for the winters could get rough in that part of the state.

After several weeks on the trail, Frank crossed over into the panhandle of Texas, stopping at a tiny town just across the New Mexico-Texas line. Frank wanted a bath, a haircut, and a shave. Then he wanted a meal he hadn't cooked over a campfire. He stabled his horses at the livery, got some scraps from a café for Dog, then walked over to the barbershop-bathhouse. An hour later, he was both feeling and looking human again as he entered the town's only saloon for a drink before he ate supper.

No one paid him much attention as he stood at the end of the bar and ordered a whiskey. Frank was dressed in jeans, dark shirt, and waist-length leather jacket. The bartender poured his drink and leaned close.

"I used to bartend up in the Dakotas, Morgan. I seen you up there when them Calhoun boys pushed you into that fight. Remember?"

"Oh, yes, I sure do."

"Three hard-lookin' ol' boys come into town 'bout two, three hours ago. They're on the prod, lookin' for someone. They got 'em a room up over the saloon. I figured I best warn you 'bout 'em."

"Did they mention my name?"

"No, sir. But I caught their name. Real funny name. Bookbinder. You know 'em?"

"I've heard of them. And you're right: they're on the prod. For me."

"They're bad ones, Morgan. I can tell. I've seen more than my share in my time."

"Thanks. I appreciate it."

"Don't mention it. Are you lookin' for a bed tonight?"

"I was planning on it."

"You don't want to stay here with them Bookbinders, do you?"

Frank smiled; a grimace more than a humorous curving of the lips. "Either me or those three won't be needing a bed, friend."

The bartender nodded his head. "I understand, Morgan."

"But I will take that room."

"You might want to delay on walkin' upstairs. Yonder comes the Bookbinder boys."

Frank turned and met the eyes of Jules Bookbinder. Frank remembered him now. It had been a number of years, but Frank knew him. Jules stopped halfway down the stairs and stared at Frank. Then he turned and spoke in low tones to his brothers. The brothers all looked at Frank for a moment. Jules continued on down the stairs, his brothers, Kenny and Alvin, following. The three brothers walked to the bar and ordered drinks.

"Smells like polecat down at the end of the bar," Alvin said. "You smell that turrible stink, brothers?"

"Shore do," Kenny said.

Jules said nothing. He was an experienced gun-handler; he knew Frank Morgan wasn't going to get rattled by words.

Frank sipped his drink and waited for one of the brothers to make a move.

The batwings pushed open and an older man with a white handlebar mustache stepped inside. The man wore a badge on his jacket. Texas Ranger. The Ranger walked up to the bar, took a place between Frank and the brothers, and ordered a whiskey. While his drink was being poured, he gave Frank a once-over. Frank gave him a look right back.

"I know you," the Ranger said. "Frank Morgan."

"That's right."

"I recall the time you and Red Douglas locked horns down south of here. Red didn't even clear leather 'fore you put two holes in him."

"I remember."

"You on the prod, Morgan?"

"No. Just passin' through."

"That's good. I hate paperwork. Times are sure changin'. Now when there's a shootin', a lawman's got to spent a damn hour scribblin' down everything he seen. Damn nuisance, if you ask me. I'm just passin' through myself. Seen your horse over to the livery. Fine-lookin' animal. That your ill-tempered dog in the stall with him?''

"He isn't ill-tempered toward me," Frank said with a smile.

For the first time, the Ranger smiled. "I reckon not. That's all a man needs, a good horse and a good dog. A woman won't bring a man nothin' but grief. I had me a good dog once. Named him Cornelius. Best dog in Texas. I still miss him. My wife left me after ten years of marriage. I don't miss her at all."

Frank chuckled at the Ranger's words and took a tiny sip of his whiskey. The Ranger cut his eyes to the Bookbinder boys and then quickly back to Frank.

"I know that crew down there," he whispered. "The older one's Jules Bookbinder. I know he's wanted all over the place, but I don't have any papers on him. They after you?"

"Yes."

"Damn. And I thought I could make this run without havin' to do a lot of paperwork."

"Sorry to have to spoil your trip."

"Don't think nothin' of it, Morgan. These things happen. You want me to jump in or you plan on handlin' this yourself?"

"Just keep your eyes open, if you will. Jules is a big man. He'll be hard to put down."

"Will do."

"What the hell are you two whisperin' about down there?" Alvin asked, his tone demanding.

"None of your damn business," the Ranger told him. "I don't answer to worthless turds like you three."

"You callin' me a turd?" Kenny shouted.

"I'll call you a low-down son of a bitch if I take a mind to do it," the Ranger popped right back. "Now shut up your trap and let me continue my conversation with my friend here."

"Be quiet," Jules cautioned his brother. "We don't want no trouble with you, Ranger."

"Fine. What are you boys doin' in Texas anyway?"

"Lookin' for work," Jules said. "Maybe working line shacks during the winter. You know of any work?"

"Can't say as I do, boys. But was I you three, I'd try somewheres else. It might not be real healthy around here."

"What do you mean by that?" Alvin asked.

"You might say you boys have a reputation as trouble-hunters. I don't like trouble-hunters. You get my drift?"

Kenny stepped away from the bar. "You tellin' us to clear out, Ranger?"

"I ain't tellin' you no such of a thing, boy. I'm merely strongly *suggesting* it."

"Nobody tells me where I can come or go," Jules said softly. "I think you're throwin' in with Morgan there, Ranger."

"Well, now, son," the Ranger drawled, "that might be true. You see, I sorta like Frank Morgan. I *don't* like you."

"That don't mean squat to me, Ranger," Jules said. "We're spendin' a few days in this town, restin' ourselves and our horses. And if you don't like that, that's just too damn bad."

"Paperwork," the Ranger muttered. "Good Lord, I can see paperwork in my future."

"What'd you say?" Alvin hollered. "Are you talkin' 'bout us? I don't like people whisperin' things 'bout us."

"Boy," the old Ranger said, "I don't much give a tinker's damn what you like or dislike. Now just stand over there with your brothers and enjoy your drinks and shut the hell up!''

"I'd do what he says, boys,'' the bartender told the trio. "That's Ranger Keller. He was a Ranger when they was carryin' Walker Colts. Leave him alone is my advice to you.''

"Who the hell asked for your advice?'' Kenny said. "Mind your own knittin' and tend to polishin' your glasses.''

The bartender shrugged and looked down at Frank and the Ranger. "I tried,'' he said.

"Some folks is just plain hardheaded,'' Ranger Keller opined.

"You are callin' us names!'' Alvin said. "You 'bout a meddlin' old fool, that's what you are.''

"Boxes and boxes of paperwork,'' Ranger Keller muttered. "Oh, Lord, I can see me scribblin' for hours and hours.''

Frank slid his gaze sideways and smiled at the Ranger's expression. "Well, Ranger, if we get it over with quickly enough, we'll still have time for supper.''

The Ranger smiled at that. "Well, I suppose I could take some comfort in that. Are you ready?''

"I stay ready, Ranger.''

"Yeah . . . I reckon you do, boy. I really reckon you do.'' He looked over at the Bookbinder brothers. "You boys back off and leave me be. That's the only warning I'm goin' to give you. You best heed it.''

"I ain't never killed me no big-ass Ranger,'' Kenny said.

"You ain't goin' to kill this one either, boy,'' Ranger Keller told him. "Now I give you a fair and open warnin'. Whatever else happens is on your head.''

"Hell with you, Ranger!'' Kenny told him, and grabbed for his gun.

Ranger Keller may have been past his prime in age, but

his gun hand was still quick and smooth. He drilled Kenny in the belly just as Frank pulled iron and gave Jules Bookbinder a .45 round in the chest. The older brother was slammed up against the bar, his pistol just clear of leather.

"Bastard!" he yelled at Frank as he lifted and cocked his six-gun.

Frank shot him again, then once more. Jules staggered and went down on the barroom floor, still cussing.

Alvin threw up his hands and yelled, "I'm out of this, boys! Don't shoot no more. I'm done."

"Oh, Lord," Kenny groaned, hanging on to the side of the bar. "I done messed up bad this time."

"I'd say so," Ranger Keller told him.

"I'll kill you both," Jules gasped. "I'll kill you."

"No, you won't, boy," the Ranger told him. "Just be quiet and die easy."

"I ain't gonna die," Jules said. "Not by a long shot."

"I wouldn't take no bets on that," the Ranger replied.

Frank jerked Alvin's gun from leather and tossed it on a table.

"I need me a doctor," Kenny said. "I mean, I really do."

"You and your brother need a preacher and an undertaker," Ranger Keller told him. "In that order."

Kenny lost his grip on the bar and fell to the floor, stretching out beside his brother. "Is you still alive, Jules?" he asked.

Jules stared at his brother with wide-open yet lifeless eyes.

"I believe that does it," Ranger Keller said.

"What am I gonna do?" Alvin hollered.

"Ride a mighty lonesome trail, I reckon," the Ranger told him.

"Are you arrestin' me?" Alvin asked.

"Nope. I ain't got nothin' to hold you on. You didn't pull on me. Your brothers did."

"It's a-gettin' dark!" Kenny said. "Is it nighttime so soon?"

"It is for you," Ranger Keller told him.

"Oh, Lord!" Kenny hollered.

"You mean I can go?" Alvin asked.

"Right after you see to the plantin' of your no-'count brothers."

"I can do that. We got money."

"You don't seen too almighty broke up about their passin'," Ranger Keller said.

"Well, I'll miss 'em, for shore."

"That's mighty big of you, boy," the Ranger observed, just about as dryly as the desert at high noon in July.

"Well, I never really got along with either of them. They kinda drug me into outlawin', you see."

"Yeah, I'm shore they did," the Ranger said.

"I need to see a preacher," Kenny whispered.

"You need a hell of lot more than that, boy," the Ranger said.

"I want to go to heaven and see my mama and papa."

"You can wave up to 'em," the Ranger said. "That'll have to do."

"I think I'm done for," Kenny said.

"Can I have your guns, Kenny?" Alvin asked. "You know I've always admired 'em."

"Take 'em and go to hell with 'em, you whiny piece of snake crap," his brother replied.

"Such affection is truly heartwarmin'," the Ranger said, pouring himself a drink.

"It must have really been a close family," Frank replied.

"How about your horse?" Alvin asked.

But Kenny didn't reply. He was stone dead.

Alvin quickly took off his brother's gun belt and started to reach for his Colt, thought better of it, and looked back at Ranger Keller and Frank.

"Go on," Frank told him. "Get it and clear out. You make me want to puke."

After Alvin had dragged his brothers out back, Ranger Keller said, "You'll be seeing him again, Morgan. He'll probably try to back-shoot you. He shore ain't got the sand to meet you eyeball-to-eyeball."

"I'm sure you're probably right. But I'm used to checking my back trail."

Keller smiled. "Ain't we all, boy. Ain't we all."

Thirty-four

Frank spent two days in the small town, provisioning up, resting, and enjoying meals he didn't have to prepare himself. Dog ate and slept in the stall with Stormy. Frank and Ranger Keller rode out together, but parted at a crossroads a few hours later.

"It's been a pleasure, Morgan," the old Ranger said. "Watch your back."

"Same to you," Frank replied.

Weeks later, with the weather turning definitely toward winter, Frank rode into Fort Worth. He checked into a hotel, got himself cleaned up while his suit was being pressed and his shirts laundered, then went to a Wells Fargo office to see if he had any messages. He had several from his attorneys.

One of the messages advised him that he was several thousand dollars richer due to some highfalutin stock deal his assigned broker had pulled off in New York City. Another message was that a Miss Judith Barnes had settled in Kansas City and was now teaching school. Another message advised him that his son, Conrad, was now touring Europe with some lovely New York City society woman.

"A real playboy," Frank muttered. "Well, good luck to you, son."

Frank and his son did not get along, and seldom saw each other.

He stepped into a saloon and ordered a beer. No one in the crowded place seemed to recognize him, and Frank breathed a sigh of relief for that. He sipped his beer and looked around the large interior of the saloon. Painted ladies working the table, and a banjo player, a fiddler, and a piano player were hard at work entertaining the late afternoon crowd.

A man stepped into the space beside Frank, and Frank cut his eyes to the man. A Texas Ranger.

"Morgan," the Ranger said.

"That's me."

"We got a wire from Ranger Keller. Said he met you and you and him came out on top in a shootin' scrape. He said you was a man to ride the river with. Comin' from an old salty dog like Keller, them words is mighty high praise, believe you me."

"I believe it. Keller impressed me."

The Ranger looked at Frank through hard eyes. Then a smile formed on his lips. "I'll tell Keller you said so. That'll tickle him. Finish your beer, I'll buy you another."

"Thanks. You had supper?"

"Not yet."

"After our beers I'll treat for supper."

"Now, that's mighty white of you, Morgan. Mighty

white." He stuck out a hand. "I'll shore take you up on that offer. Name's Pat Mahoney."

Frank shook the hard and callused hand. "Pleasure."

The two men stood at the bar and drank their beers and chatted of men they had known over the years. Good men and outlaws.

"But you know, Morgan," Pat said, "sometimes a man can be an outlaw and still be a good man."

"And vice versa," Frank said.

"You got that right. Half the lawmen in the country think you're part outlaw. But Keller knowed right off you wasn't no such of a thing."

Frank and the Ranger stood at the bar and talked for a while longer, then had supper: beefsteak, boiled potatoes, fresh-baked bread, and apple pie for dessert. Later, standing outside the café, they shook hands and parted ways. Frank could not remember when he had had a more pleasurable evening.

Walking back to the hotel, he became quickly aware that he was being followed. He chanced a quick look behind him and saw one man trailing him. The man lifted a hand in greeting. Puzzled, Frank stopped and stepped into an alleyway.

The man paused at the darkened mouth of the alley. Still on the boardwalk, he said, "I don't mean you no harm, Morgan. I swear it. You done me a good turn back at the Crossing. You probably don't remember it; that was a few years back. But I remember it."

"What's on your mind?"

"I used the money you give me back there for a grubstake. I panned out enough to leave that damn place. I come here and opened me up a leather and saddle shop. Been doing all right."

"Glad to hear it."

"You familiar with a gun-handler name of Ben Clark?"

"Yes. He's a killer. Hires his gun out. Been killing homesteaders up in Oklahoma Territory."

"That's him. Big ugly bastard. He heard you was in town. He's lookin' to make a bigger rep for hisself."

"By killing me?"

"You got it."

"He's a damn fool."

"I know it. But he's done made his brags now. He can't back out."

"Or he thinks he can't."

"Whatever. But he ain't gonna back down, Morgan. He's gonna come after you. I wanted to warn you. I done it. Take care."

The man walked swiftly away.

"Damn!" Frank swore softly. "Just once I'd like to light somewhere for a few days where somebody isn't trying to shoot me."

But he knew that wasn't likely to happen. At least not until Frank became an old man. And he also knew the odds of his becoming an old man weren't all that great either.

Frank walked to the livery to check on Dog, then returned to the hotel. The night was chilly, so Frank built a fire in the potbelly to warm his room, then sat for a time, smoking and thinking.

It was too late in the season to make the ride back to his valley in New Mexico . . . property he had picked up for a bargain. He had obtained the land at a steal for several reasons. One, because most people didn't know it was there. Two, because those that did didn't want it, not recognizing its potential.

Someday Frank would return to his valley to live out his remaining years. Someday . . .

Thirty-five

Frank lounged around Fort Worth for several days, letting his animals rest, for his horses were tired and Dog was all pooped out from weeks on the trail. Frank bought provisions, a bit at a time, and played some poker at a saloon several times and won five hundred dollars. He gave his winnings to a very surprised and profoundly grateful lady at a local orphanage. And he saw nothing of the gunfighter Ben Clark.

Sitting in his hotel room one night, drinking coffee and relaxing, Frank had an idea. The next morning, first thing, he wired his attorneys, then waited around for a reply. It came back quickly, and read: ARE YOU SURE YOU WANT TO DO THIS?

Frank wired back: YES.

The reply was: WE'LL SET IT UP PER YOUR INSTRUCTIONS.

Frank left the telegraph office smiling. Many, many years

later, long after Frank's death, the nation's press would be startled to learn that one of the West's most famous (some would say notorious) gunfighters had, over the years, anonymously given thousands and thousands of dollars to orphanages all over the nation.

After Frank's acts of kindness became known, one reporter noted in a column: "This act of compassion should remind us all that one should not judge a book by its cover."

On the evening before he was to head out for El Paso, Frank's luck in avoiding a face-to-face meeting with Ben Clark turned sour. Frank was coming out of a leather shop with a sackful of paw boots he'd had made for Dog when he spotting Ben Clark coming out of a café across the street. Ben was just as big and just as ugly as Frank remembered him being . . . maybe even more so, since it had been a few years since last they'd met. Ben spotted Frank and stopped on the boardwalk, staring at him.

The street was busy with foot traffic and wagons and riders. Far too busy for any gunplay, and Frank hoped Ben would see it the same way. But the instant Ben's hand dropped to his six-gun and he slipped off the hammer thong, Frank knew his hope would not be realized.

"Not here, Ben," Frank called.

"Why the hell not?" Ben shouted. His shout caused many to stop and see what was going on.

Frank dropped the sack to the boardwalk. "Too many people, Ben."

"They can get the hell out of the way, Morgan."

"Morgan?" a man called out. "Hey! That's Frank Morgan over yonder."

"I'm not looking for trouble, Ben," Frank called across the wide street.

"Too bad, Morgan. Your time has come."

"My time for what, Ben?"

Ben stepped off the boardwalk and into the street. "I hope you like Texas, Morgan. 'Cause you gonna be buried here right shortly."

Frank stepped into the street. "This doesn't have to be, Ben. Think about it."

"I been thinkin' about it for a long time, Drifter. Ever since you whupped me up in Wyoming that time."

"You had it coming, Ben."

"That don't make no never mind. I ain't forgot it."

Each man took a couple of steps toward the other, closing the gap between them in the side street.

The street was now nearly devoid of people. Most had taken refuge in stores and in the alleyways. A few of the braver or more foolhardy had merely stepped back, away from what they hoped would be the line of fire.

"Five dollars says the big one can take Morgan," a man called.

"I'll take that bet," half a dozen others echoed.

"Where is the law?" a woman questioned.

"Nowheres around here," a man told her. "Not with Frank Morgan fixin' to drag iron."

There was now about forty feet between the two men. Frank stopped and so did Ben.

"I say again, Ben," Frank called, "this does not have to be. Neither of us have anything to prove."

"It ain't a matter of provin' nothin', Drifter. For me, it's a matter of money. I kill you, my price goes up."

"Money's hard to spend in the grave, Ben."

"Well, Drifter, you'll be in hell a long time 'fore me. You'll have to tell me all about it when I get there." He grinned at Frank. "You ready to feel the fires, Frank?"

Frank's returning smile was tinged with sadness. "It's your play, Ben. Drag iron if you've a mind to."

It was over in a heartbeat. Sunlight flashed off cold steel suddenly turned hot and the day was split with gunfire. Ben staggered, regained his balance for a few seconds, then abruptly sat down in the street, the front of his shirt staining with crimson as his heart pumped.

"Damn!" Ben said. "You're quick, Drifter."

"So I've been told," Frank said dryly.

Ben tried to lift his six-gun, but the effort seemed to require too much strength. He dropped his pistol as numbness crawled into his fingers. He smiled at Frank. "Sometimes I reckon a man tries to chew more than he should. Right, Frank?"

Frank said nothing as he walked closer to Ben Clark.

Ben looked up at him. "I had to try you, Drifter. I just had to."

"I know, Ben."

Ben fell over in the dirt. "I got money for a stone," he whispered. "Will you see to that, Frank?"

"I'll see it gets done, Ben."

"Mighty decent of you. Mighty decent." Ben Clark closed his eyes for the last time.

"Somebody get the law," Frank said. "Let's do this legal."

Frank changed his mind about El Paso at the last moment, and pulled out for San Antonio instead. His horses were ready to go, and Dog got so excited when Frank began saddling up, he ran around in circles, barking and chasing his tail.

Frank was under no illusions about the gunfighter Cory Raven. Before he pulled out, he had Ranger Mahoney send out a couple of wires to friends of his. The reply came back quickly. Word was that Cory Raven had been hired to kill Frank Morgan. But no one seemed to know who hired him or why.

"I'll just be sure to keep an eye on my back trail," Frank told the Ranger.

"For a fact, Morgan," the Ranger said. "You do that. Cory Raven is a bad one."

Frank took his time, for he certainly was in no hurry. No one was anxiously awaiting his arrival. Hell, no one knew where he was going. Frank wasn't even sure he wouldn't change his mind halfway to San Antonio and head out in another direction.

He spent the night in a hotel in Waco and kept mostly out of sight, avoiding any saloons and eating his supper in a small café just off Main Street. He pulled out before dawn. The days were pleasant and the nights cool, great for sleeping, wrapped in his blankets, his saddle for a pillow.

In Austin, Frank stabled his horses in a nice, well-maintained livery, got some scraps for Dog, and filled a bucket with water, setting it just inside Stormy's stall. Taking his bedroll, his saddlebags, and his rifle, Frank went in search of a hotel.

Frank sent his suit out to be pressed, a couple of his shirts to be laundered, and his good boots to be polished. While that was being done, Frank visited a barbershop-bathhouse and got himself slicked up. So far, no one had recognized him.

That welcomed anonymity did not last long.

When Frank walked down the hotel stairs to the lobby the next morning, there were several newspapermen and two photographers waiting for him. He missed breakfast that morning, and never did learn who had recognized him. For several hours, he patiently answered all their questions and allowed several pictures to be taken of him. During a break,

Frank slipped back to his room, packed up his possessions, and headed for the livery. An hour later, he had put Austin several miles behind him. Frank headed west, deciding not to try for El Paso because of all the publicity there would be when the newspapers hit the street the next day. And for sure, the telegraph wires would be humming about him. West Texas would be his best bet. Out there, all he would have to worry about was bandits, Indians, a few Comancheros, and rattlesnakes.

Frank spent several peaceful and very restful days in the German town of Fredericksburg. The marshal there knew who he was but left him alone, as did many of the locals, who also knew who he was. While he was there, Frank ate his fill of traditional German foods, including some of the best breads and pastries he had ever eaten. Dog gained about five pounds.

The time spent traveling out into West Texas was the most relaxing Frank had experienced in recent memory. He almost forgot about Cory Raven.

And that slip in vigilance almost cost him his life.

Thirty-six

"Keep your hands where I can see them, Morgan," the cold voice said from the bluff above the creek bank. "And don't turn around."

Frank paused, the bar of soap still in one hand.

"I like a man who washes up before he eats," the voice said. "A fellow can get awful dirty on the trail."

"Cory?" Frank asked.

"You got it, Morgan."

"Now what?"

"Now you die, Morgan."

"You going to shoot me without telling me who hired you?"

"I don't know who hired me, Morgan. All I know is a voice comin' from a dark hallway told me seein' you dead was worth ten thousand dollars. Somebody must hate you mighty powerful, Morgan."

"I reckon so." Frank cut his eyes, looking for Dog. The big cur was nowhere to be seen.

"But I want to see you sweat and beg, Morgan."

"That will never happen."

"Oh, I think it will."

"So you're going to shoot me in the back, Cory? You don't have the guts to face me?"

The hired gun was silent for a few seconds. "Oh, I'm better than you, Morgan. I don't have any doubts about that. But why take the chance of something happenin'? This way is easier."

"The coward's way. Cory? I've always heard you were a brave man. I guess I heard wrong."

"I got my share of guts, Morgan. Don't you ever think otherwise 'bout that."

"I think you're yellow, Cory. You're nothing but a low-down, back-shooting coward."

"Don't you call me that, Morgan! Damn you! Don't you say I'm yellow."

"I have one request, Cory."

"Name it."

"Don't hurt my dog. Let Dog run free."

"I can do that. Where is that damn dog?"

"*Dog!*" Frank yelled.

"I think that damn mutt is as yellow as you, Morgan," Cory said with a laugh.

Cory did not see or hear the big cur coming up fast behind him, running hard on silent paws. Frank heard a grunt and a yell and he spun around, Peacemaker leaping into his hand.

Dog had leaped and thrown his entire weight on Cory. All four paws hit the gunman in his back. Cory's pistol flew from his hand, and the man lost his balance and tumbled down the short bluff, rolling butt over elbows. Frank was on him in a heartbeat. He hit the man a short, chopping right that connected solidly with Cory's jaw, stunning the already dazed man.

Frank's fists were big, hard, callused, and flat-knuckled. Fighter's hands. Frank hit Cory half a dozen times. The last blow broke Cory's jaw and dropped the hired gun into unconsciousness.

Frank looked up toward the bluff. Dog was sitting there, looking down at him.

"Good boy," Frank said.

Dog stood up, wagged his tail, and barked.

"I owe you," Frank told the big cur. "I really owe you."

Frank pulled Cory's gun belt from him and tossed the man's pistol into the creek. Then he walked around until he found the man's horse, and stripped the saddle and bridle from him. He led him to the creek and let him drink.

Frank quickly got his own gear together and swung into the saddle. He looked down at Cory Raven. The man was still out.

"I'll see you again, Cory," Frank told the unconscious man. "But the next time, I'll kill you."

Frank drifted for several weeks, avoiding all human contact. Finally, almost out of supplies, he rode into a small town in West Texas. He was unshaven and trail-worn.

His part in the rescuing of the kidnapped children and the smashing of the Val Dooley gang had long faded from the news, and Frank was happy about that. Frank stabled his horses and made sure Dog had water to drink. No one seemed to recognize him as he got a room in the hotel. The clerk merely gave his name a quick glance and a nod as he handed Frank the room key.

A bath and a haircut and shave later, Frank was feeling better, even with the knowledge that he could not chance staying more than a couple of days in the town. Any longer than that and someone would be sure to recognize him. That always seemed to be the case.

Frank had a relaxing meal at a café, and was enjoying a cup of coffee and a cigarette when two lawmen entered the café. They glanced at him, took a longer second look, then walked over to his table and sat down.

"Frank Morgan?" one asked in low tones.

"Yes."

"You on the hunt for someone, Morgan?"

"The only thing I'm hunting is peace and quiet," Frank replied.

"Well, this is a peaceful and quiet town," the other lawman stated. "And we intend to keep it that way."

"And that means what?" Frank had to ask, even though he knew perfectly well what was coming next.

"It means you go."

"You have any objections to my finishing my coffee and getting a good night's sleep in a real bed?"

"Not a bit, Morgan," the older of the two lawmen said. "You can even have you some breakfast in the mornin'. Just be gone right after that and stay out of the saloon tonight."

"Oh, I can do that, boys, with a great deal of pleasure. And my horses and my dog thank you for letting them get some rest."

"What kind of a dog is that mean-lookin' dog of yours?" the younger lawman asked.

Frank smiled. "He's just a dog. But I have some suspicions that he might have some wolf in him."

"You'll get no arguments from me about that. He didn't growl at us, but he wasn't all that friendly either."

Frank laughed. "He's a good watchdog, for a fact." Frank

decided against making any mention of the run-in with Cory Raven.

The older man smiled at that. "I am sorry about givin' you the boot Morgan. But trouble seems to follow you."

Frank returned the smile. "I do know that for a fact . . . far better than you."

The lawman signaled the waitress for coffee. "We'll just sit here and palaver with you for a time . . . like old friends. That'll ease any curiosity of a couple of jabber-mouths here in the café."

"Good idea. What I don't need is any publicity or gunplay while I'm in town."

"Glad you see it that way."

The three men sat and drank coffee, smoked, and chatted of men they had known, good and bad. The older lawman asked, "You know a man by the name of Cory Raven?"

"I've met him."

There was a definite twinkle in the lawman's eyes. "We got word that Cory rode into a town a good ways east of here with a busted jaw. Said his horse throwed him. You believe that, Morgan?"

"Stranger things have happened, I suppose. Maybe his horse got spooked by a snake."

"Yeah," the lawman said dryly. "That throw give Raven a black eye too. And several bruises that looked to the doctor like maybe someone beat the crap out of him."

"Cory probably deserved a good beating," Frank said. "They tell you what direction Cory took out of town?"

"North. Told the doc he was headin' for Denver."

"Of course Cory has been known to tell a lie now and then. Or so I've heard tell."

"I reckon so. He wouldn't be after you, would he?"

"Might be. I've got a lot of men who would like to see me dead."

"Well . . . if he shows up here, I'll tell him you headed south toward the border."

"Much obliged for that. If he shows up here."

"Where are you headin', Morgan?"

"I honestly don't know," Frank replied. "I'll see which way the wind's blowing in the morning and head that way, I reckon."

"Way I hear tell it, you got enough money to buy you a mansion in the city and live right nice, if you was a mind to."

Frank chuckled softly. "Would you want to live in the city?"

The lawman frowned. "Hell, no!"

"Me, neither. So . . . I reckon I'll just live up to my nickname then. I'll just drift."

For a sneak preview
of Bill Johnstone's next book—
CODE NAME: QUICKSTRIKE
coming from Pinnacle Books
in May 2003
just turn the page. . . .

One

New Orleans

As the car turned west onto Decatur Street, John Barrone caught a glimpse of the sunset and saw that the sky was the color of liquid fire. To his left the Mississippi River made a large bow of molten silver on its circuitous journey to the Gulf of Mexico. In the heart of the city, steel and concrete towers loomed dark purple against the crimson sky, their windows reflecting a grid of melon-colored light.

The car window was down, and when they entered the Vieux Carre, going north on St. Peters, John could hear the sounds of New Orleans. Muted trumpets and wailing saxophones, played by musicians with shining black skin and dark, soulful eyes, spilled out onto the crowded sidewalks from the nightclubs. This was the haunting symphony of blues and jazz, the Crescent City's major contribution to American culture.

Through the open window of the car, John could also smell the distinctive night fragrances: the rich aromas of exquisite cooking, green bananas and pineapples just off the boats, as well as the delicate flower scents from the honeysuckle, jasmine, and wisteria that climbed along brick walls and overhung the elaborate grillwork balconies of the Quarter's elegant old homes. A different perfume was given off by the French Quarter's painted ladies, who lounged in doorways or on street corners to practice their trade, marking the night with their own sweet, sensual musk.

The habitués of the narrow, winding streets of the French Quarter were, with the setting of the sun, just now beginning to awaken. By day they had slumbered as trucks plied the alleys and twisting thoroughfares, off-loading their cargoes of vegetables, meat, whiskey, and beer.

There were four men in the car: John Barrone and Bob Garrett, who were both members of a privately funded and very elite organization called the Code Name Team. The other two passengers were their prisoner, Mehmet Ibrahim, and Lucien Beajeaux, the driver of the car.

The Code Name Team to which John and Bob belonged was made up of ten people, seven men and three women. Their job was to ''take care of things'' that fell through the cracks. Terrorists, murderers, drug dealers, etc., who often got away with their misdeeds because of the technicalities and niceties of the law, were fair game for the men and women of the Code Name Team.

The Code Name Team had no government connection. Indeed, since they were extralegal, they were often at cross purposes with the government. On the other hand, there were certain individuals within the government who knew what the team was actually doing, and from time to time those people would turn a blind eye to the Code Name Team's operations. On rare occasions they would even help the Code Name Team.

In order to get things done, the Code Name Team needed some sort of operating cover. Thus, they often functioned as a private detective agency, a personal security firm, or a bail-bonding operation . . . whatever was required to give them the operating authority they might need.

The Team was sponsored by an international consortium of billionaires and multimillionaires. Though most were from America, other sponsors were from England, France, Germany, and Italy . . . with perhaps two or three from the Scandinavian countries.

As a result of their 'extralegal' status, everyone who joined the Code Name Team did so knowing that there was only one way out, and that was in a body bag. And because they had made a lifetime commitment, their loyalty, dedication, and support of each other bound them together as closely as if they were of the same blood.

Lucien Beajeaux was a private detective from New Orleans. Although Beajeaux was not a member of the Code Name Team, Bob Garret, who was John Barrone's partner on this particular job, had vouched for him. Bob had worked with the former New Orleans policeman when Bob was still with the National Security Agency.

"How long it gonna take you to get to Chicago?" Beajeaux asked, speaking in a heavy Cajun accent.

"We'll get into Chicago at ten A.M. tomorrow," John said.

"Whooee! You be on the train all night? It more better you fly," Beajeaux suggested. "You fly, you get there in a couple of hours. That what I'm goin' do when I go to Chicago one of these days.''

"Ha!" Bob said. "Now just what the hell would a Creole boy like you do in Chicago?"

"Hoo boy, ain't no tellin' what all I might do, I go there," Beajeaux joked. "Maybe I show those Chicago ladies somethin', I bet. 'Darlin',' I'll say, 'you ain' had no lovin' till you been loved by a Cayjohn man from N'arleans.' ''

"I'll bet those Chicago women are just waitin' on that," Bob offered dryly. John laughed.

When they reached the depot, the train they were to take was already standing in the station. It was a long, sleek, Amtrak train, painted in silver, red, white, and blue. As it sat at the station, the humming of electric motors was clearly audible, and wisps of vapor drifted away from the air-conditioning vents that were individual to each car. Some passengers were already inside, and they could be seen through the windows, reading, talking, or simply sitting there with their heads back against the seat headrests, waiting for departure.

"Park over there," John said, pointing to a parking spot near the station platform.

"Yes, sir, you the boss man," Beajeaux said, pulling into the parking spot John had indicated.

"I'm going to feel a lot better when we get Ibrahim on the train."

"You won't have no trouble," Beajeaux said. "The others think you fly to Houston."

"Yes, well, I hope the others took the bait when we bought those airline tickets," Bob said. "Otherwise, we will have spent all that money for nothing."

"What are you worrying about the money for?" John asked. "It was Gil Bates's money. Bates has thirty billion dollars. He could've bought the entire airline and not felt it."

"Yeah, I guess so. Still, it seems a waste."

"It won't be a waste if we get Ibrahim out of here in one piece. We'll go by train to Chicago, then fly him to Houston. It is a circuitous route, I will admit, but it's the best way to go, because they won't be looking for anything like that."

"I am not a citizen of this country," Ibrahim said from the backseat. "You have no right to take me from here against my will."

"Hey, if it was up to me, I wouldn't take your ass anywhere," Bob said. "I would have dropped the hammer on you as soon as we found you."

"Drop the hammer?" Ibrahim asked, puzzled by the remark.

Bob held his hand in the shape of a gun, snapped the thumb forward as if shooting it, then shouted, "Bang!"

Ibrahim jumped, and Bob laughed. "Scared you, huh?"

"I do not fear death," Ibrahim said. "I am a warrior for Allah."

"A warrior my ass. You put a bomb on the Dynasystems's executive jet last year. Thirty-seven people were killed, including Mr. Bates's daughter."

"That happened in Sitarkistan," Ibrahim said. "The Sitarkistani court found me not guilty. I have been cleared of that."

"Yes, well, you haven't been cleared in Mr. Bates's personal court."

"You are being foolish. Private citizens in America, even those as wealthy as Gil Bates, do not have a personal court."

"Yes, well, you can tell that to the judge," John said. "Judge Gil Bates," he added, laughing.

"Anyway, you will not take me from here. My Islamic

brothers will find me. They will kill you, and they will rescue me.''

"They may find us," John said. "But I promise you, they will not rescue you."

"Think we ought to check things out before we take him to the train?" Bob asked.

"Probably wouldn't hurt," John replied.

"I know my rights," Ibrahim said. "I demand that you take me to the Sitarkistan Consulate."

"Funny thing, isn't it, John, how all the assholes who are trying to destroy the U.S. start quoting the rights they think they have?"

"Yeah," John said. He looked at Ibrahim. "In the first place, you towel-headed bastard, you've got no rights as far as I'm concerned. And in the second, even if you did have any rights, I would remind you that we are not with the police, FBI, CIA, or any other governmental agency. We are private citizens. That means we aren't bound by any of their restrictions."

"You . . . you aren't really going to take me to Houston, are you? You are going to kill me before we get there."

"Yeah, we might," Bob said.

"You cannot kill me!" Ibrahim said.

"Why should that bother you? Didn't you just tell us that you are a warrior for Allah, that you don't fear death?" Bob asked.

"Beajeaux, keep an eye on him, while Bob and I check things out," John said.

Beajeaux pulled his pistol and pointed it at Ibrahim, then smiled. "I will do that," he said. "More better he try to run, I think."

John and Bob got out of the car and looked around carefully. When they were convinced the coast was clear, they turned back toward the car.

"Okay," John said. He opened the car door and motioned for Ibrahim to get out. "Let's go."

Ibrahim got out of the car, his egress somewhat awkward because his hands were handcuffed behind him.

"Ibrahim, walk straight toward the train," John ordered quietly. "Don't look around, don't do anything to draw attention to yourself."

John, Bob, and Ibrahim started across the platform toward the train. Just to the left of the platform, on a track siding, stood a single boxcar. Suddenly the door of the boxcar slid open and four men jumped down onto the bricks. All four were wearing ski masks. Three were carrying AK-47s; one was carrying a shotgun.

"It is my brothers of the Islamic Jihad Muhahidin! Allah Akbar, I have been saved!" Ibrahim shouted.

"Bob, look out!" John warned.

The four armed men stood in a little semicircle and began firing, their guns blasting away as they swept the barrels back and forth.

Ibrahim started running toward them, a wide smile on his face. Then the assailants did an amazing thing. They stopped firing at John and Bob, and turned their weapons on Ibrahim.

"No!" Ibrahim shouted when he saw them aiming at him.

All four opened up at once, and Ibrahim went down with wounds in his chest, neck, and head.

There were several bystanders on the platform. Some were passengers getting ready to entrain, while others were there to see people off. When the first shot was fired, the civilians added their own screams and shouts to the bedlam as they started running in a mad dash to get out of the way. Some dived for the ground, others ran for cover. Beajeaux got out of the car and began firing across the top of it, at the four masked shooters.

The machine guns and shotgun chattered and roared. Bullets whistled all around John, Bob, and Beajeaux. John dived for the platform, then lay on his stomach on the bricks, his gun stretched out before him. From this prone position he pulled the trigger, and the gun bucked up in his hand, kicking out an empty shell casing as it did so. He was gratified to see his target grab his chest and fall.

Bob was hit in the thigh and the side, and he went down as well, but continued firing.

The firing continued unabated for about thirty seconds, though to John it seemed an eternity. A bullet cut through the sleeve of his jacket, but didn't actually hit him.

Suddenly, a black Ford Bronco roared out onto the station platform, and the two gunners who were still on their feet rushed toward it and jumped in. The driver whipped the vehicle around in a tight circle, the tires squealing in protest against the bricks. Once back on the road, the SUV began to roar away. John stood up to get a better shot at the speeding vehicle, and in anger and frustration, emptied his pistol at the back of the speeding Bronco, though he knew he probably wasn't hitting anyone from this distance.

After the SUV left, John stood there for a moment, holding his pistol down by his leg, the breech open, indicating that it was empty. Scores of spent shell casings covered the brick platform, a visual indication of the number of shots exchanged during the shoot-out.

"Bob, are you all right?" John called.

"I was hit a couple of times," Bob answered, his voice slightly strained, "but I don't think it's anything serious."

"How about you, Beajeaux?" John called. "Are you all right?"

When there was no answer, John turned to look toward the New Orleans PI who had helped them.

"Oh, damn," he said when he saw Beajeaux. "Bob, we lost Beajeaux."

Beajeaux was lying across the hood of the car, his head resting in a pool of blood, his right arm dangling down, the gun hanging by its trigger guard from his index finger.

"Those sorry bastards," Bob said. "Beajeaux was a good man."

Looking back, John saw Ibrahim lying facedown and absolutely motionless in a pool of blood slowly widening beneath him on the brick platform. Two of the shooters were also down and motionless.

"If they were here to rescue Ibrahim, they did a piss-poor job of it," Bob said.

"I think they did just what they wanted to do," John said.

"What do you mean?"

"Ibrahim most have known some things they didn't want him talking about."

By now, cautiously, as if expecting another attack, the bystanders who had bolted to safety at the opening shots began to reappear. They were drawn by morbid curiosity to the little islands of death that were scattered about the station. Some stopped at the bodies of the two men John had killed. Others stood over Ibrahim, or went over to examine Beajeaux.

"Get away from him!" John shouted angrily as he saw the morbid begin to close in on the former New Orleans policeman. "Get the hell away!"

Frightened, the crowd backed away.

John went over to Bob, who was sitting on the ground, leaning against a light pole. Bob was bleeding from wounds in his side and his thigh. The thigh wound was still bleeding, and he was holding his hand over the bullet hole, trying to stem the blood flow.

"Damn, why didn't you tell me you were hit that hard?" John asked in concern. He took off his belt and looped it around the leg above the wound. Tightening it, he made it into a tourniquet.

"How about the wound in your side?" John asked.

"It's not that bad," Bob answered. "I was pretty much just nicked there. Not even bleeding that much."

One of the onlookers wandered over to John and Bob.

"Mister, what the hell was all this about?" he asked.

John didn't answer. Instead, he took out his cell phone and punched in 911.

Even as he was dialing, though, he heard the sirens of approaching vehicles, and as the first police car pulled up onto the platform, he closed the phone. Two policeman jumped out with pistols drawn.

"Get your hands up now!" the first policeman shouted.

John held up his hands. "You are a little late, officers, the party is all over," he said. "What we need now is an ambulance."

"One is on the way," the other policeman said. Both policemen continued to point their pistols directly at John.

Four more police cars arrived then, as did an ambulance. The emergency medical technicians started looking over the bodies.

"Don't waste your time with them, they're all dead," John called to them. "This is the only man who needs your attention."

By now there were well over a dozen policemen on the scene, and one of them, wearing captain's bars on his epaulets, approached John cautiously. Like the other policemen, the captain had his gun drawn.

"Who are you?" the police captain asked. "And what happened here?"

"We were taking a prisoner back to Texas," John said.

"We were about to board the train when four men jumped down from that boxcar over there and attacked us. I think any of the witnesses here will verify that."

"That's right, Officer," one of the bystanders said. "The other fellas started shooting first."

"You were taking a prisoner to Texas on this train?" the policeman asked. "This train is going to Chicago."

"It's a long story," John said without going into the explanation.

"Where is your New Orleans police escort?"

"We didn't have one."

"If you had extradition papers, you had to have a police escort."

"We don't have extradition papers."

"No extradition papers? Then would you mind telling me how in the hell you planned to get this man out of the state?"

"We don't need extradition papers; we are bail bondsmen," John said. He started to reach into his inside jacket pocket.

"Slowly," the police captain warned.

Moving slowly, John pulled out an envelope, then held it up. "Here is our license, and a letter, signed by a Texas judge, authorizing us to take Mehmet Ibrahim back to Texas."

"You're in Louisiana," the police captain said. "You need a Louisiana judge."

John shook his head. "No, we don't. There is a reciprocal agreement. Louisiana recognizes the rights of Texas bail bondsmen to return bond jumpers, just as Texas affords that same right to Louisiana bondsmen."

The EMTs picked up Bob and carried him back to the ambulance.

"I'd like to go with my friend," John said, pointing toward Bob.

"You're not going anywhere until we get this all cleared up," the captain replied.

"It *is* all cleared up," John said. "You've got my license, my letter of authorization—oh, and you'll also find a weapons permit in there—as well as my story of what happened. And as I said, any eyewitness here will back up my story."

"Cap'n, you know who this is?" one of the other policeman called from the car. "This here is Lucien Beajeaux. Remember him? He used to be on the force."

"Yes, of course I remember him," the police captain said. He looked at John. "Did you shoot him?"

"No, he was on our side," John said.

The ambulance pulled away, its warning signal making a honking sound.

"I'm going to take you down to the station," the police captain said. "If everything checks out, I'll let you go."

"All right," John said.

"Cuff him," the captain said to one of his officers.

Sighing, John put his hands behind his back as the officer applied the handcuffs.

The Last Gunfighter Series by
William W. Johnstone

Coming In October 2003, <u>The Burning</u>

William W. Johnstone
The *Ashes* Series